SISTER OF MINE

SISTER
OF
MINE

LAURIE PETROU

HarperCollinsPublishersLtd

Sister of Mine
© 2018 by Laurie Petrou.
All rights reserved.

Published by HarperCollins Publishers Ltd

First edition

HarperCollins books may be purchased for educational, business,
or sales promotional use through our Special Markets Department.

HarperCollins Publishers Ltd
2 Bloor Street East, 20th Floor
Toronto, Ontario, Canada
M4W 1A8

www.harpercollins.ca

Library and Archives Canada Cataloguing
in Publication information available upon request.

ISBN 978-1-44345-428-5

Printed and bound in the United States of America
LSC/H 9 8 7 6 5 4 3 2 1

A sister can be seen as someone who is both ourselves and very much not ourselves—a special kind of double.
TONI MORRISON

For
Judy & Phil Petrou,
Jay, Eli & Leo,
and
Nicole Bell

SISTER OF MINE

SHE BREAKS INTO A RUN AS SOON AS SHE CLEARS the flames. Tripping and falling through trees, galloping like a confused animal, head turned over shoulder, fire in her eyes. She hears a window break like a firecracker, branches snap against her shoulders. Her knees scraped, her hair singed, her breath sour and pressing, pushing out foul words and curses, knowing that she has done it now, goddammit, she has really fucking done it now.

She runs through the forest behind the property, out to the back roads, ducking into hedges with every sound of a car approaching. Eventually she hears fire trucks screaming dimly behind her, where she can see a thin column of smoke if she strains her eyes, lifting her chin and squinting over poplars in the dark sky. A deer startles her, leaping over shrubs, its tail in the air. Her long, thin summer dress is muddy at the bottom, torn in places, a lacy hem pulling away from the skirt. She pushes fingers through her hair. She swears and pants and refuses to cry.

Blocks away, she knows that her sister, curled in her tangled sheets, is waiting. The old clocks ticking, the big old house holding its breath, about to take in another secret. Can her sister hear that siren start to wail?

Mouth dry, body hopping with ragged energy, she takes a familiar route though a laneway, passing light, metal fencing wound up with a dead vine, and moves quietly to the back of the old house. Like when they were young, and would slip in after curfew. Not so long ago. When she was silly and bad, but not as bad as this. Not as good as this. She reaches into the bird feeder in the apple tree and pulls out a key, a magic ticket, shaking off sunflower seeds like fairy dust. She opens the back door, letting the screen butt against her leg, into the quiet of the lower hallway. She breathes in the flowery, soapy air of her childhood.

She climbs the stairs, and tells herself she's been there all night; that she had been there in the early evening, just before supper—washed the lettuce in the sink and wrapped it in a towel, pushing out the moisture with the heels of her hands. She tells herself they had eaten and gone to bed early, that if she says this enough, it will be true. She passes the kitchen, her heart slowing down at last. One of the wooden chairs is pulled out from the table, the newspaper lies open. A whole life that took place before now. And then just like that, she wonders what it feels like to burn, to be caught in smoke and flames, and she has to stop and hold the door frame to support herself. It comes so fast. This is it; this is how it will be. Get used to it. Push it away. Douse the fire.

A creak from a bed, the sound of someone sitting up and listening. She takes the second flight of stairs with purpose. She speaks, and hearing her words for the first time in hours makes her aware of her voice: scratchy, soft, scared.

"It's me. I'm home."

PART ONE

CHAPTER 1

THERE ARE PEOPLE WHO, WHEN YOU HEAR THE thump of their car door close, when you sense their feet on the steps, make your body tighten just a little. Even when you love them. Especially when you love them. You find yourself wishing them away, praying that a bluster, a breeze, a patron saint of snatchers will nip them off the porch and leave you be, without them—without who you are with them—for just a little longer. And if you have a freckly fire-haired sister who breathes in all the air of any room she enters, well then, all the more.

Hattie burst into the house. Officer Moore was with her, smiling at her back, his hair trimmed neatly, his pants pressed.

Hattie stopped when she saw me.

"Oh! Hi, Penny," she said, her smile wavering, dropping her purse on the bench where the purses of all the women in our family have been dropped over the years. Her keys jingling, an impotent wind lifting the hem of her skirt behind her as she closed the door.

A year after the fire. A year of her entrances in this two-person, sister-only life raft of a house.

I nodded in mock formality. "Hattie. Officer Moore. This is a pleasant surprise."

He smiled awkwardly. "Hello, Penny. It's Iain, you can call me Iain, of course. Nice to see you, too. Sorry, I was just," he looked at Hattie, "I just bumped into Hattie, and was walking her home. I was heading in this direction anyhow." He brushed his hair from his forehead, self-consciously. In his civilian clothes—khaki pants, button-down shirt—he looked like any other young man in our small town. Plain, baby-faced, his neck red from the sun.

I needed to remind him he was *Officer* Moore. That he shouldn't be here, mooning over Hattie. He could cause us trouble. I didn't underestimate the threat he posed, baby face or no. I thought, as I always did when I saw him, of the very first time we'd met. How my hands had shaken then; I remember holding them behind my back. *Would you like some tea, Officer Moore? We're not coffee drinkers, I'm afraid.*

I waved him off now. "Please don't let me interrupt your visit. I've got business in the kitchen anyway." I fixed Hattie with a bland smile and moved into the next room. I heard her, speaking loudly for my benefit.

"Well. Thanks, Iain."

"My pleasure. I—" I heard him say, quietly, "I enjoyed seeing you."

"Me too."

"I'll call you later?"

"Of course. Anytime. I've got a busy few days, but yeah, let's see."

"Okay, I'll just work around you."

I knew she was blushing, smiling.

The door closed behind him, and the room shrank to the size of an acorn. I called through to Hattie.

"Why is he here again, Hattie?"

"No beating around the bush for you, I see." She joined me in the kitchen.

"Seriously. How many times?" I stood watching her, cornering her. "It's a bad idea. I think I've been pretty clear on that."

"I'm not doing anything wrong, first of all—and it's certainly not an 'idea.'" She paused. "It's been a year, Penny. And—he's nice to me."

"I don't want him coming here."

"You've said."

"And what do you mean, 'he's nice to me'? Tell me you're not that desperate for attention. If it's nice you need, I can start bringing you flowers."

"I'm not like you, you know."

"You can say that again," I said, darkly.

"Look, I like being with people, okay? It's a distraction. I actually like to leave this house once in a while. You used to understand that."

"I do understand that. He's the wrong person to do it with."

"He's not that bad."

"No? Well, then he's definitely too good."

"Maybe it's wise to have him onside. Have you thought of that?"

"Onside is one thing. *Inside* is something else altogether."

"Jesus, Penny. Fine. I'll—I'll let him down easy." She shrugged, as if she didn't care about ending the friendship, as if it were her choice.

I paused, knowing that while she may not do it right away, she would sooner or later. She would do what I asked.

"You hungry?" I was heating up some leftover soup.

* * *

7

WE SAT DOWN AT THE LARGE CHERRYWOOD DINING TABLE that our mother had bought at an auction when she was pregnant with me. The story was that she had cravings for antiques the way other pregnant women crave pickles. The house was riddled with them: crocks and old farm equipment, wash basins and mismatched chairs. I loved to imagine her, body full to bursting, perusing antique auctions and estate sales, overlapping birth and death. We never really redecorated. I had always insisted, despite Hattie's attempts to usher in some new style, that we honour the house, our own grand madam of the town of St. Margaret's. The odd chair or couch was reupholstered, but the house was a snapshot of our lives as children, of a life that our mother had pieced together. It had become our sanctuary and our prison. As I've often reminded my sister, change isn't always good.

We sat near each other, but there was no denying the table's size, its ornate carvings casting their own presence.

"What'd you get up to today?" I asked.

"You know, not much. Perm, trim, updo. Really exciting."

"Getting any time to read while you're there?" Hattie had a voracious reading habit, always had done.

She smiled.

"When I can, when I'm on break. I'm loving *Jane Eyre*. All those English moors and twists of fate. Beats the hell out of washing someone's hair."

"Good. That's good. I'm proud of you, Hattie."

A look, a chink in the armour.

She smiled again, a shy thing. I returned it, careful, though I was proud. She was smart and lovely. I almost reached out to her, across the abyss of highly polished wood and a whole lot of years, but held back. Saving for when it counts. We silently ate our lunch. She leaned over her bowl of soup, the steam in her face, and I saw white scalp glowing from her centre part, waves of orange bursting from that most pale divide.

When we were kids that last summer that our childhood was sunny and bright, Hattie was sometimes called Little Red. Mostly by other kids' dads, to whom she became a diminutive version of our dad, Big Red; cigarettes between their teeth, ruffling our small heads as they passed us on the sidewalk where we played, heading into our house. *What's the buzz, Little Red?* Our bare feet burning up, Hattie's skin going pink and her freckles revealing themselves like a seasonal invisible ink. My black hair a magnet for heat. Hattie looked like our father in miniature.

What were they talking about, all those men, with our father? I would watch them, a sharp-eyed eight-year-old, while my five-year-old sister played mindlessly beside me. He slapped their backs on their way out, chuckling and shaking hands. I wanted his attention for myself. He was funny and silly and generous. He was often on the road, and when he returned, he would lift us into the air and tickle us until we begged for mercy. Later, he dodged our mother when she asked him things: about money, about bills, about deals and promises he'd made. I learned, from listening near doorways, that deals fell through sometimes, that sometimes they were big and involved strangers, and other times were casual, between friends and neighbours. I heard snatches of familiar last names. Our mother didn't trust that things would "work out," something he always told her with a grin, and I scoffed, like he did, at her lack of imagination, her inability to believe in him. They fought often, quietly and in heated whispers, thinking we couldn't hear. Sometimes he leaned in and kissed our mum, teased her and made her laugh, but those times became further and further apart. There was a lot of talk of money. But to me, my parents were perfect: my mother a queen, and my father, a magician.

But then, like a trick, he disappeared.

It was after Hattie, Little Red, tried a trick of her own.

I remember it so clearly.

Hattie and I. Curled in bed together, under warm sheets. Her breath like a puppy's, her eyes wide.

"Penny?" A whisper. A husky morning call. My eyes adjusting to her face inches from mine.

"Penny? Are you awake? It's morning." A tiny lisp. Sometimes I hear it still, hear it on the wind, all those sweet *s*'s of hers, gone with growing up. Zipped away by cigarettes and swearing, which never sounds right with a lisp.

"I'm awake."

"I have a surprise for you."

Awake now in earnest. My ears went up, up, up. But grouchy still. Older sister sneers and cherishes the chance to lord age over love.

"What kind of surprise could you have? You are too little for real surprises." I pulled away from her.

A pout, quivering lip. She turned away from me, her hair wrapping her face in a red mask. I waited. Knew she would lie down in front of death for me.

A surprise?

"Okay, okay. What is it?"

She rolled back. She took my hand in hers and pulled it under her chin. She often got to sleep this way, with my arm tucked against her, hand under little chin. We had our own rooms, but Hattie always asked to sleep in my bed. She said she liked my room better. My bed, under the window, offered a view of our giant maple tree. Hattie followed its progress through the seasons with diligence. She was a restless sleeper, though, a dream-twitcher, and often I woke in the night with her feet at my back or in my face. Sometimes she was right flat against the headboard, like she was keeping vigil for the maple itself.

She snuggled against me now. Opened my hand. Opened her own sweaty palm and rolled the contents into mine. Two sparkling emerald earrings. They shone, and dazzled, and I looked, shocked, at them and then Hattie. Our mother's earrings, which she had told me I was too young to wear. That she only ever wore herself for very special occasions. She kept them in a box in her top drawer, to which we were only given brief glimpses as she readied for a night out. Once, as she pulled a long silky tangle of nylon out of the drawer, I asked her to see them. Never imagining that anything so formal and striking could belong to her.

"When you're older, you can wear those, Penny," Mum had said. "They are only for really special occasions. Like meeting the Queen." A smile, closing the box with a slight snap. And now, here they were in my hand.

"For you, Penny. I got them for you!"

"Hattie," I whispered. "We can't."

"It's okay, don't worry. You will look so pretty in them. We will only wear them here, at bedtime, okay?"

"Okay," in a trance, the treasures glinting in the sliver of light coming from under the blinds. I have treasured those earrings my whole life. After Mum died, I wore them sometimes, on days when I especially missed her. They became like a secret light I sent out for her alone, given to me by my sister.

"I love you, Penny." Hattie squeezed my neck with her tiny arms, and closed her eyes again. "Do you love me?"

You little minx. I hugged her back, nodding. Saying nothing, but nodding, which is not the same. But I did. I do still. Even after it all.

* * *

OUR MOTHER NOTICED THEY WERE MISSING, OF COURSE, and with a directness that shocked me, accused our father of selling them. We could hear them clearly, their voices rising up and out the windows. Hattie and I, in the backyard, froze. We locked eyes. *See?* I was saying with mine. *You never should have taken them*. But I didn't tell her to return them. I didn't slip them back into her jewellery box, or even tattle on Hattie myself.

Days passed. The fighting continued. It morphed into other things. Years of resentment and fear and embarrassment bubbled up, our mother's voice breaking. And still: the earrings sparkled in my mind but stayed hidden in my drawer. Hattie and I remained silent, creeping about with our secret, avoiding our parents. We saw a suitcase in the hall. Our father told us he had to go away for a while. And then, in the morning, he was gone.

Weeks passed, then months. I knew that he wasn't coming back. Then our neighbours and his business associates began to drop by the house, my mother serving them coffee in the living room, her hands shaking the cups in the saucers. They left angrily, the front door rattling like a jaw snapping shut.

"You did this, Hattie. He left because of you," I told her one afternoon.

She looked confused, not quite up to the task of pinning it back on me. She hung her head and her eyes welled. I turned away to not to have to see that.

BY THE FALL OF THAT YEAR, THE SEASONS CHANGED FOR us. The town, which had seemed like an open, sunny place until then, turned its back, and we were shivering in the shade. Our house, once a hub of activity and laughter, stood alone, a cage. The fathers of friends no longer ruffled our heads, but ignored us completely. No one came around, kids or adults. No more neighbourhood girls to hold up the other end of the skipping rope for double Dutch. We just took turns skipping alone.

"Your dad's a crook!" one boy shouted, launching a string of spit at us as he raced past us on his bike. We went inside the house, leaving our skipping rope on the sidewalk.

The phone, on the other hand, was the conduit of people's private furies. It rang often and we came to associate its jarring rattle with our mother's whispered apologies. And then, eventually, she told us not to answer it, and it rang and rang and rang.

Our mother got a job at Simpsons. I would see her sometimes, walking towards the house in her uniform, a cigarette in her hand, her face tired and worried, but by the time she opened the door, she had reverted to her old self: sunny and bright, making jokes and hugging us fiercely, asking how we were.

I was often left in charge of Hattie. I learned how to boil water for hot dogs and pull them out with a fork. I barely spoke to her. She was confused and sad, and tried to fill my silence with her chatter. She told me boldly, one day, that she wanted to be called Red. The name, our father's nickname, sent a shiver through me, and I lashed out, shoving her to the ground.

"Never," I snarled.

I called her Harry instead, until I tired of it, running my hand down her thick red hair, and yanking it hard when I reached the bottom, like ringing a bell. I hated her hair, so like his. My own wiry and thick black mop, my soot to her fire, my long straight nose and the gap in my teeth conspired as elements to make me striking, if not beautiful. Black Irish. That was what our grandmother muttered, brushing my coarse hair in those early years. *Black Irish*, she said, as though it were a curse, a kind of black magic. There was a ginger majority in the family, our grandmother included, her hair fading from wild red to silver. Our father's mother, like so many others, had forgotten us when he left. Eventually the phone went silent. The three of us on our own to fight for ourselves, amongst ourselves, our shouts and laughter and tears bouncing off the walls of our stalwart house, becoming an echo chamber and a mausoleum of memories.

A SUNDAY IN JULY, A YEAR SINCE OUR FATHER HAD DIS-appeared. A year of gossip and teasing, a year of making our world smaller.

Outside, the sun shone while we, in our itchy wool dresses, were condemned to the inner sanctum of the church basement. From the limbo of the tiny chairs in the Sunday school room, I could smell burned coffee and cigarette smoke, with an under-tone of paste and manila envelopes. *Anima Christi.*

Hattie was called to endure the punishment of doing chores for God and Mrs. Walker, as we often were on Sundays. A kind of agreed-upon penance that the Grayson girls deserved. She'd been hauled off almost as soon as we'd shuffled into the room. Mrs. Walker, that strict madam of ministry, that call girl of Catholicism, saw in our small family a host of sins. She prayed for, and preyed on, Hattie in particular. There was something in Hattie's soft innocence, her hair colour, that infuriated the Sunday school matron, and Hattie often spent Sundays cleaning baseboards with a toothbrush or scrubbing the diaper bucket from the nursery, gagging into her black velvet Polly Flinders shoulders. I waited, numbly, with the other children, for Mrs. Walker to return. I knew I should bail Hattie out, but too often I thrilled in seeing her punished. But still, I could hardly concen-trate when she was gone. She was a magnet to me and I to her; I hated that I couldn't help but love her, hated that this love made me feel obligated to protect her. Sometimes wishing I was an only child.

Time stretched out on this morning, and the other kids began to goof off, joking and whispering, but ignoring me. I kept an eye on the door, wondering where my sister was now. There was a scrape of feet and the creak of pews from above us in the sanctuary, the muted chorus of parents and grandparents coming through the floorboards. I looked out the half-window, which afforded a glimpse of the parking-lot asphalt. Time ticked by. Hattie wasn't usually gone this long. I was uneasy.

I looked out the doorway again and pushed out my chair.

"Where are you going?" snapped one of the older girls who was left in charge. "You aren't allowed to leave without asking me."

I ignored her and left the room.

I kept walking, down the hallway towards the storage room that doubled as Mrs. Walker's office. Ran my finger along the cold concrete brick wall that was painted a glossy white. In the groove, my finger going up and across, through a maze. I heard a *whap whap* as I approached the room. Mrs. Walker sometimes had Hattie bang out the blackboard brushes, which was something I actually loved doing. *Whap whap whap.* That sound, and now a whimper coming to my ears as well. What a baby. My patent leather Mary Janes were digging into my heels. *Whap whap whap.* Harder and louder. I rounded the corner to the storage room, the smells of dust and craft paint and old costumes rolling over me.

I saw Mrs. Walker, hunched over, her coarse black hair, streaked with wiry white, hanging in her eyes. And Hattie, palms up, her face red and wet.

"Penny!" she squeaked.

Mrs. Walker turned, a wooden yardstick in her hands. There was a strand of hair stuck to her lip.

"What are you doing here, Penelope?"

"I—I—" Hattie's hands were swollen and bright pink. Mrs. Walker was out of breath.

"Your sister, if that is what you're here for, defiled the belongings of this church. And of God."

"What do you mean?"

She wiped her hair from her face and threw down her yardstick. Grabbed a children's Bible from the table beside her, its bronze cover starting to tear, the name *Harriet Grayson* printed in crooked child's writing on a piece of masking tape curling from the front cover. Mrs. Walker opened it to the first page, where there were two circles drawn in pencil, little dots in their centres, and a triangle below.

"This." She shoved it under my nose, and I looked at the drawing.

Hattie, sniffling, said in a whisper, "It's a face."

I could see how she meant it to be a face, but to the trained eye of a curious kid like me, and apparently a grown-up like Mrs. Walker with an eye for judgement, it was a naked lady.

Mrs. Walker scoffed. "It's a sick depiction of a woman's nude body, and it will not be tolerated." She took back the Bible and muttered, smoothing her skirt, "Least of all by a little minx who has clearly learned a host of habits from her father." Hattie hung her head, knowing that this must be some kind of insult.

I lifted my chin up and said, "I did it."

Hattie looked at me, confused, her red hands at her side, palms still facing out.

Mrs. Walker regarded me carefully. "You expect me to believe that?"

"It's true. I did it. And it is a face, that part is true." I added that as an extra touch. Every lie needs an ounce of truth. "And leave our dad out of it."

"Harriet, get back to the Sunday school room so I can have a word with your sister."

"Yes, Mrs. Walker." Hattie's lip trembled, her teary eyes finding mine. I nodded, and her little shoes clip-clopped out of the room.

Once back in the Sunday school room, I refused to look at Hattie, who scooted her chair right next to mine. I smiled when another child picked on her. I could only go so far in love.

But later we compared hands. I liked how mine felt, and liked even more the feeling I'd had marching back to face all the other kids, my head high as the brave sister. I had stood in my sister's stead. Protected her, but also stole the spotlight, painful though it was. Hattie and our Sunday school classmates had stared at me with wonder, and it felt good. At home, we held icy cold cans of Coke in our hands and did not tell Mum, who made us cinnamon buns after church like she always did.

"Anything interesting happen in Sunday school today?" Mum wiped down the counter and ran the dishcloth under the tap. Hattie looked to me, her eyes wide. I shook my head sharply.

"We learned about Abraham and Isaac," I said, taking a bite.

"Hmm. I always found that story disturbing. Strange choice for children."

"Mrs. Walker says it's about sacrifice," Hattie piped up. I rolled my eyes.

Mum smiled at Hattie. "Well, sure. Isaac *was* the sacrifice."

"But he didn't do it," I said, meaning Abraham. "He just almost did it. Maybe he was never going to do it at all."

"Maybe," said Mum, filling the kettle. "But sometimes it's the thought that counts." She took a deep breath that signified a subject change, and sat at the table with us, pulling her cigarettes out of her apron and lighting one. "So! What are your plans for today? It's a gorgeous day out there."

"I want to go swimming!"

"That might be fun, Hattie. Penny, do you think you could take Hattie to the pool?"

"I guess."

"Did you have other ideas?" Eyebrows raised, Mum smoothed my hair down with a smile.

"I dunno. I wanted to ride my bike."

"Well, you two can ride your bikes there."

Hattie grinned at me, and I dampened it with a blank face until she looked away.

"Can't I just stay home with you, Mum?"

"No, honey. I've got lots of tidying up to do. Laundry and other exciting things far too fun for kids. I'll take a walk over later and watch how your dives are coming along, though, okay?" She squeezed my reddened hand, shooting pain up my arm, and I loved her.

Later, at the pool. Hattie puffed out her cheeks and sank her head beneath the water, her hair like red seaweed waving around in slow motion. She gestured and bugged out her eyes and mimed a tea party, begging me to join. I pretended not to understand her, pretended I didn't want to play, even if part of me did. Took to the ladder and walked proudly to the low diving board. My skin goosebumped, my hair matted in a black clump, I climbed the silver steps, looking for Mum. She was there, in a lounger, a long flowered dress hitched up to her knees, talking to another mom, smiling gamely and nodding her head. I caught her eye and she waved enthusiastically, dropping her cigarette in a puddle beside her chair. She threw up her hands and laughed at herself. The

other mother stared, unmoved. I walked across the pebbly diving board; the whole pool seemed to freeze. Mum clasped her
hands together and nodded. *You can do it*, she mouthed. I almost
lost my nerve. I waited. The kid behind me muttered under her
breath. I put my toes on the edge of the board and felt a shiver.
Hattie was climbing out of the pool in front of Mum. Her eyes
moved to Hattie. I took one bounce, and jumped, making as big
a splash as possible.

THAT NIGHT, HATTIE CLIMBED INTO MY BED AND WE
carefully pressed our hands against each other, fingers to the sky,
and I remembered why I loved her. How I couldn't help it, just
like no one else could. She smelled like fresh soap with an under-
current of chlorine, her post-bath, wet hair soaking my pillow.
She looked at our matching hands.

"Like we are praying," Hattie whispered, and her innocence
chafed against my newly hardened heart, and still softened it.

That year and those after, we prayed. For our father to return.
For everything to go back to the way it was before. And later, for
friends, for boys, and boobs. But then everything changed again,
and prayers didn't work where fists and flames did. Prayers got
lost when we whispered them up into the air, they got caught in
the branches of the maple tree in front of our house. I've spent the
past few years trying to shake them free, hoping that one of them
will flutter upwards and be read by the wind.

CHAPTER 2

I ENCOURAGED HATTIE TO TAKE EXTRA SHIFTS AT THE
salon, and urged her to read lots, after the fire. She needed
to be kept busy, distracted. We were together again, stuck in
time like bees in amber. One day she looked up from her book
while I was straightening up the sitting room.

"Leo Tolstoy said there are only two kinds of stories: man
goes on a journey, or a stranger comes to town."

"Oh yeah?" I looked at our mother's wingback chairs and
shifted the position of one.

"Yeah," she murmured, turning a page. "If only that were
true. No one ever comes here."

TOLSTOY WAS RIGHT.

A stranger did come to town, and it was like the moon
dropped out of the sky and broke open like an orange. By then
we had become St. Margaret's dangerous darlings. We were
young and pretty and had been touched by death and tragedy,
and the people of St. Margaret's, some with long memories, and
others without knowing why, avoided us like we were cursed.
They watched and whispered, but we had very few friends other

than one another. Because I was the widow, people largely left me alone. Hattie had initially let Officer Moore in, buckling under his kindness, his soft persistence. I noticed how his tender blue eyes, like so many others, had lingered after her when she left a room, trying to will the red mist of hair back as it swung out of sight. Her beauty like smoke that I hoped had clouded his judgement, but she got rid of him. Keep your enemies close and your sister closer. We might have been adult orphans now, but we'd learned enough growing up to know that secrets can't be split in more than half or they start to crumble, and you find pieces of them all over town in everybody's pockets, drifting up against the curb when the snow melts.

He changed everything, that stranger. Jameson Leung. And if I could turn back time now, I would still open the gate, leave the door open, I would usher him in despite it all. All over again.

"He's different," Hattie would say later. "Different from everyone else in this place."

I couldn't argue with that. He was. He was funny and strange and charming but also plain and good and true. Like he'd swallowed the sun. And, well, the sun had always favoured Hattie. She was the light in the corner, the warm side of the bed. I had been the darkness. We had a balance. But then it listed sideways.

The daycare where I worked as a director was attached to the public school: Arrow Park PS. *PS: You're still here. PS: You're never leaving.* It had been a small schoolhouse where our mum had gone as a kid, and Hattie and I after that, but had since grown with an addition and added portables in the back. We had waged the war of childhood there, and now I was an old general back from the front, with a torn uniform and scars the recruits couldn't see. I kept watch over the faded wooden playground with its bouncy bridge and the mock stained-glass pictures made with coloured tissue paper taped to the windows. When the weather was warm, and the windows were open, I watched toddlers in the yard as the chipper young women who worked there dusted sand off chubby bums. I listened as the children in the school sang the national anthem and said the Lord's Prayer, chairs squeaking against the plank floor when they returned to their seats.

Jameson was the young new teacher. He was taking over for a teacher going on maternity leave, and so joined just as the year was coming to a close. He was, as our mother would have described with a sparkly wink, *extraordinarily handsome*, with just the right lack of symmetry—in his case, his left arm ended at his elbow—to make him curiously exotic to the townspeople. Jameson Leung. He was as beautifully strange as anyone who had come to St. Margaret's in a good number of years. Mrs. Carr called him the Oriental Teacher with One Arm; one of my workmates called him the Knockout. As with most newcomers in a small town, people mainly watched him and talked about him incessantly to each other. He kept to himself, and was left largely alone. I, too, had been carefully keeping an eye on him for a couple of weeks before I took the plunge.

I introduced myself as Penelope Grayson, realizing at that moment that I had returned to my maiden name. I blushed as I said it, and Jameson shook my hand, saying, "Well, that's a nice name."

"Everyone calls me Penny."

"Okay, Penny. Everyone calls me Jameson."

Jameson: projecting loudly to the children in his classroom, running around, kicking a soccer ball, flying kites, cheering on the slower kids in the field behind the school. Getting on his bike at the end of the day and riding one-handed to wherever it was he lived, calling goodbye to me, and the daycare kids, on his way. At the end of June, while he was cleaning out his classroom, I invited him over for dinner.

I was overly cheery and nervous, conscious of the echo of my shoes on the floors. He turned when I knocked, a corrugated border in his hand, stepping down from a ladder. The left sleeve of his light blue dress shirt was knotted under his elbow. The sun was high in the sky, and a breeze moved everything in the room around, made it alive. Something about the room or the weather or Jameson made me feel giddy, and like taking risks. And so, I asked him to our house. *The house I share with my sister, Hattie.* He'd love to come, what could he bring, where did I live? An errant eyelash that stuck to his cheek caught my eye when I turned to leave. The breeze swirled around me. Blow it away. Make a wish.

I told Hattie what I was planning, and she'd raised an eyebrow.

"You never invite anyone over here."

"Yeah, I know. I dunno. I guess I felt sorry for him. He's nice, and he doesn't seem to have any friends." She was right, I knew. And immediately after asking him, I had felt a surge of anxiety. But it was too late for that now.

"You'll like him," I said.

"If you say so," she said, smiling.

"HELLO!" HATTIE NEARLY SHOUTED, ANSWERING THE door and taking Jameson's summer jacket, hanging it on the large gothic coat stand at the front door. "I'm Hattie—welcome!" She was so jolly, I noticed, alive and vibrant, so happy that the outside was coming in. I felt the panic return: a rush of regret for welcoming someone, even briefly, into the fold. But there was Hattie, filling up the house with her voice, her hair, her big laugh. She was so intoxicating. Sometimes shy and coy, other times boisterous and fun: she seemed to know which way to turn, like magic. Something slipped inside, and I knew I was already behind.

Jameson was laughing straightaway. I watched from the doorway of the kitchen as he took Hattie in, surprised and charmed by her brazen dissimilarity to me. I can pivot, too; I can adapt and change, but not like her. Never like she could. Jameson followed Hattie through the large front foyer into the kitchen, where I was making a salad. Seeds and dried fruit scattered on the cutting board, hands red from slicing beets, hair damp against my forehead. Hattie caught my eye and gave me a face of girlish approval.

"Jameson," I said. "So glad you could come. Beer?" And I wiped my hands on my apron, cracking open the bottle and handing it over, fingers touching.

Hattie, one step ahead already, clinked bottles with us both. "Want to eat outside?"

IT WAS THE PERFECT EVENING. BOTTLES FILLING THE centre of the table while we nibbled on the remains of the meal, and fireflies sparkled in the hedges around us.

Jameson lifting a bottle. "You two are so polite. I know you're wondering about my arm, so let's just have it out."

Hattie and I exchanged nervous glances and she giggled.

"No, not at all. I mean. You don't have to share it with us."

"Right." He smiled. "I'm sure you're right. It's not interesting." He sipped his beer. Hattie clasped her hands together like a child.

"No! Please tell us!"

"Hattie!"

"What? He started it!"

"I think you guys should just guess. Go ahead. I'll let you know if you're right."

I closed my eyes in embarrassment while Hattie's widened with excitement.

"Construction!"

"Car accident?" I ventured.

"Logging! Carpentry! You fell down a well!"

"Biking?"

Bold, cutting over another; Jameson grinning and shaking his head.

"You know this is really disrespectful to disabled people. Down a well, I ask you. And you call yourself a student of literature, Hattie. Where is your imagination?"

"Virgin sacrifice gone wrong!"

His smile a twitchy switch for us both, lighting the night, his aftershave and the summer scents mixing like a spell. I leaned back in my chair, watched a raccoon that was tight-wire tiptoeing over the fence at the far end of the property. Slowly moving along the edge with purpose.

"It was a hiking accident. A rock came away from part of the cliffside where we were hiking, my brother and I. It came out of nowhere and pinned my arm. My brother rolled the rock over with incredible—dare I say superhero—strength, and ran three kilometres to get help. It was too late to save my arm, but he did save my life with some quick-thinking first aid."

Jameson smiled, and silently lifted his smaller arm up and down. Shrugged his shoulders.

"Oh my God," said Hattie.

"What did you think? When you were waiting for him to come back?"

LAURIE PETROU

I was overcome with the urge to touch his arm. I felt myself touch my own where his ended. A spider dropped down from a hanging vine and skittered across the table.

Jameson paused, and then his face broke into a wide grin.

"Pathetic. Both of you." He laughed. "I was born this way. Never knew any different. Never wanted a prosthetic. It's incredible what we can adapt to. This is my arm, not a tragedy. Although, it's also amazing how people who suffer from trauma adapt." And what could we do but agree? I felt Hattie look at me quickly, and I was reminded of her love, her protection, our secrets. I looked into my lap and saw a long, red hair folded there like a promise, like a threat. Hattie's voice rang out.

"Well, now you're even more exotic to the women of St. Margaret's!" She poured the remains of her beer into her mouth. Winked. Jameson nodded his head in thanks, his neck going quite red. He glanced back at Hattie, and I saw their eyes meet. She didn't look away.

The night was clear and humid, and the three of us thrived in the warmth of the season, laughing and sharing stories and topping one another with witty barbs and outrageous anecdotes. Hattie was lovely and vivacious, and the night just made her more so: she bloomed like she couldn't help herself. But I knew she could. I felt a bubble of anger, and I thrilled in the familiar feeling before I pushed it down. I knew I had to concede, then: take myself out of the running so at least I had some feeling of control. Let her think this was my idea. Something lurched in my stomach. I had been here before. I had seen the eyes of some- one I loved shift towards my sister. I recognized the boiling hate that would start as a simmer but become a fire. I stamped it out. Refused to let this happen again. And so, I told myself it was what I'd wanted all along, Hattie with Jameson. I could trust

Jameson. He was an outsider like us. I could keep them close. Yes. It would be good for her. Almost like a gift to her. I let out a breath, and smiled.

SHE MET ME IN THE KITCHEN A LITTLE LATER.

"Wow, he is *great*," she said.

I laughed and nodded. "He seems to like you."

She looked worried. "No, not at all! He is totally into you."

"Hattie." I levelled my eyes at her. "Please. Don't bother with the act. It's already done. He's all yours. I actually, you know, think he might be a little too goody-goody for me."

"Sure?"

"Sure. But Hattie," I put my hand firmly on her arm, "he can never know. Never."

Hattie took a deep breath, and nodded seriously.

"I promise," she whispered. And then, in a blink, she was smiling again. Took a deep breath like she was ready for it, ready for something wonderful.

"Okay. Wow, you know, he is so great." She looked out the window at Jameson, his back to us. "What are the chances? I mean, this could be something, you know?"

I watched while she put a grape in her mouth, eyes twinkling.

"Steady on, girl," I said.

She snuggled up to me and kissed my cheek, and her gratitude threatened to relight my irritation. I shook my head, smiling, shook off my frustrations.

WE STAYED OUT ON THE PATIO LATE INTO THE NIGHT. Eventually I rose to leave Hattie with Jameson. Her eyes on him, her face rosy, her hands moving as she spoke. I pushed my chair back against the stones, making a choice. I went inside without a word and didn't come out again. Washed a wine glass carefully, my hand fitting into the fragile bowl, knowing what a dangerous mess it would make if it shattered.

I heard Hattie's voice through the open window over the sink, mentioning my name, and I couldn't help but listen, my body frozen like a bloodhound.

"Her husband, Buddy, died in a fire."

CHAPTER 3

BUDDY IS GONE, BUT HE VISITS ME AT NIGHT. He did then, and he does now. It would be easier if he were angry in my dreams, but with his rough tough love, he tries to convince me that it wasn't justice, that it wasn't justified. It was.

He crashes about my subconscious, his boyish face looking irritated, which was always a short jump to anger. He was sometimes the life of the party—loud, fun and affectionate—but could just as easily be sullen and short-tempered. He was an unpredictable drunk, something his friends knew well, but that I knew better. I had to be ready for when he might slip into the worst side of himself.

I wasn't all that bad, Penny, he mutters in my dreams. *You make me sound like a monster. I mean, didn't we both get carried away? Did you really need to go that far? Did I deserve to die?* He smiles and rubs his stubbly face, grinning, like it was all a game. *You could be such a bitch, Penny.* He laughs, gruffly. *I love how you think you're such a fucking saint.* Smiling, rolling up his sleeve. *We were good fighters. Like Sid and Nancy, isn't that what Mac used to call us? Scrappy. We fought all over town, didn't we, Pen? Come here.* Reaching out, smiling. Smile fading. *I said, come here.*

In the early months after the fire, I often dreamed of being stuck in a room with him. His huge body blocking the doorway. Hattie on the other side.

Sometimes I woke in a sweat to Hattie sitting at the edge of my bed.

"He's gone, Penny. It's okay, he's gone." Running her fingers through my sweaty short hair. "Go back to sleep. You're safe."

"You don't know what it's like to have these nightmares, Hattie." My fingers reached to touch an earlobe, where an earring would be.

She would pause for a long time.

"I dream about fires, Penny." Covering me with a blanket and turning out the light. I would watch her silhouette retreating from the doorway.

"But when I wake up, they have always gone out."

THE NIGHT JAMESON CAME TO DINNER, I FELL ASLEEP quickly, but was soon awake again. I tossed in my sheets. Convincing myself I'd had too much to drink, I stumbled to the bathroom to get a wet cloth for my face. The window was open and I stood still, damp terry cloth on my cheeks, listening to the cicadas chirping rhythmically. Taking deep breaths. It was summer. My favourite time. I was safe. I was right.

THE NEXT DAY, JAMESON SOUGHT ME OUT IN THE CHILdren's cubby room. He looked a little pale, standing among the rubber boots and sun hats, the handprints and photo collages, but was smiling and I knew that Hattie was at the bottom of it, sloshing about with the beer and wine. That morning she had giggled her way through breakfast while I rolled my eyes, asserting myself as older and wiser and not putting up with nonsense. I thought I'd try the same with Jameson.

"Well, helloooo there," he ventured, sidling up to me while I tied my outdoor shoes. Giving me a nudge with his elbow. I laughed.

"How are you feeling?"

"Ah, you know. A little fragile, a little tender, thanks to the Grayson sisters and their magic elixirs. You two are trouble." He deadpanned, "Really, I blame the town of St. Margaret's. No one warned me. There was nothing in my welcome package."

"Ha. Maybe one of us is more trouble than the other."

He nodded, a goofy smile spreading on his face.

"Yes . . . ?" I looked at him with the same impatient look I'd given Hattie that morning.

Jameson laughed. "Oh! Right, right. Uh, okay, here it is: Would you mind if I asked out Hattie? There, I said it."

"Please do. Really." I stood and patted his shoulder, like he was doing me a favour, and pushed that jagged shard of jealousy into the breast pocket of my wounded heart. "You two really hit it off."

He grinned, and looked away, happy.

Later on, Hattie was taking laundry off the line outside.

"He's different, Penny."

"You said."

"Seriously. He made a very good first impression."

"So did you. First class, Harriet."

She grinned and sniffed a towel. "Don't you love the smell of stuff that has dried in the sun?"

"There's an earwig on that towel."

She screeched and shook it out, laughing hysterically.

THAT FIRST NIGHT BECAME A SERIES OF THE SAME, FOR that threesome of bosom buddies that was Jameson and Hattie and me, lounging and listening to the sounds of trees and insects and feeling the yawning space between reality, and the dreamy, sticky draw of new love, of sisters, and of friendship closing like a lazy trap.

Sometimes it felt like our lives were made up of summers. My memories of early childhood, before our father left, of growing up and out, opening my arms to possibility like Maria from *The Sound of Music*: all the action took place on the hot and sunny days. Something about the heat and the humidity made us rash and impulsive. Summers held a spell on us that winters never could. In our drafty old house, a season that brought the clanking furnace and heavy blankets built up unshed energy that we could hardly wait to blow off come the spring. All the big things happened during the summertime, like the Fates were saving their strength in the cold, pooling their resources to let loose a spark of events after the thaw. The summer was our season: open windows and doors, breezes blowing right through the house, bringing all manner of mischief with them.

In the ways that young people are so good at, Hattie and Jameson and I slept late, started the ritual of summertime partying early, drank and sang and twirled our hair in our fingers; we made exotic food and still settled for potato chips, told awful jokes, bumped into each other in the middle of the night, and did the whole thing again the next day. For Hattie and me, work ended each day while the sun was high in the sky, and soon Jameson was done teaching for the year. Often we came home to find him in the kitchen, making a mess, half in the bag, happy as can be. Music was loud but always perfect, the beer was always cold, Hattie's arms around his waist, and there we were: children playing parts, sweet summer fruit dribbling down our chins.

Hattie and Jameson were falling in love right in front of me; we were always together, but somehow, she and I were cut loose from each other.

Maybe I didn't need to watch her so closely anymore. She didn't seem to need me as much, or require me in the same way, she didn't seem so unpredictable. Secret safe. Game, set, match.

Late one Saturday afternoon, when the three of us were trying our hand at making fancy cocktails, there was a knock at the door. Jameson went to answer it.

"Hi," I heard him chirp cheerfully.

"Oh—hello."

Hattie and I exchanged looks, and she hurried into the hallway, wiping her hands on a towel.

"Iain, hi!" she trilled.

I watched them from the doorway, lifting my hand in greeting to Officer Moore.

"I was just," he cleared his throat, "just nearby. Thought I'd pop by to say hello, but, I see," he looked at Jameson, who had put his arm around Hattie casually, "that you've got company."

Jameson removed his arm from Hattie's waist and shook Officer Moore's hand, introducing himself, inviting him in. Iain ducked his head and, mumbling an excuse, made his exit, walking almost silently down the path. Hattie looked at me, a faint smile on her lips.

I shut the door, thinking foolishly that our worries were behind us. We returned to the frivolity of the kitchen; the sweet, minty drinks all the more refreshing for the interruption.

* * *

IT WAS A TRICK. OUR HAPPINESS COULDN'T LAST, AND sure, part of me knew that even then, but I needed to believe that I could be free. I let the summer wash over me in a flood of music and late nights and long talks. It was just the three of us. The sisterhood, the secret club, had widened its membership, but only by one. We had let Jameson in, wholesale—nothing gradual—and shut the gates with a clang, turning up our boom box in the garden, grape leaves hanging down into our conversations, while down the street the local pub rang out the same hits for people from our high school who were playing darts and forgetting us until the gossip came around to our tragic loss. But Jameson wasn't from St. Margaret's; he was a cut above, just as I'd always, frankly, considered myself, and even Hattie, to be. We were different from our peers, from those people we went to high school with who never had a kind word to say about us anyway. They could have their stag and does, their nights at the Legion—I had tried it all once already, with Buddy. I would take our house over that life any day.

"IT'S CRAZY TO THINK THAT WE'VE BEEN IN THIS HOUSE our whole lives," I mused one day, while we were peeling peaches in an eleventh-hour bid to do some preserving. Jameson lifted the lid on the canning pot to inspect the sterilization process. Hattie was sitting at the table reading. She lifted her head.

"This house has seen a lot." She gave me a tiny smile.

"I bet," Jameson said. "Were there a lot of kids on your street, growing up?"

"Sure," I said, glancing at Hattie. "Our house was kid headquarters for a while."

She nodded, dropping her eyes. There was a time, she and I both knew, when everyone stopped coming. At first out of our control, and later, much later, by our design.

I thought of young Hattie now, in those early days.

"God, Hattie, you were irresistibly cute. Jameson, we'll have to show you some pictures. No one could say no to her, even then."

"No doubt." He kissed the top of her head.

Our childhood: its sweetness, its sourness. Two sides of it.

A late afternoon hauled up from memory. She was ten and I was thirteen. I was curling my hair in the mirror. I looked at her in the reflection. She was a little leprechaun, I used to tell her. All except the luck. She was bad luck.

"Penny, is it because of me that he didn't come back?" her image asked me.

I regarded her coolly.

"Sometimes I think so, yes," I said. "I mean, I'm sure you didn't mean to, but he did leave right after, didn't he? I just wonder," I brushed my large curls to the side, "if he'd have stayed if you'd never taken those earrings."

Hattie twisted her fingers.

"Yeah." She looked at me, and offered her hand for the curling iron. "It looks good. Want me to do the back?"

I handed it to her, and she worked silently. We could hear Mum in the kitchen, chopping something for dinner. The smell of pasta sauce and meatballs wafted down the hallway. She was singing from the kitchen. Out of tune, happily opening and closing cupboards. I looked at my reflection, solemnly assessing my likeness to a grown and sexy woman. My eyes kept straying to the red-headed kid in the background.

I often asked about our father, hoping each time that my questions would reveal new information that I could collect and store away. Our mother rebuffed my questions, changed the subject, making up for his absence in many large and small ways.

Hattie and I were lucky—blessed, doted upon, challenged and truly loved by our mother, who had done a bang-up job of making up for our father's abandonment of us. This didn't stop me, though, from tormenting Hattie, who I blamed for everything. Sometimes I let her find me, crying dramatically in my bed, and I would tell her I missed Daddy.

"You wouldn't understand," I said. "You didn't really know him."

I was both the tormentor and the tormented. I felt insecure at times, like a failure; I didn't know where to put my arms, I sucked my thumb too long, and hated my hair. Hattie was a pain and a drag and got all the attention, and I loved her and hated her. Life was a tricky balance, but in the end, I knew I could curl up in Mum's lap at any time and listen to her slow heartbeat and voice while she stroked my hair at the temples.

We told Jameson all about the happy parts of our childhood, and willed it back to clarity. This house, which had only ever seemed to have the capacity to hold three: Mum, Dad and me, Hattie, Mum, and me, and now the three of us. Jameson listened, soaking up the memories we chose to tell him, like he was learning a language. Jars of peaches bubbled in the pot, and our faces got sweaty and smiley.

"Remember when Mrs. Donkersley was pregnant and on bedrest?"

"They wheeled her in a bed through the summer solstice parade!"

Moms and dads on the street brought cold drinks and watermelons and chairs that folded out in bright nylon criss-crosses that had begun to fray. There were two sets of wooden bleachers, side by side. I remember the weight of stepping down through them, coming from the top, the sound of my sandals hitting the washed-out wood. I'd wobble and grab a seat to right myself, a splinter occasionally slipping into my skin. There were games all day and into the evening. Races and tosses and watermelon-eating contests. Parents cheering from the stands, drinking from cans of beer, the sun reddening their shoulders. Three-legged and potato-sack races, egg tosses.

But then, after, we didn't go to the summer parties. It was an unsaid rule that we weren't welcome anymore. Mum would have a picnic for us in the backyard to distract us, but nothing could take away the sounds of the parade, the games, the noise of people whose lives hadn't been rocked by small-town scandal. Eventually we would go inside, and watch TV in the darkened den, turning up the volume to drown out summer.

I saw in that summer with Hattie and Jameson something of the old happy whimsy, the appeal of an unstructured game played outside, the avoidance of something dark behind the clouds. I know now that these things can't go on, and maybe I knew it even then, that you can't truly stop anything the Fates have in store, that the wind changes and a chill blasts through even the most enthusiastic summer plans with the force of a bottle rocket. It would come. But I will forever look back on that time and see us, crystallized in youth, and when I see Hattie in my dreams, it is that Hattie: the one with the hearty laugh, the blazing eyes, the gall.

I HEARD SOMETHING RATTLING ABOUT ONE SUNDAY AS I turned over in my bed, pulling the covers to my eyes to push away the chirping birds in the still-dark morning. It was coming from downstairs. Thumping, the occasional giggle, at first moving into my pre-waking dreams, that slippery limbo of real noises and subconscious stories. There was a crash, and I pulled off my covers, heart beating, and moved quickly to the hallway.

"Hattie?" I called.

There was a small gasp, then Hattie said, "Sorry, Penny! We didn't mean to wake you!"

I groaned and rubbed my face. There was no crisis.

"What the hell are you doing down there?"

Jameson now: "We're gonna go fishing. Do you want to come?"

"Absolutely not." I turned to go back to my bedroom when I saw Hattie coming up the stairs. She was wearing a large green fishing vest with bright things hanging off it. Grinning like a fool.

"Come on, Penny! It'll be so fun. We have all Grandpa's old equipment and Jameson has some stuff, too. We're all sorted. We even have hip waders!"

"Huh. Do you think maybe you could have gotten it all out before bed last night instead of, say, now?"

"Sorry. That noise was the fishing rods. I don't know why Mum stored them so high." She grasped my arm.

"Probably because no one has ever used them before. Hattie, just let me go to bed."

"Sorry, can't do that. I really think this is something you need."

"I do not need this, trust me. Come on, Hattie." I moved towards my bed. But she was like a small yippy dog, and nattered at me until I agreed, angrily, to join them. We piled into Mum's old car, and I spread out on the back seat as I had so many times as a child. Jameson drove us to the lake, minutes away, although I had fallen back asleep by then. Tires on gravel. We walked along the dock of the marina, where other fishermen were pushing off and starting their mornings.

"Do we even have a boat?"

"A friend of mine said we could use his. It's not much of a boat, really, just a row boat—ah, here it is." Jameson located a rusty old red rowboat that looked like it belonged hidden in some reeds at an old cottage and not at the marina with all the yachts and large motor boats. He heaved our bag of bait and other fishing odds and sods into the boat and it rocked alarmingly.

"Is that going to fit us all?" I asked, hoping I could go back home.

"Oh yeah. We're not leaving you, Penny. And come here." Jameson took my hand and helped me in. "I've got some special coffee for us."

Even for a tea drinker, Baileys in coffee makes for a much more interesting fishing trip. The sun coming up bright and warm, soon we were laughing in our cups with fish flapping around in the bottom of the boat long enough to make us scream and scare the rest away. We threw them all back, their slimy tails in our hands for just a moment, we three cackling and causing a ruckus. Scowls from other boats.

Eventually we tired of fishing, and lay lazily, rocking gently, Jameson at one end and Hattie and me at the other. My arm dangled over the side and made a trail through the cold water. My eyes closed, the Baileys easing me into a sunny morning cat-nap. Light playing colourfully behind my eyelids. Hattie's and Jameson's voices blended into the lapping water. There was a childlike safety in being with them, never feeling like a third wheel but more like a coddled youngster; they were both so afraid of leaving me out that I was at liberty to do what I liked in their company without criticism or judgement. For now, anyway.

* * *

I WOKE WITH THE SUN PRICKLING BRIGHTLY. HATTIE WAS sleeping, head on arm. I sat up, and cleared my throat. Jameson turned around and smiled.

"Morning, Sunshine."

"I forgot where I was," I said, rubbing an eye.

"I'm so glad you came." Jameson reached over and squeezed my arm. "You make everything better, Penny. And . . ." he turned to root in his tackle box, "I think it's a goddamn shame that you haven't heard that more often."

I was quiet. He was talking about Buddy. Hattie had told him about Buddy's hands on me, his fists and fury.

He turned back to me and took my hand. His was soft and warm. "You are loved, Penny."

My face went hot and I was overcome. I wanted him, all of him. I wanted to push Hattie out of the boat and take him away. It flitted in my brain like a fish jumping out of the water. Next moment, Jameson was breaking the tension with a joke about the one-armed fisherman, because frankly, despite his best efforts, fishing was not a sport that came easily to him. Desire dove out of sight. I pulled myself back. Kindness. Love. Hattie stirred and yawned and I remembered who I was: older sister, best friend, guardian.

CHAPTER 4

I N THE TIME BEFORE MUM DIED, BEFORE I MET BUDDY, Hattie and I were navigating who we were, and where we each stood on the moving map of growing up. I got a call, in the city where I was living. Far from St. Margaret's, but not far enough.

"I'm coming down to visit, Penny."

It was Hattie. She was sixteen, and her loud voice broke through the phone like an electric shock.

She was so bold now, her confidence growing with her years, and it was unnerving. I didn't feel quite so self-assured, trying on my different selves like masks. I dreaded the thought of my younger, increasingly attractive sister bursting onto my carefully constructed scene.

"It's really not worth it, Hattie. There's nothing going on tonight."

"I don't care. I have to get out of here." I heard her inhale.

"Are you smoking?"

"So what?" Her voice holding in the smoke and letting it out in a dramatic relief.

"Jesus. Hattie, don't come down. I don't think it's a good idea." I thought of my friends, alternately doting or being turned on by my pretty little sister, with her radiance alive like a man-eating plant. I was being protective, but I didn't know of whom.

"I'm not asking your permission, I'm just telling you." She paused. "Anyway, Mum says it's alright." I heard a scramble and noise in the background. "Mum! Do you ever knock?"

I heard Mum. "Good Lord, Hattie, are you smoking in here?"

"No. Can you tell Penny it's okay for me to go visit?"

"It's okay, Penny! Try and knock some scholarly sense into her, will you?" She shouted in the direction of the phone.

I rolled my eyes and lay back on my bed. "Fine. Just—just try not to get out of control, okay?" This was my life, after all, and if anyone was going to let it go to shit, it was me.

I left St. Margaret's right after high school. Said goodbye to small-town gossip, judgement and Hattie. I had been growing my hair for five years, and it was long and lusty and black and I was ready to fling it over my shoulder while dancing and drinking cheap beer in the city. I had been accepted at university to study the Romance languages, and dreamed of living in France one day. I moved downtown immediately, months before school started. At that moment, my aspirations were more about shaking off what it meant to be one of the Grayson girls. I'd grown resentful of St. Margaret's, a place that had turned its back on me. I wanted to reinvent myself, as so many teenagers do. *Ha ha*, I had laughed at the rear-view mirror, checking my eyeliner and kissing the wind as it blew by, my hand at the wheel of an old, unreliable car I had bought myself as a graduation gift.

I got a job straightaway at a bookshop, to help me pay for my crappy apartment, tuition and books. I moved in with four other girls in a tiny apartment downtown, near Heaven, a disco bar that would eventually exchange its glitter balls for glam rock and hair bands, but for now lit up in mirrored optimism. We shared the rent and the rooms, enacting a repeating and overlapping cycle where at any given time an unconscious girl could be found beside a high one near someone making food, and another primping her hair. Then we'd switch, round and round we'd go.

School started, and I buckled down during the weekdays, after months of partying. I soaked up everything my professors said, desperate for my education and grades to be the currency of change in my life, if not the world. I wrote letters home to Hattie, telling her about other students, about lecture halls and crazy librarians, painting a picture of vaulted halls of learning, trying to impress her, but of course, the letters were accidental lures, and she was the big fish.

Hattie, sixteen and wild—trying to be like me and different from everyone else—began visiting constantly. She borrowed our mother's car, smoked all the way, arriving coughing and hacking through a cloud of hairspray and smoke. She'd open the door to my apartment with her arms wide open, laughing loudly, hooting like an old friend, drinking and trying more, but wearing and caring less than I did. *Who's Red?* people would ask me, while I sat one out, leaning against the corner of a dirty bar. I'd squint into the smoke, not wanting to see the girl of my childhood. She had no interest at that time in following my dreams of higher learning, but opted instead for just getting higher.

When I'd found her making out with a much older musician who happened to have come back to our apartment, I pushed her towards the front door, grabbing her knapsack and purse on the way. I shoved her keys at her and opened the door, hustling her outside.

"Out."

She looked at me, furious, and pointed at my ears, where I was wearing Mum's earrings. I touched one of them self-consciously.

"I see you didn't leave home without your prized possession," she scoffed. "Too bad you forgot everything else important."

I ignored this comment. "Hattie. Please. You're just acting out to get attention. You and I both know it."

I closed the door and turned up the volume.

I told her she couldn't come anymore, told Mum I needed to focus on school, and that Hattie was out of control, a distraction, a nuisance. The next day Hattie screamed into the phone at me that I had ruined her life, that she hated me, and hated Mum, and hated me all over again for telling Mum to keep her at home. I let the phone ring when I thought it might be her: it rang and rang, and I tried to ignore that fiery sister who was scowling into her pink phone a childhood away.

It was a blazing hot autumn, fall trying to wear summer's clothing. The weekend after I banned Hattie was unseasonably warm. I remember this because I can't help it.

When something changes your life, you remember everything. The colours are brighter, the sounds louder, the emotions greater. And you keep those things, all the small things, in your memory, for years. I'm sure Hattie has a different version of events, but I'm not interested.

That afternoon, Hattie, pouting about staying home, was parked in my old room in front of a fan, with her earphones on and the music blasting her brains out. She didn't go outside, where the sun was dripping like a juicy peach, where Mum was wiping her forehead and drinking in the sweetness of gardening on a dopey fall day that thinks it's summer. Lazy bees flying drunkenly around in the twilight of their days. I remember this, I swear I do. I wasn't there, but I know what happened.

A bee. A swollen, overfed, over-the-hill soldier took a break on the grass. And in that tiny moment, a moment the size of a bug, Mum leaned back—I can see it in my mind's eye—and put her hands down on the grass behind her. Her palm flattening the big little bastard.

Hattie was inside, listening to records I'd left behind, feeling so damn sorry for her poor self that she could hardly even get up. The unfairness of life weighing her down like a lead blanket.

Outside, there was a yelp, I imagine. A yelp, and a quickening of her breath. Oh, but if I had been there to hear her. A last word, a tiny murmur, a plea for help, anything.

Maybe everything jumped into focus for her, too. She knew Hattie wasn't coming. She knew she was on her own. If I'd been home, I would have sprung into action, I would have sucked the stinger out of her hand and held it tight all the way to the hospital. And Hattie, upstairs, now and always, aware of nothing beyond her perky nose.

What did my mother see as she lay in that garden, an expanse of green and red and pink and yellow? The Russian sage waved *no no no* and the sumac hung its head. The sunflowers leaned right over as if to lift her up, but by then her throat was swelling like a tomato full of the heat of the day and if only someone had bitten in, she'd have had some relief.

"WHAT SONG, HATTIE? WHAT FUCKING SONG WERE YOU listening to when you let her die? What. Fucking. Song?" I had grabbed her thin shoulders.

"Penny, please. Please stop. Please." She was sobbing. "I didn't know. I'm sorry, Penny."

I pushed her away.

"Fine. Don't tell me. It'll haunt you for the rest of your fucking life anyway."

45

When you are sixteen, like Hattie was, you are in between. You look like every grown-up tries to look for the rest of their lives, you are in full bloom. You are legs and boobs and hair and skin. But only five years ago you were holding your mother's hand, ten years ago you were sucking your thumb. And if, when you are sixteen, you are the absent witness to the death of your mother, who lay in the dog-tired tomato plants for far longer than she should have, then, well, it's no joke, that will fuck you up forever.

But when you're nineteen, and your sister couldn't unplug the curly black cord of her own self-absorption long enough to save the one person who was like a real live saint in your life, well, you can't help but be full of a reasonable amount of hate, can you?

CHAPTER 5

AFTER OUR MOTHER'S DEATH, I WAS IN CHARGE of Hattie. I became her guardian. I should have rushed to her side, but I didn't. I left her in the house alone. I made her lie for me when people asked after me, told her to tell people I was tying up loose ends in the city. Sometimes she stayed at our neighbours, the Carrs, and I told myself she was fine. That I was, too. But I know now I wasn't. On the outside, I put on phony smiles the way I caked on make-up. Fake it till you make it, right? That's what they say. They don't know.

And one day, a guy walked into the bookshop, and he looked familiar and big and good-looking and like he didn't give a shit about music or books or art or anything cool, which was exactly what I was looking for.

"Hey," he said gruffly, a bit of a frown on his face. My stomach jumped. "Do you guys sell maps?"

"Sure. Are you lost?" I smirked, sure I knew him from somewhere. His brow furrowed at the jab, but just for a moment. Then he smiled and looked me up and down, and I reddened a little. That face, those youthful dimples that belied the huge frame. Goddamn, he was cute. I was done for.

"No. Well, I'm hoping to avoid that. I need to get to McCaul Street."

"You're close. You look familiar. You live near here?" I laughed at my mistake. "Right, obviously not."

"I recognize you. You're one of the Grayson girls, right?"

St. Margaret's had found me in the city, and rather than repel me, that drew me to him. I wanted to be wanted by this guy. I wanted him to carry me through doorways in his arms. I wanted to be under him and on top of him.

"Penny. I'm Penny."

He put out a meaty hand. "Buddy Collerfield. I think I was a few years ahead of you at school."

I nodded, recognizing the name. Shook his hand. Large, soft.

And went home with him. All the way home, back to St. Margaret's.

BUDDY SEDUCED ME, MIND, BODY AND SOUL. HE WAS unpolished and a bit defensive, but good-looking and sexy, and didn't want anyone else looking at me. It was intoxicating. As I got to know him, I saw that he was also proud, competitive and argued too much with his friends, especially Mac, a man who was more like a brother, who brooded and snarled, fighting dirty like the runt of the litter when they got into scraps. I thought Buddy's passionate personality was conviction, found his temper sexy and commanding. He flirted and flattered me. He often pulled me tightly to his body, moving his large hands all over me, hushing me when I tried to protest.

"You're too smart for me," he said one night, while we sat on the hood of his truck and looked out over the town from the top of the hill. "I'm a little more," he ran a finger up my arm, "basic in my needs." He sipped from a bottle of beer from the case beside him.

I looked out over the town. The city had, in spite of my dreams, left me feeling untethered, unanchored. In all the years of fighting against the suffocation of St. Margaret's, I had come to depend on it. It was what I was used to, for better or worse. I was resignedly glad to be back. This was familiar, if not entirely good.

"You're wrong," I said, scooping myself under his arm and shivering. "I am just the right amount of smart for you."

He chuckled and kissed me hard, and I melted into him.

Down there, in the sleepy town, was my house. Waiting patiently. And my sister, who was also waiting. But I didn't see them. I saw hair that fell into Buddy's eye, and pushed it aside.

"I have to make sure you don't go leaving me for any of those university nerds," he said, gently, his face clouding over in a way I was now familiar with.

"Never," I soothed, stroking his large arms.

"I have to keep you. I love you, Penny Grayson," he said, his voice catching. In that moment, the hill could have eroded under us, taking the truck and the trees and destroying the town beneath us. And I would have floated above it all. Youth. Love. Grief. Put them together, and it is the most dangerous elixir. His strength and protectiveness would become bullying and violence, but I couldn't imagine that then.

He had lifted me out of the well. Out of my grief. And because of that, I avoided Hattie. In her, I saw only sadness, and I couldn't go back down there. Instead, I pushed her away so I could breathe. She'd held on to me in solidarity, assured that I would raise her and save her; I shook her off, and made promises to myself instead. I got a job back in town, at the daycare. I spent my days doting on children, a cozy future on my mind.

Buddy asked me to marry him. It was not unusual for people to marry straight out of high school in St. Margaret's, and so we fit right in. I didn't mind being typical. It appealed to my new desire to be part of everything about Buddy's life. More, I suddenly saw school as expensive, when compared to the chance to start a real life with someone who loved me, who wanted me with him. I no longer wanted to be an outsider to St. Margaret's; I saw the comfort in being back in the fold. Quitting school felt right: I needed to be home with my soon-to-be husband, to care for my family, and yes, for Hattie. I was proud of my decisions; they demonstrated my selflessness, my duty and my larger-than-life love. I ignored nagging doubts that picked at me like an itch, making plans to move in with Buddy, into a home just for us. I told myself that we would be close enough to Hattie, that she would be fine in our old house. Buddy had assured me that we would all be family, but that he needed me.

"You're going be my wife, Penny. Your sister can take care of herself. It's not right for her to live with us," he looked at me firmly, "I just won't have it." I liked that he wanted me all to himself, then hated myself for it later.

HATTIE WALKED ME DOWN THE AISLE ON MY WEDDING day, clutching and crying. A couple of sad beauties in the eyes of our town. Later, Hattie, the maid of honour, drunk and grinning her pain away, twirled on the wooden floor at the wedding reception, all eyes on her. I sipped flat Champagne and looked at my new husband, who, I noticed, was watching Hattie also. Buddy's bright blue eyes, already getting that look I had learned to recognize as his drunkenness, fixed on the pixie schoolgirl. I smiled, thinking that he was proud of his new family.

* * *

"YOU'RE SO LUCKY," SAID HATTIE, WATCHING ME PACK
the last of my things. I hadn't stayed often with Hattie in the
house before the wedding, but she had gotten used to my being
around again. She wiped a tear, and I looked the other way. The
late summer sun came through the window, brightening the room.

"You're gonna be okay here by yourself, Hattie."

"Sure, I guess. I mean, are you sure you and Buddy don't
want to move in here? There's lots of room."

"Yeah, I know. But, you know, we just got married. We want
our own space. And," I looked around, "I need a break from this
place."

"Yeah. Yeah, okay."

"We'll come over all the time, though, I promise."

"I know."

"Maybe we should get you a dog or something." We. We.
We. I wore my marriage like a badge, and didn't see myself for
the child that I still was.

She laughed and turned away, rolling up a poster that lay on
the bed. "No, that's okay. Not right now."

"You'll be so busy with school soon, and going out with your
friends, that you'll hardly miss me, I promise."

Hattie fiddled with a loose thread on her bedspread as she
watched me.

"I'm sorry, Penny. I'm sorry Mum missed your wedding."
Her voice was breaking again, and I gave her a quick smile and
turned away.

I couldn't look at her. "We didn't know, right? She was bound
to be stung eventually. She was always outside, but we just never
knew she had a bee thing." I clenched my teeth, put my head into
my closet and grabbed a bunch of hangers.

"Yeah." She hiccupped a sob back. "Um. Maybe, Penny, we could have dinners here? I'm not that good at cooking, but we could order in food or whatever."

"For sure. Great idea. I'll tell Buddy, I'm sure he'll love that."

AND HE DID, ACTUALLY. HE HELD MY HANDS TO HIS lips. He reassured me that any family we had would include Hattie.

"She's my little sister, too, Pen," he said, his husky voice like a love potion. I know he meant it, and that he did love me, for whatever it's worth now. In my deepest, smoking heart I know. He wasn't all bad, or even mostly bad, but the part that was, was terrible. Finding that part of him was like stumbling into a trap and discovering it had teeth only after its jaws were around your ankle.

True to his word, we often had Hattie over to our house, which was walking—or running—distance from our family home. Our house—mine and Buddy's—was a small bungalow set beside an unused barn. The property was larger than we'd ever need. I loved it, and I loved seeing Hattie kicking up the dusty country road in her sneakers, playing grown-up by bringing a bottle of wine, or a dessert from the local baker. In the winter, she appeared out of the white, a snowy vision. Bustling into the door with a burst of icy wind behind her, her cheeks and nose bright pink.

"Hattie, you look frozen!" Buddy would rush over, helping her out of her coat. "But beautiful, of course." She laughed into his face like he was the best older brother.

"Right, the snotty nose is really a great look. Hi, Penny!" She'd call in to me. "Smells great in there!"

Everything seemed fine then, in those snatched moments. I wish our mother could have seen how things were falling into place, how we looked out for her, made room for her. Those days and nights. Playing cards and laughing. Buddy's hand on Hattie's back as he moved past her in the kitchen. Lingering looks, kindly ones on her face. Making a home. A family. There was a kinship between them, that was all, I told myself. I was lucky they were so close.

Then, always, at the end of the night, I looked at my watch, and Hattie blushed and said she should be getting on her way. Buddy offered to drive her home and I said that she was fine to walk; her agreeing quickly. Not calling for a while. Knowing she was okay, all by herself. I was trying to make a new life. I was trying to get on. New love. But nothing stays new.

Closing cupboards too hard. Muttering. Sarcasm swirling in my glass. I hated myself when I felt this way.

"What's the problem, Penny? I was just being nice."

I wanted to believe him. That it was just me, being jealous.

"You said to make her feel at home here!" Rubbing his chin in pretend confusion. "Jesus, Penny, I do not understand you sometimes."

"Well, no kidding," I mumbled.

"You're drunk."

"I'm not," I said, but wondered if maybe I was.

"You're acting crazy. I'm going for a walk."

So many nights. Words bigger and meaner, twisting my thoughts, each trying to top the other, trying to blow each other away.

And when words weren't enough, shoves, elbows, slaps to make me see. Make me understand.

There are days I wake up and am sure I can smell smoke.

CHAPTER 6

THE DAY AFTER THE FIRE.

"I'm going to the morgue, Hattie. They want me to identify him."

"Do you want me to come with you?"

She had just hung up the phone. The local paper had called, wanting details of the fire. What happened. What a tragedy. Hattie's voice had been cold and far away as she'd answered them. *Please respect my sister's privacy in this very difficult time.*

"I don't think so. I think I should go alone."

We never spoke of it. I was superstitious. Whenever Hattie began to discuss what had happened—*Shouldn't we talk about this, Penny?*—I shut her down. I was afraid our house would rat us out somehow. I was afraid that even in those hallowed halls, our secret would escape, rush up the chimney like a wind, blow around the town and into everyone's ears. I tried to pretend it hadn't happened, patched the hole in the wall of our minds so that unless you were looking closely, you would never know it had been there.

* * *

I'D NEVER BEEN TO A MORGUE. ST. MARGARET'S DIDN'T have one. It also didn't have a movie theatre or a bookstore, or any number of things people wanted. I wasn't surprised that I had to drive to the hospital in nearby Woepine to see Buddy one last time. Officer Moore had written the directions in his official police pad, even though I knew my way, and the page was wadded up in my hands as I turned the wheel into the parking lot of the Woepine Hospital, where the body, his body, in all its large and indisputable strength, was being kept in the basement on ice. I turned my car off and wiped sweat from my face. The hospital was a large, white brick building. Buddy and I had both been born there. I thought of Buddy's parents, and of Officer Moore going to their small bungalow to sit on their couch and do the same as he'd done with Hattie and me. Buddy's stern, quiet father, murmuring to Mrs. Collerfield, wild with sorrow. Her wails came my way, reaching me through the phone when I called. I cried quietly at the other end, saying nothing while they told me they loved me, that Buddy had loved me, that they insisted I come over. I deflected and hid under my guilt. I needed to be with my family. My family meant Hattie.

I followed the arrows to the basement, Officer Moore's paper still in my hand, a crumpled buoy. I saw him standing with his back to me, speaking with a woman at a reception desk. She caught my eye and smiled kindly; Officer Moore turned and nodded quickly, coming towards me.

"Mrs. Collerfield, thank you for coming."

"It's Penny, please. I never really took to being called Mrs. Collerfield." My voice was shaking. I was about to cry, and so stopped talking altogether.

"Of course." He extended his arm past the gatekeeper desk. "This way, please."

There are things that make your feet feel like they are lifting off the ground. Things that are so strange or unfamiliar or awful that you take leave of yourself. I felt, in those minutes while Officer Moore escorted me to the remains of my husband, that my tongue swelled like a thick mass, and my body hummed and hovered. My ears buzzed, and I hardly heard what he was saying. There was a bag and a zipper, and as it was coming down, the noise in my ears was deafening.

And then there he was, peeled and horrific like a scalded red and hairless beast. I once saw a photograph of a moose that had been charred in a British Columbia forest fire galloping away from a bear. The photographer had been close enough to see the burned-away skin, hanging in folds, glinting bone of kneecaps bending through stretched and mottled flesh. The bear in pursuit. Right on its heels.

I stumbled, and Officer Moore, nice and clean and mindful of protocol, instinctively reached out in my direction. I veered away, afraid of him touching me, and nodded many times, *yes, yes, yes, please, that's him, please put it up again.* Acid in my mouth.

"I'm going to do everything I can," Officer Moore said quietly, "to get to the bottom of this, to help you find peace." I stared at him, startled, and nodded.

And then we were back, back at the desk with the nice receptionist, someone moving something on wheels in another room, a clanging, a door closing, a doctor being paged. *Right here, dear, where it says Identification. And your name on the line, please. Thank you, dear. And I am so sorry.*

"Yes," I sobbed. Death is such a sad thing.

***

"What did he look like?"

Hattie met me at the door as soon as I got back that afternoon, when the clouds opened up a condemnation. She reached out to take my umbrella, her face crumpled in fear. I watched water pool on the floor and wondered about mopping it up. I didn't look at Hattie. I said nothing and went up to my room, a hand on the railing.

The funeral was something I hadn't thought of, not really. The sheer fact of it hit me with the force of death itself.

"Buddy sure had a lot of relatives, didn't he?" Hattie said, as we'd pulled up to the church. Our wedding had been a small affair at the local Catholic church, then a reception at the Legion. I hadn't met many of these people before now. I nodded in agreement, watching a young woman with an ashen face lift a toddler out of her car. So many there had that ruddy-faced, healthy look of the Collerfields. Freckles and dirty-blond hair, laugh lines and bright blue eyes. Their sorrow blew around the room and shook my balance. They cried into my shoulder. They held my face in their kind hands and shook their heads. They gripped Hattie, who looked like she'd disappear into the wool of their overcoats like a lost poppy pin.

Under the chestnut trees of St. Margaret's Catholic Church. I stood with my hands clasped, my wedding ring like an anvil, standing at the edge of the grave. Hattie's arm was around me. She was trembling.

She whispered, looking at the coffin, "Good Lord. What have we done?" I stared at her in disbelief, and she shook herself and looked around. No one was near us, no one heard. "I'm sorry," she muttered. *I'm sorry.*

Back at our house later, people filled the rooms. Talking, chasing children, laughing and wiping tears. I hadn't accounted for all of them. Buddy's mother sat in one of the living-room chairs, smiling wanly at everyone who came to offer their condolences. His dad had been steadily sobbing in the foyer, hadn't taken off his coat. Within a couple of months, they would move from St. Margaret's, to get away from the memories. I heard from them seldom, and then only in cards, at Christmas. I will forever think of them, impotent in grief, frozen in our house like spectres.

My friend from high school, Sally, was constantly asking me what she could do, how she could help.

"You don't have to be this strong, Penny," she whispered while offering another in a series of hugs. "We are all here to hold you up." I nodded, my eyes searching the room for an exit. I dodged her throughout the day, along with many other acquaintances, people from Buddy's work, neighbours and high-school peers. People wanted to share their stories, hoping I would lend mine back, using grief like currency. But where were these people during my marriage? When my body was a map of violence, everyone had somewhere else to be. Although I knew that I had been expert at hiding it, a master at make-up, prone to calling in sick to let the swelling go down.

"Thanks, Sal," I said, and thought how, in a different life, I truly could have appreciated her huge heart, her compassion, her friendship. A life where I didn't have to keep people at arm's length. "This is just how I deal with things, I guess."

She held me by the shoulders and smiled bravely. "I understand. In that case," she inhaled deeply, "let me clean dishes instead!" She grinned and headed to the sink.

"I don't think we have enough vases," Hattie said to me from the counter. We were inundated. The kitchen overflowed with flowers as though they were growing out of every surface of the house. She brandished a pair of scissors and cut stems, filling every vessel we could find with water. I uncovered sandwiches and fruit trays.

"You have to go out there, Penny," she said quietly as she passed me.

"I know, Hattie. Just let me be."

But I went into the foyer, through to the living room, where the first person I saw was Buddy's best friend, Mac Williams, laughing bawdily while tears streamed down his face. He was loudly telling a story about Buddy to a quiet classmate of Buddy's—Gary Fagan, who had withstood a lifetime of being called "Faggoty-Anne" by Buddy and Mac—while downing a can of beer in huge gulps. Other people sat in chairs and on the arms of sofas, speaking quietly to each other; children weaved around people's legs. I noticed the crust of a sandwich ground into the rug. It was hot in there, and I waved a condolence card I'd been holding in front of my face like a fan.

"He was such a son of a bitch, honest to God," Mac howled, shaking his head.

Gary caught my eye and smiled weakly. "Hi, Penny."

I waved my fingers, and Mac turned, lurching immediately in my direction.

"Penny, babe," he said, arms opened wide. He enveloped me in a massive hug, all flannel and aftershave. "I didn't get to tell you at the church, but I am so sorry for your loss." He began to sob in earnest again, wiping his face and coughing. "I can't believe it, Penny. I mean, you know better than anyone: Bud and I had our moments. He could be a real prick, am I right?"

I raised my eyebrows and smiled at Mac nervously. "Sure, I guess."

"You guess?" He chuckled, and there it was, his shared tendency with Buddy to turn his tack, change his mood on a dime. "Yeah, right. *You* know! He could be such an angry son of a bitch, anything could set him off. But man, he was like a brother to me, Penny. Honest to God. I can't believe it."

People were staring. I put a hand on Mac's enormous forearm. "I know, Mac. He loved you, too."

"I mean, God, we fought sometimes, you know? Like wild dogs. What do I mean, sometimes?" He chuckled. "A lot! I mean, *you* if anyone know what he was like. Eh? Right?" His mouth curved into a sad smile, and I wished the floor would swallow him up, shut him up, but he kept crashing through with it. "Sid and Nancy, you two, right? But my God, he had a heart of gold. I know he woulda taken a bullet for me." He downed the last of his beer and looked around immediately, hoping to replace it. "Like a goddamn brother." He staggered from the room like a confused bear, and I heard him in the kitchen, calling to Hattie, telling her how sexy she looked, his attention turned from grief to flirtation like the flip side of a drunk's coin.

There were a lot of people from our childhood there. A couple of high-school teachers, a lot of young men and women who we hadn't seen since our mother's funeral, but who we knew the way you know the landscape of your town. They worked in shops and factories, their parents had known our mother, their stories were woven into the fabric of this place. They stood like props on the set of this phony funeral. Officer Moore arrived, and I nervously watched him: his finger in the delicate handle of a teacup, speaking quietly with a woman Hattie and I had gone to school with. What was he asking? Hattie had reminded me that he used to mow our lawn for Mum when we were younger, mostly after I'd gone away to school. And seeing him there, in regular clothes, jogged some faded memories for me. He had been heavier, quieter, from what I could remember. Now he was fit, and his face had lost the chubbiness that had dogged him through youth, but I could still find that baby face in the man that stood in my living room. He had turned to watch Mac embrace me. I had smiled at him, almost sheepishly, when Mac had lumbered from the room, trying to share acknowledgement of "those guys"—the guys we'd known to rule the town, showing up late and drunk at festivals, tearing down banners and pulling stunts. Officer Moore had made a career of responding to noise complaints from Mac Williams–style parties. But he hadn't returned my smile; he held my gaze for a moment before looking away.

The mourning went on for days. I forgot that people would swarm us with their good intentions. And we didn't have enough vases, not by a long shot, so I brought up all the mason jars from the cellar. Flowers all over the house, on tables and sideboards, the mantel, and counters. They kept coming. Every time I turned around, the doorbell rang and the same flower delivery guy was standing there looking like he wasn't just sorry that Buddy had died, but sorry he had to keep coming over. I wanted to throw them out, but then I didn't, but I didn't refresh their water either. I let them die, and their sweetness turned to rot.

I had forgotten, really, that other people would factor in. I hadn't thought of anything other than starting over. I forgot that most of the work would come after. That there would be grief-stricken parents, and people dropping off food and bags of clothes, cards clogging up the mailbox like hair in the drain, half of them from people we'd never heard of, the other half from people who had abandoned us in earlier days. Each card written in a spidery hand, *Mrs. Collerfield,* sticking me to him all over again.

Another day. I clipped flower stems and watched the rain. It had been raining all morning, lines on the window. There were petals in the sink, their edges curling into brown lace.

LATER, I RECLAIMED MY OLD ROOM. I POLISHED MY childhood bed until its black iron was shining. There were figures of fairies sculpted into the frame; spindles and knobs surrounded the mattress and crafted the safety net for dreams. Hattie returned from errands to see me putting the few old belongings I'd had from the basement into the room, trying to make it mine. She fussed about, trying to help bring items from elsewhere in the house, but already I was distancing myself from her. A small part of me saw her love and hated her for it. I wordlessly asked her to leave me in peace. She stood for a moment looking at me, tripped up by the sameness of the scene all these years later, the light coming through the large windows and shining on her hair. She walked through the door and pulled it shut.

CHAPTER 7

AIN MOORE CAME BY AGAIN," HATTIE TOLD ME A few days after the funeral when I'd come in from shopping. I'd been making excuses not to be at the house, which smelled like death to me with all the flowers.

"What? Why?"

"I dunno. He said he just wanted to check in and see how we were doing."

"Did he say anything else?"

"Well, he's a decent guy. Do you remember him now? From before?" Her neck reddened.

"Yeah . . . kind of."

"I used to talk to him after you went away to school. He helped Mum doing jobs around the house. Sometimes he let me up on the ladder while he cleaned out the eaves." She paused. "He even came by to help after she died, a few times. It was nice, at the time, having someone to talk to." She picked at her sweater wistfully.

I tried to get her back on track.

"Did he say he's coming back, or anything else? Did he say anything about Buddy?"

"No. He just brought some banana bread and said he was offering his condolences again. He wasn't even wearing his uniform."

She followed me upstairs to my room. "Do you think it means anything?"

"I have no idea." I thought about his kind face. "But he's the police, Hattie. Don't forget it."

I HAVE A MEMORY OF MY MOTHER AT THE KITCHEN COUNTER, cutting an apple in her palm, the knife curving towards her, telling me that it's challenging to have an impulsive personality.

"I know you do rash things, sometimes, Penny. You make choices quickly. Try being thoughtful. Think like someone building a house. Measure twice, cut once. You can't turn back the clock." I had watched her, mesmerized by her hands, her short red nails, and the knife. "There." She dumped the apple slices into a bowl and handed them to me with a wink.

When I made the plan, the terrible plan, I pictured Hattie waiting for me. Distracting herself, folding laundry, her hands shaking. Tucking sleeves behind backs, bending socks into pairs. And maybe she looked a little excited, a little pleased with herself. And yet. *Please understand. I needed her, Mum. I needed her, and she was there. The sun was low in the sky, and Mum, I know you could see what I couldn't.*

A fire and a plan, a match struck and a change coming.

After it was done, we cuddled like in a storm under an old quilt. Both of us shivering. Hattie put her arm around me, and I winced at her kindness. Wrapped around us was smoke and dirt and clean sheets and a whiff of regret. She touched the black baby hairs at the back of my neck and she loved me like only a sister can. We were bound now, twisted together in a braid of badness, neither side so different from the other anymore. I fell, almost immediately, into the dreamless, safe sleep of the almost, nearly, just-escaped dead. And when the knock came, when Officer Moore came for the very first time, my sister was ready.

Hattie had been lying there, waiting, and when she heard it, she sat up and threw the covers off, bolting out of the bed before I knew what was happening. It was still dark out, the middle of the night, or at least a far cry from morning. She shook my foot.

"Penny! Penny!" A tiny whisper, smacking my clammy skin. And then I was awake; eyes snapped open, hands rushing to my mouth in childlike nervousness. "The door, Penny!" she said, the thin edge of panic sneaking up and out in her voice. And she flew down the hall, bumping down the stairs to meet our fate. Right to the tips of my fingers, I felt it, my mouth hot with acid.

I heard her open the old front door, a suction-like sound as it pulled in the cold spring morning. I climbed out of bed and listened. Walked to the hallway, looked down the stairs. He was standing there, just like I thought he'd be, the police officer. He was a little different than what I'd expected. So young, his cheeks red. He was handsome, in a baby-faced way. Around our age and sort of familiar, and so it felt pretend, kids in a play, unreal.

"Yes?" Hattie said, her voice shaking.

"Hattie?"

"Yes. Iain, is that you? What's the matter? Has something happened?"

"H-Hattie, it's Officer Moore now. I'm here because—uh, may I come in?"

"Why, what's going on? Just tell me." She put her arm out and held the door, and from where I was standing, I felt the breeze up my sleeve. He looked past Hattie, and saw me standing on the stairs.

"Officer?"

"Penny—I mean, Mrs. Collerfield."

I came down the stairs, nodding.

Did I imagine it, or did he breathe in deeply? Sniff the air, almost imperceptibly? I was suddenly conscious of the smell of fire all around us.

"May I come in, please?" He scratched his cheek, which looked razor burned. He looked over his shoulder nervously. I wondered if this was the first time he'd done this kind of thing. He couldn't have been more than twenty-two. Hattie stood aside as he walked past her. There was something on his shoulder. Ash. My knees shook. He held his hat in his hands like sad police officers are meant to do. I gestured to the living room, where we all sat down. Hattie and I beside each other in wingback chairs. She was white. A flicker of a realization of how young she was: just eighteen to my twenty-one. A marriage of only two years, but a world of pain. Oh God, to think of it now.

Here it comes. I watched him swallow.

"There was a fire, Mrs. Collerfield. At your house."

No screaming out or crying right away, no questions. My mouth fell open and I reached for Hattie's hand. She gripped mine, stuttering through words of shock, *when* and *what do you mean* and *how?*

"Your husband, Penny," the officer held my eyes, ignoring Hattie. "Buddy. Mr. Collerfield. He perished in the fire."

It worked. He died. He was dead. In my thick-tongued shock, there was a pulse, a heartbeat of relief. Dead. It was over. It had just begun.

There was more. He had details, but he kept them tight, letting them slowly trickle out. And even though this was all coming to me as sure as anything, even though I knew the story better than this officer did, I was crying for real. I gagged and sagged and held my face, sobbing like the widow of a kind man. Grief and guilt do tricky things. I was sick about it all, and so filled with relief and self-disgust and an armload more, and maybe that's why I was crying so. The completeness of it. Done. Hattie looked at the police officer, his hands turning his hat in his lap.

"Are you sure?" she asked. "Are you sure it was him?"

"Quite sure. Although we would really appreciate if Penny would identify him. When she's ready." Hattie squeezed my hand. I didn't respond. I was shutting her out, turning inward, even in those early moments. Regret, retreat, repeat.

"Your neighbour, Mrs. . . ." and here the officer read from a notepad, "Neufeldt, told us that you were planning on spending the night here at your sister's." A nod at Hattie.

"What is your name, Officer?" I asked him.

His face went red. "Moore. Officer Iain Moore." He looked down. "I'm sorry I didn't say so, I thought you knew." He fumbled around for his badge.

I regained my composure, shakily at first. "Yes," I lied. "I'm sorry I didn't recognize you. This is a terrible shock. Would you like some tea, Officer Moore? We're not coffee drinkers, I'm afraid."

Tiny sugar spoon, clinking cups, saucers and the sun just starting to rise. I stared out the window, daring the day to begin, daring the officer on our couch to pry. Hattie stirred her tea loudly; kept repeating that she was shocked, tears running down her cheeks, sitting there in her flowered pyjamas, and I wanted to hug her, push her, tell her to shut up, tell her to get out, to stay. This was mine, this grief, whatever it was, and it was mine to deal with, but I couldn't do it without her. And there it was, here we are.

The officer, young Iain Moore, pulled his blue pressed pants up at the knees and sat on the sofa opposite us, on the uncomfortable line between two cushions. He told us how the fire appeared to have started with a cigarette, and that it seemed that Buddy had had a number of beers, and that the fire alarm was out of batteries. That this sort of thing was unfortunately quite common, and that even in his very few years on the force, he had seen a number tra-gedies as a result of poor household safety and drinking.

"Of course, we all have to unwind. I mean no disrespect, Mrs. Collerfield."

"Penny is fine."

I looked at him and thought of how my life would have been so different if I had hooked up with a sweet-faced boy like Officer Moore instead of Buddy Collerfield. I nodded, yes of course, thank you. And then he gently asked some questions: what time had I come here, was there anything unusual about the night, had Mr. Collerfield and I had a fight, for instance, how had I gotten to Hattie's—questions I had expected. Maybe it was standard police stuff, but I knew there was also a chance it was small-town gossip. Maybe our privacy hadn't been so private after all. But I had answers for all of them, because it was so simple, what had happened. No argument, no, I made him dinner and put it in the oven for him for later, then walked home—to my sister's place—since it was such a nice afternoon. Of course it wasn't simple, and that was the clincher.

Fire catches so easily. Buddy slept so soundly. I thought of his snores, of a lock of hair looping down in front of his stubbly face. Flames go up, just like that. But cigarettes don't normally catch the curtains first. A cigarette won't kiss the bottoms of polyester floral like a long match will. Not when someone has had that many beers and something else, too, to make the snores deepen and the mouth loll. I moved a finger over my ear, an old habit from having long hair, and bit a chapped part of my lip, thinking of smoke and fire. I hadn't looked at him, hadn't touched him. Had frozen in that moment, looking around at that place. The wallpaper. The phone on the wall. Part of me worried that Officer Moore could see these thoughts, crazy though it was, and I dropped my eyes to the rug and studied the faded patterns under our feet. There were crumbs of Hattie's homemade granola dotting the swirling designs.

But Officer Moore, in his fine trousers, hardly seemed suspicious. He bashfully looked away when I studied his face. And there was Hattie, reaching out a hand to let me know she was there. I didn't want her, but I needed her. A nod. A secret vow. Let no man put asunder. Let no man pull us under.

AND HERE HE WAS, VISITING AGAIN, AFTER THE FUNERAL.

"Did he say he's going to come back?"

"No. But he left his card." Hattie reached into her jeans pocket and withdrew a small white card with Officer Moore's extension on it. I was right in thinking she never should have let him in. Some instinct told me that he would fall in love with her, become hypnotized the way so many did, that he would never really leave. Better to keep our doors locked. And of course, he did fall in love with her. But by the time Jameson came on the scene, she had been avoiding him for some time. He had left a few sad messages on our voicemail, but they had eventually become few and far between. I still saw him in town: at the Strawberry

Festival handing out police magnets to children, or once or twice, out of uniform, reading a paperback at Tim Hortons. Sometimes I had felt someone's eyes on me, and would turn and see him there. He was always friendly, tipping his hat or lifting a hand in greeting, and I would return it, my stomach clenched in surprise.

CHAPTER 8

TIME HAD PASSED SINCE THOSE HARRIED DAYS after the fire and funeral. Jameson had slipped into Hattie's life, and I felt, for the first time, that I had space to breathe. With the summer over now, I had withdrawn from our threesome somewhat. I wanted my own space away from my sister, now that I didn't feel the need to keep her so close. Still, I felt the occasional impulse to check in.

I walked along the main street of St. Margaret's towards the salon where Hattie worked. The bell jingled when I opened the door and Hattie looked up from her station and shouted my name like I was the prodigal sister returned. The other stylists greeted me happily, and I noticed that they all took Hattie's cue in their boisterousness. The salon was a place full of music and energy. The clients seemed to leave with more bounce and cheer than when they'd arrived, and I knew this was almost entirely because of Hattie. I sat in the waiting chairs and chose a magazine with a good-looking and tragic celebrity on the front. Soon I got lost in the folds of Hollywood scandal and didn't see Hattie standing in front of me. She smiled when I looked up.

"Ready?"

"As I'll ever be."

We walked to the sinks, where she gingerly lifted my head onto a folded towel and began to wash my hair. I closed my eyes as the warm water and her fingers seduced me into relaxation. I listened as Hattie chatted with her co-workers, who clearly loved her—laughing, singing along to the music, complimenting clients—and I tried hard to relax.

"So!" Hattie said, cheerfully. "I feel like you haven't been around much lately." She rubbed shampoo into my scalp with her fingertips.

"You leading a secret life, Penny?" asked Daniel, a sharp-looking stylist who was standing with a jaunty hand on a hip nearby.

"What? No," I said nervously, and he laughed loudly and clicked his tongue.

"Hmm. Playing coy," said Hattie's friend Jessica from her chair, where she painted highlight foils onto a teenager's long blond mane.

"I'm not!"

"Okay, guys, take it easy on her." Hattie laughed, then paused and said in a singsong voice, "However . . . Is it me, or have you been somewhere else at night? Have you got a fella?" She peered into my eyes, her hair hanging around our faces, her smile bewitching. Hattie wanted life to be a fun and romantic party, an impulse from childhood that not only hadn't been dulled by tragedy but had emerged stronger than ever.

"A fella!" the other stylists screeched, and I squeezed my eyes shut.

"I haven't got a 'fella,' Hattie. I've been—staying at the property. At the barn. You got me. I confess." I raised my arms in surrender. "Secret life." I saw Hattie struggle to remain chipper with the reminder of that place. Her larger-than-life work persona was thin, and I knew that a more delicate Hattie was

72

just below the surface. She recovered quickly, for the benefit of her pals.

"Ah, yes, the barn. There's a lovely little place on Penny's old property that survived the fire," she explained, as they nodded interestedly. She looked at me, prompting. "You fixed it up so it would be livable, I hope? You wouldn't be hanging out in some decrepit ramshackle building, would you?"

"Of course not," I said, playing along cheerfully. We both knew better. The barn was more than just a relic from the fire; it had been my refuge during my marriage. After violent nights of fighting with Buddy, knowing I would never go to the hospital or to a friend's, I often went out there, sometimes even in the middle of the night, and found in the place a kind of solace that I sorely needed.

"It's her special place to get away from her sister." Hattie laughed. I smiled, thinking of the barn. The land itself perched up on high and forested ground, the properties surrounding it used as vineyards or left alone for tall trees and wildlife. I had bought a tent and a sleeping bag and spent the first of many nights on my land almost entirely awake, listening to the sounds of coyotes and birds, dreading the footsteps of a stranger or worse, and finally falling into a fragile sleep before the sun came up. But that is how beginnings start, after all. I tried again. And kept returning, sleeping inside the barn itself if the weather was temperamental. Wind swept dust, pieces of hay and sticks from the rafters, forlorn doves cooed in their nests, and I lay staring up at the high ceiling of the thing, hearing creaks and feeling swayed.

"No, Hattie, I just like my alone time." I kept my eyes closed while she combed my hair.

"Okay, okay. But is it safe?"

"It is now."

When Hattie finished my hair, and it was fun and light and I looked like someone I wished I could be, I asked her, "Do you and Jameson want to come to the barn tonight? We can have dinner there."

"Seriously?" She looked at me in the mirror and her smile faded. She lowered her voice so only I could hear. "I don't know if I want to go back there."

I watched her, her small pale face. "No time like the present. It really is a great little place now."

ST. MARGARET'S ISN'T A HARD PLACE TO FIND PEOPLE who know how to fix things. In fact, there is an embarrassment of riches in terms of handymen, and like everyone else, some are better than others; some full of bravado and puff, and others humble and kind and, for all the lot I knew, terrible at what they did. With some of the money from the insurance settlement on the house, I hired three men from My Brother's Handiwork, a company in which the brothers Murphy did just that: refinished floors and installed kitchens and drywalled basements, and yes, righted tilting barns for young widows.

"I heard about your loss," said Jack Murphy, dropping his eyes while he shook my hand in a grasp that swallowed my palm. I met him and his brothers at the property on a shining day in early August. All three men were tall with different versions of the same face: long nose, sunburned skin, a tangle of facial hair. Like a trio of lumberjacks. They were older than me, but that means nothing when it comes to a small place, where gossip just runs downhill. They had a sister in Hattie's year, Joni, who they claimed had been broken up by the death of my husband, you know, since it was such a tragedy. I inhaled and pushed away the feeling that Joni had been just Buddy's type. I smiled tightly, and we all looked around at the state of the barn, which I had turned into a kind of squatter's hut with my tent and sleeping bag in the corner under a blanket, some cooking implements piled up beside.

"Has someone been living in here?" Jack's brother Davy asked me. He lifted the blanket and inspected a pot.

"I've spent a few nights here."

He dropped the blanket quickly, reddening as though he'd been holding my underwear, and shook his head. "You shouldn't do that, Miss Grayson—I mean, Collerfield. This place isn't safe." His brothers murmured agreement while nodding gravely at the splintering walls.

"Well," I said. "That's why you're here."

There is something called a comealong, a glorified winch system used for righting tilting barns, among other jobs. Watching the Murphy brothers anchor the comealong to a large chestnut tree in the front of the barn and work to slowly pull up the walls, a couple of delicate inches at a time, was a moving event that I took not at face value, but as a grin-worthy symbol that my life was going to improve, that I would stand on my own. For not the first time, I would fall victim to poetic fallacy. I could hardly help applauding when it was done.

My Brother's Handiwork fixed the old barn, adding new and safe infrastructure, holding it up and supporting it, adding beams and slats to keep out the elements. They asked if I wanted it sanded and stained, and were confused when I declined. Are you going to raise cattle? Sheep? I shook my head, smiling, giving them cash for their fine work, and sent them on their way. I stood in the centre of the barn and laughed out loud, my happiness echoing. It was my place. It was drafty and old and perfect.

* * *

AND NOW, I HAD A NEW HAIRCUT AND JAMESON AND Hattie were coming for dinner. Feeling light and cautiously carefree, I went grocery shopping to buy some food for that night. I wheeled my cart through the aisles, my mind elsewhere, and then I realized someone had called my name, an old name.

"Mrs. Collerfield."

I turned to see Iain Moore coming towards me. I smiled.

"Officer Moore." I nodded. "It's Penny." He stopped and our carts were side by side, taking up the aisle.

"Okay. How are you?" He looked uncomfortable to see me. Irritated, almost, if I had to give it a word.

"Very well. And you?"

"Fine, thank you. It's nice to see you. I've been thinking of you and Hattie lately."

"Oh?" I kept my voice light, already shifting my cart, my body, to signify that I was done talking.

He nodded. "I've driven by your old property a few times. I see you fixed up that barn."

"I did, yes," I managed, startled.

He paused and looked at me thoughtfully.

"Well, I—" I gestured at my cart apologetically and turned away. "I have to get going. Have a great day, Officer."

As I reached for some crackers a few minutes later, I noticed my hands shaking slightly.

I PUT UP LANTERNS AND A TABLE IN THE BARN, TRIED TO make it homey. When Jameson and Hattie arrived, she hung back, almost like her legs wouldn't work, and I watched her over Jameson's shoulder as he marvelled at the soundness of the barn's rebirth. She was looking at where the house had been.

"Hattie!" I called. "Come here!" She looked up and smiled resolutely, and marched over to the barn, giving me a big hug.

"It looks great, Pen."

She was shivering despite the warmth of the evening.

Nothing music and booze couldn't fix. The night cantered on, and we resumed our familiar practice of eating and drinking and telling stories, singing, dancing to a battery-run boom box and music pulled from a shoebox of tapes. Somewhere around midnight, Hattie looked at Jameson and grinned. His eyes were glassy and there was an exchange that I took to mean something lusty and lovey, and it irritated me. Hattie cleared her throat.

"Hey. So," she looked at him, "we have something we've been trying to tell you. You know, if you hadn't gone off the grid, you weirdo."

"Oh yeah?"

"Yeah. Um." She looked at him and he nodded happily, encouraging her, and I dimly registered how handsome he looked in the lamplight.

"Jameson and I are trying to get me pregnant." She laughed and burped spectacularly, reaching for a wedge of cheese. They held hands, and I started at the shock of this news.

"Don't you think it's a little soon?" I asked, and they shared a glance that told me they'd expected this.

"No," Hattie said, boldly, "we don't. But I'm guessing you do." Jameson smiled bashfully, and I had the feeling he'd been talked into something.

"Yes, I do, I mean—"

"Then lucky it's not you doing it."

There was a pause, and the woods around us chattered.

"Well." I cleared my throat, trying to recover myself. "Then that's that." I poured a glass for each of us, and we toasted to a future baby.

I watched them stumble home, arms around waists, and felt a cold snap raise the hair on my arms. I rubbed them closely and turned to blow out the candles, only to discover that a gust through the door had done the job for me.

We were harvesting beets in the backyard, putting the garden to bed. It was bright out, with a cool, telling breeze. My shirt lifted at the back and my skin was goosebumped. Hattie banged a beet against the wooden side of the raised bed to knock off the dirt and a stubborn slug. I looked at her beautiful, youthful face, so much like she was as a child. Unchanged in some ways.

She was so keen about the baby that I had to fall back and let her be. She read books, ate all the right things, took vitamins and researched the hell right out of the serendipity of conception. I busied myself with other things, tried to stay above the fray, out of the house, in the sand, because as happy as I was for them on the surface, something was itching inside me. Something old and familiar. *Lucky it's not you.*

CHAPTER 9

AND THEN, IT HAD BEEN A YEAR. THERE HAD been no more police visits but there was no full belly either, no glowing skin, no fuller hair, no crib in Mum's old room, which was earmarked as the nursery. Jameson had officially moved in, and that had failed to live up to their expectations for their new adventure. I heard urgent whispers and quiet anxiety through the walls. I wore headphones and listened to music to fall asleep, the curly black cord that plugged into my stereo invariably tangled around my arm by morning, a deep purple mark left on my skin.

In the mornings, I would lie awake and stare for a few moments at an old framed picture across from my bed. It was an embroidered portrait of Saint Margaret that had hung in my room since childhood. I had loved the picture always, spending many nights staring dreamily at the patron saint of our strange little town, its eerie Catholic mysticism so seductive to me as a girl. But now she seemed, like the rest of St. Margaret's, to be watching us. Waiting for us to stumble.

Hattie was frustrated, delicate, moody. She made me nervous. She was erratic, and seemed to have moved, almost overnight, from sweet and happy to unstable and irritable. She wanted me around all the time, and while I knew that the closer I was, the more I could be sure to keep her in check, her moods threw me, and I avoided her when I could. It was fall, and Jameson had returned to the demands of the school year, the heady summer of fun slipping seamlessly into the season of grown-ups. She was flailing, trying to tempt Jameson and me into late nights and shaming us when we demurred and declined her increasingly urgent invitations. Sometimes, crossing paths during the preparations for bed, meeting in the doorway of the bathroom, Jameson and I would exchange knowing and sympathetic smiles, and I caught something between us. We were in this together, somehow.

One night, after I'd had a bath, I stopped in the hallway, wrapped in a towel, my cheeks flushed and my hair curling against my face. I saw him through the open bedroom door, lying in bed, book in hand. He noticed me and lowered his book onto his lap. He lifted his hand in a small greeting, our eyes locked. There was a noise downstairs as Hattie dropped something, breaking the spell. I felt my face burn and finally looked away, going into my own room beside his.

With every month of not becoming a glowing woman with child, my sister became more childlike. She came close to tantrums when her period arrived, taking to her room and skipping work at the salon. Tear-streaked face, demanding to know why we looked so happy, why Jameson and I had come home together. *Are you two talking about me on your little trips home from your 'real jobs'?* She required constant reassurance, exhausting Jameson with moods that took her from cute and whimsical to sarcastic and paranoid in the changing direction of the wind.

One afternoon when we were alone together in the house, she stood wringing her hands while I folded laundry.

"What is it, Hattie?"

She took a deep breath.

"I think we should maybe think about going to confession. You know, at the church."

I dropped the shirt I was holding and turned to face her.

"Hattie," I said calmly but firmly, "that is *not* an option. I understand how you're feeling—"

"What if I'm being punished, Penny?" She wailed, suddenly. "What if God doesn't want me to have a child because we are evil? If we just confessed the secret, it maybe wouldn't be stuck inside, like a growth or something—"

"Hattie, NO."

"Penny, I just—" She flopped on a chair and held her face in her hands. I scooted beside her, and wrapped myself around her while I stared ahead, terrified of what this meant.

"I know, honey. I know. I am so grateful that you have kept this between us. I am. My life depends on it, and I don't take that lightly. But, I also don't for a second believe that you are being punished by God. If that were the case, I'd have been struck by lightning by now."

She chuckled and wiped a tear.

"It'll happen for you, I'm sure of it. You crazy kids will have a baby. These things don't happen instantly."

She nodded, sniffling like a child.

"And listen, if you want to go to church again, I'll go with you. Just not to confession. Okay?"

"Okay." She looked up at me. "I'm sorry, Penny. I'm sorry I've been acting so nuts."

"I love you, you nut." I gave her a squeeze.

* * *

I EVADED HER, SPENT AS MANY NIGHTS AS I COULD IN the barn, even as colder weather would invariably interrupt the warm fall.

On a balmy October afternoon, a few weeks later, I saw Mrs. Neufeldt walking at the boundary of the property close to the trees, through piles of orange and red crisp, crackling leaves. I watched her lift her arm and wave at me, and then, when I hoped she'd move on, she waved me over. I crossed the tall grass, a few pieces slipping under the cuffs of my jeans and scraping my ankles. Tall cedars were casting shadows across the dry ground, and not for the first time, I thought of fire. I wanted to move on, to push past this, and quickened my pace. I was out of breath when I met Mrs. Neufeldt at the deer fence. She looked ruddy and freckled, more lined than I'd remembered, but still the same kindly woman who had greeted Buddy and me when we'd first moved there.

"Hello, dear," she said, and, "Look at all the work you've done here. I think it's wonderful!"

I thanked her and asked after her family, her husband. She offered kindly platitudes, small health-related bits of news, comments on the weather. I thought we might be finished, and smiled and nodded cheerfully, turning my body ever so slightly. *I'm so glad to hear, that's great, please give them my best.*

"Dear," she paused, "I know you've been staying out here lately, and I just wanted to make sure you were safe."

"I am, Mrs. Neufeldt, don't worry."

"Yes, well," she paused, then continued, "I have seen, when I'm out walking, someone coming here occasionally, when you're not here."

I froze, the smile fading. I unconsciously grabbed the fence, pushed the fat of my palm into the wire. I cleared my throat, furrowed my brow.

"What do you mean?"

"I—I'm sure he means no harm, but I just worry about a young woman here alone. I think it's that—well, you probably know him: the Williams boy?"

Mac Williams. I nodded slowly.

"Sure, Mac. He was a friend of Buddy's."

"I see. Okay, well, I'm sure it's fine. He just seems to come here and drink. Sometimes he pours beer out where the house was. Sometimes he seems to be talking to someone . . ." Her voice trailed off. I pictured Mac, drunk, stumbling around the empty space where he had so often drunk and brawled with Buddy, slamming the screen door when he left Buddy alone with me, driving out the back way from the property, through the overgrown road, leaving Buddy somewhere to place his rage.

"Okay. Thank you, Mrs. Neufeldt. I'll keep an eye."

"Right. Okay, dear. I also mentioned it to that young officer Iain Moore, the one who was, I guess," she paused again, searching for words, "investigating things after the fire. I ran into him in town. I'm sure he'll look out for you also." She smiled, thinking this would be welcome news, while I just felt it as another complication. I needed the past to be simple, but it refused to comply. She continued, "You know, Penny, love, I owe you an apology. I have felt terrible, for so long, for not reaching out to you. For not offering our home to you, just for somewhere to take a break, or for someone to talk to." She looked at the dirt between us. "We just pretended that there was nothing wrong, but I knew, dear. I knew that he wasn't treating you right." Mrs. Neufeldt's eyes were welling up, and I put up a hand, the fence between us, trying to smile.

"Oh no! Please! Don't get the wrong idea. I mean, we had our moments, Buddy and I, but he was a good man." Almost choking on these words, teasing them out. "He was good to me.

Truly. Please don't for a second worry about me." I needed to get out of there, away from there. Smiling, smiling, sweating, my mouth drying up. I waved away her worry.

"Don't give it another thought. I do have to get back, though, I have a rose bush that isn't going to wrap itself in burlap." *Ha ha*. Reassurances, changing the subject, sending love to family. *Yes, yes. Bye now.*

I hurried against the tall dry grass as it whipped about my legs, and felt panic course through my body. Into the barn, I rolled up my sleeping bag and hurriedly packed up my things in a clattering, banging whirl against the cooling afternoon as the sun ducked behind the roof beams of the barn. I was afraid to even think, my secret might betray me somehow, might be on my face, my breath, but my mind took me back to that day, to the plan, to the foolish foolproof nonsense I had drafted in my furious brain. This goddamn town was so small.

I thought of leaving St. Margaret's altogether, of really leaving this time, reclaiming the life I felt I was owed. Taking off somewhere far and foreign, and hoping that I wouldn't leave a smoke trail of my misdeeds, of mindlessness and murder. I squeezed my eyes shut and shoved my fists in them. Buddy's huge body a red and peeled thing, his skin like puckered fruit, his hair burned away to his scalp, which curled up like pigskin. I cried out for him and for me, and gulped the air around me. What a reckless thing. Why hadn't Hattie talked me out of it? I wondered if she would stand by me still, if we had to do it all over again. I shook my head fiercely. It was right. It was right what I did, it was right. And then I swear I smelled his cigarettes, those goddamn Belmonts right there in the barn, and I tripped, I stumbled getting up, left all of my belongings and ran to the car in the burgeoning darkness, gravel kicking up around me.

**

THAT EVENING, HATTIE ASKED ME.

I sat on my bed, frozen with a cold and nervous fear, Saint Margaret's portrait regarding me from across the room. I thought about Hattie's desperate idea to return to church, to try and appeal to a vengeful God, and how little she had changed, in some ways, from the girl she used to be.

Guilt. It didn't come to me often, but when it did, it was overwhelming. I had done the largest thing. The biggest thing we cannot undo. And not just me, Hattie was wrapped up in it as well. She had tried moving forward, but was forever changed. She was scarred. If we had only known that we were forging an unbreakable bond wrought from fear and justice. That we could never leave it, or each other, behind. I am not a murderer. That is not me. That is not us. All around us, people were busily living their lives, and we worked so hard, every day, to live ours.

Coming back to the house hadn't calmed my nerves entirely. Hadn't smoothed down my panic. My breath was quick, and I needed to sit on the edge of the bed, head between my knees. This will pass. It will pass. I'd been telling myself the same thing since the fire, but it was taking longer, it was harder than I had ever imagined.

Elsewhere in the house, I heard Jameson scoff loudly, swear to himself, then the front door open and the walls reverberate with his leaving.

I heard the stairs creak as Hattie's small feet carried her up, and soon she'd turned the doorknob and come in. I sat up and tried to smile. I was so accustomed to putting on a face that wouldn't belie my thoughts.

"You'd think after all this time that you would know to knock on another person's door," I said, as she appeared in the doorway.

The setting sun was shining in from the bathroom behind her, and at first she was in shadow, a small pixie spectre. But then she shifted, and came in, and there she was, my little sister. She was also wearing a forced smile; she could never fool me. I readied myself.

"Hi, Penny," she said, sitting on the bed with a whimsical bounce. "What are you up to?"

"Nothing. Jameson's gone?"

"He just left. Has some stuff to do." Her smile was causing her some difficulty, I could see.

"Everything okay?"

She took a deep breath, rearranging her expression to one of a sister caught, gave me a knowing look, and I swear she almost batted her eyelashes. And I'll always remember how she looked, sitting there in my room as the sun fell away to evening and the taut cord of debt pulled between us. The sun now glowing almost through her, stray hairs bright and skin translucent. Like some kind of saint.

"Penny, listen. I need you to help me with something, and I want you to know I've put a lot of thought into it."

I sat up.

"Okay," I said, "I'm listening." What wouldn't I do for my sister?

"As you know," she fiddled nervously, then looked at me, "I've been having trouble getting pregnant." She waited for me to nod, to encourage her along. "Well, I can't take it anymore. I know it's because of me, that I'm the trouble." She leaned in. "Jameson has gotten a girl pregnant before—back in high school." She waved it off. "She had it taken care of—and so. It's on me to fix. And, frankly, you."

"I don't know what you mean," I said.

86

She cleared her throat and scooted forward towards me. She grabbed my hand and squeezed it and I felt, in her clammy small hand, a fierce desperation.

"What I mean is," she said, "I want you to carry our baby."

And so there it was, lying between us: that gasping fish of payback.

I stammered, "What does that even mean? I know what that *means*, but what do *you* mean, Hattie?" I pulled away, remembering the door slamming after Jameson. Thinking of his finely composed face, and feeling my own face flush.

"I know you and Jameson really care for each other, and," she put up her hand at my interjection, "there are easy ways to do it. I've read about it. Sounds nuts, but you know, those turkey basters, they actually can work. And no gossipy doctor or nurse to get involved." Her voice was raised now, as I was trying to make myself heard.

"No. Hattie, no." I shook my head and pulled my legs up and away from her. "This is a bad idea. And weird." And inside, something squirmed, something wriggled and tried to be set free.

"Penny, please. It's not weird to me! I promise! I've told Jameson the same thing. He had the same reaction as you to begin with, but maybe if you both think on it—"

"Where did you come up with this idea?"

"Penny, come on!" She looked angry now. "Everything I've done has been for you!" She lowered her voice. "Don't you feel like you owe a little back to me?"

And there it was. That was what she needed to say, and she knew it. There was the rub, there was the trick. *You owe me.* But I didn't owe her. We were even. I levelled my voice.

"Hattie, I know. And you know I would, too, but I think you would regret this. I think we all would."

She shook her head fiercely, long red hair coming untied, some catching in her mouth. She looked furious for just a second, and a kind of madness flitted over her features.

"No, I wouldn't. You're talking about you again, not me. I need this, Penny. This is what I want. What I deserve."

I sighed and tried to think of how to shake her. "I'll—I'll think about it, okay? I'm sure I'll have no choice now but to," I grumbled. "But my position is this now: I love you, but that is a crazy idea. You are not thinking straight. You've been a little . . . off-centre lately, kiddo. You don't want me to be your kid's biological mother. It's just too weird."

She smiled. "Okay, okay. I get how you feel," she said, turning strangely back to her chipper self. "Just consider it. That's all!" She shrugged, not bothered, casual. "Just think about it. Keep an open mind." She leaned over and gave me a kiss on the cheek, and I smelled her soapy skin, her tea and the hint of a burgeoning sense of justice.

CHAPTER 10

I AVOIDED HATTIE THE NEXT MORNING, WAITING FOR sounds that she had headed off to the shower before emerging to have my breakfast. I took my cereal out to the front porch, and sat in a large, wooden porch swing my grandfather had made before his own early death, and reflected on how we had long been the Grey Gardens of St. Margaret's, and wondering how much more we could bear. The two weird sisters, growing into caricatures, dodging the ghosts of scandalous stories, insisting on living together in their dead mother's home like women from a ghost story or a biblical parable.

What would the good people of St. Margaret's think if they knew what we had done, and that Hattie was asking me to carry the baby of her handsome lover in order to bear her a child? My face reddened as I waved half-heartedly at a neighbour pushing her plump baby in an umbrella stroller on the sidewalk past our house. An image of Jameson's arm wrapped around my waist emerged suddenly in my mind, and I burned further with embarrassment, banishing the thought. I loved Hattie, I did. But my life had never been my own. Everything I have ever loved has been sucked into her vortex. Just when I felt I could stand apart, stretch, reach up and out and away, take the important steps away from her, from our home, I was back in a tangled embrace. It's not enough to have my life, she wanted my body as well. And Jameson. I couldn't stop my mind from creeping in his direction. Did he think of me, too?

I castrated my curiosity and reminded myself of what Mrs. Neufeldt had said the day before. Mac, drunk and lonely like a dog whose owner has died, returning to the place of Buddy's death. It made me nervous. There were too many pieces that needed to stay in place, like holding a paper chess set in the wind. I clenched my jaw—a habit I'd had as a child. Fucking Hattie. Two girls and a match, but a world of difference in what it looked like after that. A forest fire of debt.

HATTIE WAS HOME, READING IN THE LIVING ROOM WHEN I got back from work that day. She looked at me, and dropped her eyes into her book, her foot twitching hyperactively. I went to the kitchen and filled the kettle, watching the activity in our birdfeeder out the window. A male blue jay dominated the thing, knocking it over in his greed, the bully of the yard, but it was hard not to be charmed by his beauty. Squirrels ran about on the ground, scratching at the fallen goods. The kettle whistled and I filled my mug, returning to the living room. Afternoon sun poured in the large windows, and lit upon Hattie's hair.

"Hattie, listen. I'm sorry." I came into the room and sat across from her. "I thought about what you said all day, and I just can't do it."

Hattie lifted her face to meet mine, a tight smile and neutral eyes.

"You can't." Her face hardening.

I pushed ahead.

"You guys will have your own baby—you're so young."

She was shaking her head now, in disbelief, chuckling.

"'Sorry, Hattie. I *just can't.*' Wow. You just can't."

"I can't do it, okay? I'm not comfortable with it."

"You're 'not comfortable'? Are you hearing yourself?" She was practically shouting now. "Because jeez, you know, gosh, Penny. I just can't imagine what that feels like."

I closed my eyes and nodded. "Right. Of course. I see." I met Hattie's gaze, her face furious. "You're just not thinking straight," I said. She scoffed but said nothing, opening her book again.

I thought of Jameson. That he had rejected the idea gave me pause. I blushed in spite of myself for thinking that he might have considered it.

I looped my finger into the afghan on the large chair I sat in, remembering that long-ago morning when we had united against reality to grieve in pretend shock: Buddy, gone. My tea steamed against the sun. Hattie's foot jiggled and I knew that she was reading the same line over and over again.

"I think I'll stay at the barn tonight, okay? Looks like a nice night."

She said nothing. Waiting for me to leave.

I DID STAY AT THE BARN THAT NIGHT, AND THE NEXT number of nights, stopping at home only to shower and eat before work. As the weather got colder, I held myself close, my unbidden thoughts sharpening. I stayed. I had an all-weather sleeping bag and felt well-protected, warm and safe. I kept a light on all night—a plug-in tungsten-style lamp that made use of the outlet the workmen had installed for me. I had encountered some teenagers on one of my first nights there and wanted to ward off any more. They had been bashful and apologetic, their stilted sex burning on their faces as they plodded off in search of a private place to smoke and sweat and explore.

I brought a sketchbook with me, along with my journal and some pencils. I began to draw. I wrapped a blanket around my shoulders as I rested the sketchbook on my knees and recorded with tentative scratchings the wildlife around me. Rabbits and birds, the odd deer at the fence, a hawk on a post. My drawings got better, with dark, cross-hatched shading, more confident, more thoughtful. The side of my hand became grey and smudged. I'd see it on my face in the mirror at home when I'd return to shower and change, trying to plan my visits for when Hattie was at work or before she woke, the markings of a private life I was trying to draw out, moving from black-and-white to that grey area where I often landed. It made me feel whole, making these drawings, making something at all. Part of something fragile and innocent.

It was getting too cold to stay at the barn much longer, but I was unsure about going home. Hattie had offered frosty silences when I saw her in passing. Jameson was also keeping his distance, I had noticed, and we hadn't really seen each other since we'd both rebuffed Hattie's request. I thought of him often. Hattie had stolen into my mind and left an idea to fester. And it wasn't the payback or the baby that drew me, but Jameson. She must have known. She had a way of twisting. She was waiting me out.

How could no one see what she was really like? People see what they want to see. It was the same with Buddy.

"Really? Are you sure, Penny? He's always so nice."

"To you," I had said, darkly. "Watch out for him, Hattie." I rolled up a sleeve to show her a bruise shaped like four fingers around my arm. She gasped, begged me to get away from him. She believed me immediately, and more: looked frightened.

But I didn't leave him. I stayed with him, our arguments became fights. Before long, they dissolved faster, quicker to get to the same end: me, huddled and scared. He was convinced that I made him cruel, that I brought something out in him.

"Why do you do this to me?" he whined one night after he had knocked me off a kitchen chair onto the floor with one swipe, like an angry bear. I believed him. I believed it was my fault, too. I was vicious with him. I was angry and jealous and spiteful. I knew he was insecure and defensive and explosive. And he became a monster right before my eyes.

The first time he hurt me, he was shocked at himself. After that, it became routine. I thought I might leave, I told myself I should. But I couldn't. I couldn't, because of Hattie. Always Hattie. I worried she'd be his target somehow.

"Go ahead," he spat at me, after a particularly brutal argument that ended with me in a corner, my head pounding from being knocked against the wall, "Leave. Leave me. Go ahead. I should have known. No loyalty. Not like your sister." He cocked his head in feigned innocence, waiting for me to respond. "Think I haven't noticed? She likes me just fine. Who do you think she'd choose, pretty little girl all alone? A kind, big man, or her fucked-up sister?" He swam in front of my eyes, and I shook my head to clear it, to shake off the mention of Hattie. He got close to my face, I smelled the beer on his breath. "But go ahead. Leave, don't leave. You decide."

I did decide.

And I pulled her under to save her from being burned.

NOW HERE WE WERE. I THREW MYSELF INTO MY WORK, focusing on the daycare's day-to-day business: chatting with parents, doing administrative paperwork, doting on children in passing with abject loyalty, checking in with the caregivers, but I found my eyes wandering over to the schoolyard, hoping to see Jameson. When the day was over, I lingered, getting into my car, before I holed up once again in the chilly barn, my sanctuary. I had hung my drawings with clothes pegs onto lines draping from corner to corner inside the barn, a kind of wholesome decoration in the face of my smoky nightmares and desires.

CHAPTER 11

MAC WILLIAMS CAME TO THE PROPERTY.

I was reading by lamplight when I heard a truck rumbling up the old path, park with a screech. The headlights, which had shone through the slats in the barn walls, flicked off. Footsteps crunched in the leaves, and I tried to quiet my fear, tell myself that I was safe. Still, though, I reached for my keys and held one between my fingers as I'd been shown to do at a useless self-defence class Hattie and I had taken in high school. I was hunched with a blanket around me, an open copy of *Jane Eyre* in my lap. The gothic moors had gotten to me, I told myself as the footsteps stopped and a man's voice called out, accompanied by rapping on the large door.

"Dirty Penny! You in there?"

Mac's voice brought back his crude jokes, the kindred cruelty that aligned him with Buddy. Brothers in flannel, most valuable piss tanks, soldiers in tattooed arms. When they weren't fishing and betting and drinking, they were brawling like street dogs. Two peas in a small-town pod. Mac was temperamental and unpredictable. Being near him was like doing a delicate waltz of trying to stay out of his way and not letting him know you were doing just that.

"Yes. Yep, I'm here. That you, Mac?" I hadn't put my key weapon down yet. Unsure what difference his answer made.

"Sure is. Open up," he said, sliding the door open before I could get to it.

I stood, and looked up at Mac, his presence an intimidating combination of huge stature and blatant drunkenness. I felt the smallness, the remoteness of the space, the familiarity of a large and dangerous man and nowhere to go but the corners of my frightened mind. I tried to stand tall.

"What're you doin' here?" he asked me.

"I might ask you the same thing."

"*I might ask you the same thing,*" he mimicked, lumbering through the doorway. He looked unabashedly at everything in the barn, picking things up and putting them down in the wrong place, flicking my drawings with a fat finger. I smelled booze on him, even from where I was standing.

"I've come by, ya know. Poked my head in a few times, but you were never here."

"It's been getting too cold."

"What are you doing here anyway?" he asked again. "It's not like this is your house anymore, *Mrs. Collerfield.*"

I ignored the question, watching him. He sat heavily in a beanbag chair I'd brought from the house, and just like often happened, he changed tack. He sighed, nodded his head a few times, working his way up to something.

"God, I miss Bud. This place is not the same without him. This is his place, Penny. Always was." He pointed a lazy finger at me. "Not yours. His. He saved up for it, worked on it, he loved this house. It's not right that he's not still here, you know."

I sat on a stool and tried to smile at him.

"I'm sure you must miss him, you two were good friends."

"You have no idea."

"That's probably true," I said quietly.

Mac looked at me as though seeing me sitting there for the first time. He stared, and the silence built up between us, and then he looked around again, caught up in his thoughts.

"I keep comin' back here, 'cause I just don't get it. It doesn't make sense. In his own house . . ." He was mumbling, more to himself. "A man's house should be, you know, sacred." He looked up at the ceiling, and around at the barn. "I remember when he bought this place, he thought it was so cool that there was a barn on the property. All the things he coulda done with this." He trailed off.

"Can I, uh, get you anything? I can put the kettle on." He started, looked at me. I got up to plug it in. He also got up, and followed me the short distance to where I kept my tea things. I smelled him coming behind me, felt myself tense. I felt his hand suddenly on my shoulder.

"How you holding up, Pen?" His hand moved to brush over my ear. "Got your hair done different, hey?"

I dodged slightly and turned to face him.

"It's, uh, been difficult. But I'm managing."

He opened his arms wide and cocked his head.

"Come here," he said.

Not knowing what else to do, and like women everywhere, I leaned stiffly into him, and he wrapped his huge arms around me.

"There, there," he murmured into my hair. I gave him a friendly pat to end the hug, but he still held me, now lifting my face up to his. "Poor girl."

I pulled away then.

"I'm fine, Mac. Truly."

"Oh," he lifted his hands in surrender, "okay." He scoffed.

"Just trying to be friendly, Penny. Share my grief, you know." He shook his head. I felt for him in that moment. I think he believed that: that he was sad, and wanted to share in that sadness, but there was something dark, something angry in him that set me on edge in a familiar way. Mac was hot-tempered, a loose cannon. His grief could propel him in any direction. I thought suddenly of all the men, all the men all over who were like him and Buddy: taking what they wanted, mad when they didn't get it. They rose around us like vicious weeds.

"Of course," I smoothed over, "I know. I just—I'm okay, Mac. But thank you."

Mac walked away from me and leaned against a wall. He pulled a cigarette from his inside pocket and lit it. Took a deep drag.

"He never told you everything, you know, Penny." He exhaled thoughtfully. "A guy has to have his"—he reached around for the word—"confidences."

"Right. Sure."

"Don't say it like that. So prissy. *Right. Sure.*" He mimicked me again. "See?" He gestured at me like I was proving something. Shook his head in exasperation. "That's exactly why. You always acted like you were better than everyone else."

I sighed. "Sorry. I don't know what to say. I didn't think that, if it means anything."

Mac made a face and blew out his cheeks. "Whatever."

"I'm sorry, Mac. I know you miss him. I do, too."

He shook his head and rolled his eyes, like everything I said proved his point. "Sometimes I feel like I'm the only one who misses the guy." He got up and wiped his nose, and headed for the door. Looked back and stopped.

"You know what, Penny?" He pointed a finger at me. "And I'm sorry I gotta say this, but it's true: you maybe thought that you were too good for him, but he was too good for you. He was gold." His voice was catching. "It is such. A fucking. Shame. You two," he slurred a little, "you two never made any god-damn sense. You were *not* good for him. It coulda been different for him."

My mouth opened and closed, and I blinked at him, suddenly afraid. And then the moment was gone. He turned on his heel and walked out, his boot crushing a stick as it hit the ground, making me jump when it cracked loudly. I heard him kick something out of his way, and it crashed into the darkness. And then he yelled out, a sob at the edge of his voice, "This is *not* your place, Penny!"

He slammed the door of his truck. I listened as it pulled away, the tires grumbling angrily, then paced the barn. I smacked the dry paper of one of my nature sketches, hating its sweet inno-cence, its stupid, hopeful naivety. It spun around on the clothes peg, tearing slightly at the top. I heard a mouse scratching in the rafters, and then suddenly an owl screeched and I started, my hands flying up to my face. I took a breath, exhaled whatever confidence I had left. I just wanted a life away from it all, away from the town, that house, those memories and Hattie. My sanc-tuary, always, this barn, wasn't holding up its end of the bargain if Mac Williams could find his way to me.

Not half an hour after Mac had left, I heard a car on the gravel again. It could only be Hattie, and I couldn't bear to talk to her right now. And sure enough, I recognized the sound of her car, could almost smell the stuffy interior.

It was Mum's old car, that bog-coloured beauty with vinyl seats that would tear the top layer of skin off your leg on a hot day. Hattie had a habit of emotional hoarding, and I sensed that it was not just practicality that had forced her to keep that thing around as long as she had. I hated it. The long back seat had been the site of too many early make-out attempts, the knobs for the windows were prone to getting stuck, the brakes never worked that well. None of this had ever bothered Hattie, who had a knack for putting things out of her mind when there was something to be gained. A door opened, closed again, and I heard the jingle of keys in a hand. And for the second time that night, I arranged my expression in preparation.

There was a knock at the barn door, and the ridiculousness of this formality happening twice in one night would have struck me as funny if I hadn't been so hopped up on nervous anxiety. I had turned this old barn into my shack-cum-house even though I had a perfectly lovely house down the road. I was now running away to this place when once I had sought refuge in the other. It was as though there were only two places in my small world, and one of them had owls living in the ceiling.

"Now you knock. Hi, Hattie," I said loudly.

"It's me, Penny. Jameson." A pause, a shuffling of a shoe in the dirt. "Sorry, I should have called. Or, right, not called, but I should have let you know. Courier pigeon. Smoke signal. Anyway," his voice faded. "Forget I came."

I did, almost, just let him go. I held my tongue because I knew that the silence was the only thing keeping my mask on, and if I opened my mouth, it would fall off, and I would be left standing there naked, apologizing for being rude, and rushing to open the door. He started to walk away, and I listened to his loafers on the hard dirt outside, but I had hardly been listening long when I gave in and hurried outside to stop him. My mouth was dry, a rough unfurling kind of quiet that had to be coughed out, my voice stammering. Jameson turned around when he heard me, and he stood there, all pressed and clean and curious-looking in a way that made me aware of my bag-lady squatter appearance.

"Sorry. Sorry, Jameson. I just—look, please don't go. I thought you were Hattie."

"Okay, sure." A look passed over his face that was half smile, half reprimand. I stood there like the wild woman of St. Margaret's. Wearing a quilt around my shoulders, my hair in all directions, I could have just as easily been pushing along a grocery cart with a stuffed parrot in it, talking to myself.

"You alright, Penny? You look a little," he scratched his cheek, "out of sorts."

I pulled the blanket tighter, my cape of denial.

"I'm just fine. How are you?" I said primly.

He ignored this question but waited me out. He hadn't turned all the way back towards me, but wasn't committed to leaving either. He gestured to two Muskoka chairs that were set up, paint peeling sadly, towards the sloping sigh of the escarpment. I realized then that he had with him a stylish brown satchel, a shoulder bag in army green, and from it he withdrew a thermos and two cups. Laying it on the grass, he pushed the chairs more tightly together and surrendered into the bucket seat of one of them, his usable arm bumping into the other chair. He smiled at me, and I joined him, offering up and spreading my blanket on our laps like a map stretched between explorers.

I didn't feel like talking or seeing anyone. He began to talk into the black hole of my silence, revealing that he had come directly from work, having had a staff meeting at the end of the day. He batted around mindless details about the meeting, the people on staff of whom I had cursory knowledge, having seen them in and out of the school, hearing the parents of older kids gossip about good and bad teachers while dressing their younger charges for home. Jameson picked at the peeling paint of the chair, and I nodded disinterestedly at his chatter. I knew it was coming, the gulf between us, that vast desert of Hattieness that had become impossible to cross; I decided to head him off at the pass.

"Jameson."

He looked at me.

"What the fuck? What is wrong with Hattie? What the hell made her think that—you know, that that 'idea'—was, was a *good* idea?"

He sighed and smiled bashfully, and I felt myself blush in my frustration.

"I dunno, Penny. Maybe it was a bad idea. It's been hard. She's in a state. She seems to think we'll never have a baby. I'm really sorry that she tried to get you involved in this. You're right, it's total fucking madness. I know you two are close, but Jesus."

"Not that close."

"Right. Pushing it a little too far." He deftly opened the thermos with his hand by holding it with his knees, and, propping the cups on the arm of his chair, poured out whiskey for each of us. It stung and warmed, and was perfect.

"Does she know you're here?"

"No," he said.

I nodded, looking out at the trees as their black shapes blended into the sky. Jameson put his arm around the back of my chair and I felt his fingers on my shoulder, making it sing and tingle. A mouse scurried in and out of the woodpile. I was blushing and full of desire for him. He cleared his throat.

"Not sure if Hattie told you, but she wants to have a big party at the house."

"She does?" I immediately felt my stomach clench.

Jameson nodded, laughing quietly. "Yes, she does. She's acting out a bit because we both said no. The only balm for any emotion, apparently, is a party. And, she said she thinks you and I are too insular. That we should branch out, share ourselves with the world. Plus pizza and beer."

I put my hand over my eyes. "God, my worst nightmare."

"And mine!" He laughed. "But . . ." sighing, with a smile, "you know, she gets what she wants, our Hattie."

"Always," I murmured.

"Think we should do it? Might make our lives more bearable?" He was looking at me so softly, I would have agreed to anything.

"Of course. For our own sakes." I grinned.

"Naturally. This is a self-preservation party."

We were quiet again.

"Even if she doesn't know that she wants me to be the DJ. I'm glad to fill in the role," Jameson said.

I laughed. "Well, sure. One can't call it a party without someone playing the Bee Gees."

"Hey!"

I giggled and elbowed him. He looked at me, and bit his lip, and we stared at each other until he looked away, smiling shyly. A flirtation simmered. He moved his arm between us and gave my hand a squeeze. He didn't stay long after that, although he did ask me to stop sleeping at the barn, to come back home to him and Hattie, who, he said, missed me.

"You need to come back. So we can keep this party to the right guest-list size: three."

"Trust me, I am not a party girl."

"That, my friend, is exactly why she wants to do this. She likes to, let's say, keep us on our toes, don't you think? Push us out of our comfort zones."

I nodded, but said nothing.

He hugged me, and I still felt his chest against mine long after he drove the car away. But something prickled at me. Worry. And a terrible thought slipped between the crevices of my mind. Did Hattie send him here? Did she think Jameson could talk me into that pregnancy plan of hers? No, of course not. That would never happen. Not because Hattie wouldn't plot that, but because Jameson wouldn't.

I stood in the chilly breeze, finally alone again. I listened to the wind licking the leaves off the trees. And in that solitary moment, I suddenly missed Mum something awful. I needed her now: she could have offered me advice, could have changed the course of things, the course of me. It really feels, after all of this time, that there is an actual hole in me. I was robbed of my father, I was robbed of my mum. What would she have told me to do? How could she have steered me differently, and would I have gone there? I touched my cheek where it had brushed against Jameson's and went back inside, pulling the door shut behind me.

CHAPTER 12

DIDN'T KNOW IT HAD HAPPENED UNTIL I LOOKED across the bed at my feet and thought a bath would be nice on a cold night like this. Then I remembered that I'd turned it on already. The roar of the water had just become background noise, like the whipping winter wind. I ran into the bathroom, slipping and splashing on the checkered tile, the water flowing over the edges of the tub. You think you will hear it if a bath overflows. You think that you'd know. It just all sounds the same until it's too late. Hattie yelled up that there was water coming through the dining-room light, and we put out a bucket to catch it until it stopped.

I look back on that moment and see now that this is what we spent our lives doing: trying to contain the flood.

I was back in the fold, home to the cage of our house, just as the weather changed and Hattie warmed me with her sisterly embraces once again. And I was grateful for her, and so glad to see Jameson on a daily basis.

Hattie was desperate to plan the party, and although my initial response was to think this a bad idea, I began to soften in the face of her excitement. She agreed to my condition that she keep the party small. I didn't want to open our door to the town, but with every discussion of the event, Hattie pushed it open further. In fact, she was happier throughout Christmas and leading up to New Year's than I had seen her in a long time.

"This house is so amazing, it's the perfect party house! We need to breathe some new life into it, people!"

Jameson and I, rolling our eyes, bonding over our shared instincts to keep things small, but doing her bidding. We looked up recipes in long-forgotten cookbooks of Mum's, Jameson doing rounds of testing different Swedish meatballs, digging out the fondue pot with the chip in it, trying out drink concoctions. The whole month of December was like one long New Year's party in stages. Hattie marched about like a cruise director, making guest lists and buying shimmering decorations, finding a seemingly endless supply of party gear in our basement.

"Oh! I remember those," I said, watching Hattie open a box of Champagne and tinted shot glasses.

"Remember the parties with all the neighbours here?"

"We were the waitresses!"

"Child labour," Jameson mused, lifting out a glass. "Think there are any local kids we could pay in meatballs?"

NEW YEAR'S EVE FINALLY ARRIVED. THE HOUSE WAS full to bursting: throw a house party in a small town and everyone comes. All manner of St. Margaret's people arrived, and they were the exact sort, in fact, who would be great fun at a stay-in New Year's Eve party during one of the first blizzards that winter. A collection of singles and couples, young and old, shy and the kind of balls-out line-crossers who would have us knocking over wine glasses and mopping up the spills with our stocking feet to ring in the new year.

I was nervous and put off joining the party until the last moment. I am not great at crowds; prefer them from the outskirts. But it was seductive, the sound of the gathering crowd, and so I allowed myself to relax into it. I teased my short hair to make it stand up, wrapped a long string of cheap pearls around my neck and drank sparkling wine from a tumbler on my vanity before skipping down the stairs, my hand on the railing of my childhood, to greet our ragtag assortment of ball-dropping misfits. The night slipped silkily downward into a kind of reckless post-Christmas frivolity that marks the best kind of parties. She had done it: it was a hit.

A mess of tapes was scattered on the rug in the family room, spilling out of a box on the floor and stacked in a tower on the stereo, which was set up beside a ceramic planter whose plant had long since shrivelled with neglect. People were dancing, twisting their socked feet into the braided rug that Mum had bought at an antique auction. Jerry, an octogenarian patron of Hattie's hair salon with very little hair to speak of, was flirting unabashedly with Hattie's friend from work, Diane. Leaning in to hear each other, they were squeezed into the end of an overstuffed chesterfield. Three young women from the daycare took up the rest of the real estate, legs crossed over each other, arms linked, giggling boozily into one another's faces. Jameson had his arm around Hattie, and he rocked her back and forth to the music, whispering in her ear, making her cackle and grin—a trick of the light, and she had a devilish pointed-toothed smile. And then it was gone, replaced by her closed red lips and happy eyes. Jameson looked at me and winked, and I blushed up to my ears. Hattie swung over, wrapped her arms around my neck and sang into my face flirtatiously. I laughed at her bravado, so pleased to see her swagger and stomp, throwing her worries away in a big, windmill-armed toss into the night. A good time. I could have a good time, right? I grinned and let myself go.

"This is better than sleeping in a barn, don't you think, Penny?"

"It is." I laughed, embarrassed to be outed. "It definitely is."

Jameson shouted out to me, "See?" while Hattie refilled his glass.

SITTING WITH MY OLD FRIEND SALLY, IN MY ROOM LATER. She hadn't been upstairs in our house since high school and had meandered about looking at my photos and knick-knacks before settling down on the carpet. Our legs crossed, a ouija board and an overflowing ashtray between us. Sally's hair was falling out of its hair-sprayed architecture, slanting sideways in faded, teased glory.

"Who do you want to contact?"

I took a haul on a joint and passed it back to her, thinking. "Well," I exhaled, "I think my mum is out. That is just too weird. Also, I'd like to think she's doing more than waiting around for calls from a ouija board. Mind you, she loved this kind of thing. And Buddy, well, that's just too sad."

I was quiet in a fuzzy, stoned moment.

"How you holding up, friend?" Sally asked, her hand on my arm. "I hardly ever see or hear from you."

I sighed for her benefit. "Hmm. Oh, you know. Alright, I guess. The nights are hard, maybe I'm not deeply, subconsciously okay, but you know: okay by day. Like a superhero!"

Sally laughed. "Grieving Widow: okay by day . . ."

"Panic-stricken insomniac by night!"

"Yeah . . . That's not too catchy."

"I'm sorry I'm hard to reach. I'm not a great friend." And for that minute, I almost meant it.

We were quiet again.

"Death sucks," Sally said, inhaling the joint.

I nodded. "Yup."

"Okay. Who, then?" I grabbed the ouija piece. "What about your uncle, the one who had to buy two seats for his ass on the bus?"

Sally nodded, giggling, and we moved our fingers together across the board, the whole effort collapsing intermittently into stoned hysteria. Eventually we gave it up for a bad job, assuming that the obese uncle was in a huff in the afterlife and was refusing to co-operate. We leaned against the legs of my bed and lapsed into silence, the music from downstairs thumping, punctuated by laughter and the occasional crash. It was nice, just sitting there with a friend, relaxing. Almost normal. Like a glimpse into the life I might have had.

"Are you glad you moved back?"

"Sure. But, I mean, I didn't really move out."

"I know, I know. You did that outdoorsy thing for a while, though. Woman of the woods. I don't know how you stayed in that creepy barn for so long. I didn't even know you were out there until Hattie called to invite me to the party."

"Yeah. Well, it wasn't creepy to me. Never was." I thought about whether I had been tempting fate to stay there alone, and I suppose I had been. I had no protection, no stashed weapons or defence plans, knowing as I did that if someone wanted to hurt you, they would find a way. Buddy had always found numerous, unrelenting ways to torment me, so it surprised me that he had never thought to ruin my barn. But I usually crept there after he'd stormed out, or passed out. I don't think he ever knew I'd spent any time there.

I shuddered now and thought of Mac Williams returning to haunt the scene of so many crimes. He was like Buddy all over again: one rising up where the other had died. I emptied the rest of my glass down my throat and immediately felt the room move. I lay my head back and closed my eyes, half-listening to Sally's story about an abandoned house and a ghost. My mind hummed. I thought of my barn, gathering snow in its rafters. I heard Hattie's laughter somewhere nearby, Jameson mumbling, stumbling, a door closing.

It was the middle of the night. I woke with a sore neck, my arms flopped out beside me, my mouth dry and sour. Sally was gone. I couldn't hear anyone else, the music was off, the house was dark. I scrambled to my feet, swayed, catching sight of myself in the mirror, wheeling about like that rickety automaton, that drunk robot version of myself. I winded my way to the bathroom and splashed water on my face, gargled out the foulness of the long-gone drinks, almost gagged, my face hot, righted myself again, and wandered into the hallway. I walked down the stairs, considered getting something to eat, but turned and walked towards the den, where I heard faint music playing. It was a small room with large, floor-to-ceiling windows and a wall of bookcases. Against the windows was a settee bed, perfect for reading.

Jameson was there, stretched out across it, one leg crossed over the other, a foot bobbing to the music.

"Hi," I said, smiling and self-consciously wiping a finger under my eye. He turned to me and offered a lopsided smile. "Everything okay?"

Jameson lifted his arm, let it fall on his lap and laughed. He was drunk also.

"Yes. Yep. I guess . . ." He laughed again, slurring his words. "I actually don't know why I'm here."

"Okay," I said, sitting beside him on the edge of the bed. He shifted slightly, trying to sit up. The room spun.

He threw himself backwards and exhaled happily. "I don't think I'd be much good at, to talk to, for talking right now." He giggled. "Great party. Hey, did you know there is a sock hanging from the light up there?"

I carefully lay down beside him and looked up. He scooched over to make room for both of us.

"Uh-huh. That's one of the guys from the salon. His sock."

He turned to look at me, his face inches from mine, his breath boozy. "You looked really good tonight, you know. Did you have fun?"

I watched him and felt my face flush.

"You, too. And yeah, I did."

He laughed and lifted his head up. "Penny?"

"Yeah."

"Nothing." He laughed and touched my face.

I reached out, putting my hand on his arm. I rubbed his skin gently.

"You are so . . ." He touched my lips. "So nice, Penny."

I watched him. I moved my hand to his chest, put my hand over his heart. He sat up.

"I should go. I'm drunk."

"It's okay. Please don't go. I love—I like you here."

"I like it, too."

I pulled on his shirt, pulling him back. He looked at me, then leaned towards me. I felt the room tip, wanted to crawl into his skin. He put his hand around my neck gently, moving his fingers through my hair, and I knew what Hattie must know. Every nerve responded. I wanted Jameson terribly. Who could blame me, then? I would do it all over again, I swear I would.

We tumbled backwards together.

"Whose idea is this," I slurred.

"I'm not an ideas man," he whispered, and bit my ear softly.

All over again, I would rush into that kiss. I would put my fingers into his shirt and feel across to where his arm ended, and know it, once and for all. His hand on my back, lifting my damp, wrinkly shirt over my head, his mouth on my breasts. The unclasping, unbuckling, unzipping, the licking and sucking and pushing. Who could blame me? I have no regrets.

The ceiling swirled above us, the plaster circles of a long-ago artisan, echoing the waves of our bodies below.

It was a new year.

CHAPTER 13

I WAS ALONE, AND WITH A TERRIBLE HANGOVER. THE kind of desperate, dried-out, after-drink sadness that lingers in the corners of your eyes, the folds of your armpits and behind your knees, that yields to nothing but sleeping the whole day away. I felt it immediately: the memory, the embarrassment and the pleasure. I knew he wasn't there but turned my head sideways to look. I closed my eyes and slept until the sun took the hint and moved elsewhere.

Much later, I stood in the kitchen, my ragged robe knotted tightly around my waist, my secret running in an imaginary stream down my inner thigh. I shakily poured tea into my favourite mug, trying to protect myself with familiar comforts while ducking from the shadow of my betrayal. I slunk around the house. Put my fingers to picture frames, along window ledges. Slowly and silently like a ghost.

I was waiting it out, waiting them out, Hattie and Jameson.

Always three. Even while I tried to start again, away from this house, in my new home with Buddy, Hattie was there in our lives. Buddy brought up Hattie whenever he could. Reminded me of how different we were.

"Have you gone frigid or something? You used to love this." Mauling at me with the hands I had once thought of as so big and sexy. "You've changed, Penny, you know? You're so uptight." He shoved me away. "Why can't you loosen up? Be more like Hattie, hey?" He got up to leave. "I chose the wrong sister."

When Hattie came to visit, she was wary of Buddy. She had an idea of what he was capable of.

"I popped by the other day," he said once, to her. "You didn't answer this time."

I stared at her.

"I—I must not have been home, Bud," she said.

"You go over there?" I asked him, quietly, and I reached up, tugging my earlobe, a nervous tic.

Buddy took a swig of his beer and shrugged. "Sure. Once in a while. Just checking in."

Later, on the phone, Hattie told me, in pleading tones, that she never thought anything of it. That she thought he was just being nice, that he'd never done anything wrong.

"He never 'did anything wrong'?"

"To me, I mean."

I hung up on her. My frightened heart hardening.

Always the two of us, always a third, secrets winding around us.

I HAD TRIED TO LEAVE BUDDY ONE NIGHT. MY TIMING was off. In these things, timing is everything. He returned home from the pub earlier than I'd expected. But he'd made great progress while there. I heard him stumbling, crashing about.

"Penny! Dirty Penny!" He called me over and over again, coming up the stairs.

I had a knapsack over my shoulder, and he came into our bedroom. He took up the doorway, cocked his head, his jaw sticking out.

"Where you going?"

I stood tall. "I can't do this, Buddy. I need—we need to . . . This isn't going to work."

"You're leaving."

"Yes. It's not your fault. I just—"

He laughed softly.

"Nope."

"Buddy, please."

"Let me put it this way: Nope. No. No way. Because," he burped, and shook his head, like there was a buzzing, "'cause I'll kill ya, Penny. I will kill you, I swear. And then who will take care of little Hattie? She'll be all alone, like that." Drunken snap.

I tried to calm myself, and by doing this, him. I nodded, held out my hands.

"Okay. Okay, Buddy. I won't go." I put my knapsack on the bed. "Forget it. It was a dumb idea." Diffuse, diffuse. There was a humming in my ears, and it was the sound of fear.

"That's a hard thing to forget, Penny." He held the door frame to support himself. "But just so you know. Just so we're clear. If you think you can sneak out. If you think you can leave one day while I'm at work. Go ahead. But I'll kill you, Pen." He had started to cry. "I swear. I will. I will. Don't leave me, Penny." He was sobbing.

My mouth dry, tears streaming down my face. He shuffled towards me, then fell on the bed, and rolled over.

"I love you, Pen," he mumbled, crying into his pillow.

"I love you, too, Bud."

Soon he was snoring like a sick child, the next day he remembered nothing, and I never left.

Until the one day that I did.

OUR HOUSE—HATTIE'S AND MY HOUSE—HAD BEEN QUIET all day, but in the late afternoon, while I was reading in a corner of the living room, my teeth gnawing on my lip, Hattie and Jameson returned to the house after a brisk New Year's Day walk. They were laughing, smiling, sharing the tail end of a tease or a joke that blew in with them. It stung seeing Jameson, back to playing house with Hattie, after being with me. I saw at once that Hattie didn't know; there was too much sincerity there for a graceful cover-up. Jameson avoided my eye, following Hattie into the kitchen as she called out to me over her shoulder, chastising me for wasting the day away. I sat silently, the fool.

"I *told* you you'd have fun if we had a party, Penny! I knew you just needed to cut loose a little bit more." I heard puttering in the kitchen. "Of course," she called out, "Sally told me you passed out before midnight. You're such a lightweight."

I let her prattle on. I felt sick. I had done a terrible thing, hadn't I? The biggest betrayal, of the person closest to me. But I also felt hurt, stupid, ignored by Jameson's blatant desire to move forward. I steeled myself. It was good he hadn't told her. She could never know. That sort of thing could drive a person mad.

I listened as Hattie called out plans for dinner.

SINCE MY BARN WAS COVERED IN SNOW, I FOUND AN apartment almost immediately after the party. I told Hattie that I needed a little space, and that I thought they might also. Jameson continued behaving as though nothing had happened, and seeing him was an aching reminder of what we'd done, and how little it had meant to him. I needed to get out.

The apartment was over a store on the main drag of our little town. Above a key carver and general repair shop. There were often clocks in there, lying abandoned on the counters, dismantled with their guts strewn about. The gentleman, Joseph, who owned the building—he was exactly the kind of person you would call a gentleman, complete with tweed vests and newsboy hats—greeted me on our first meeting with such warmth and familiarity, despite not knowing me at all, that I almost wept. He touched my hand, in which I held the ad for the apartment, with his own liver-spotted and papery one, and told me that I looked like just the sort of gal who should live in that place upstairs.

"You'll shake things up, I can tell. I can tell just by your short hair. Some gals don't like short hair; hell, pardon my French, some guys don't either, but I think you look real sharp, Penelope. And what a name! You move in whenever you want, okay, honey? And if you ever need anything, just come on down or call me. I'm home most nights and I only live in the back of the store, there."

He studied my face, and I squirmed and looked away.

"You're not having any trouble, are ya, Penelope? Boyfriend or someone giving you a hard time? That why you're here?" He smiled and I laughed in spite of myself.

"Just a meddlesome sister," I said.

"Oh yeah, I know what you mean. We're gonna get along just fine."

I moved in right away, three days into the new year. I took with me a number of boxes and laundry hampers full of things. Because I was officially moving out, I was herded by Hattie, who wrung her hands, vacillating between snapping at me and imploring me to change my mind. We stomped through the snow in our impractical boots, my neck bristling at the breezes while I held a box on my hip and unlocked my car door. Hattie gabbed away at my side, begging me to call when I got to the apartment, which was a mere five minutes away. Jameson had cheerily loaded most of my things for me, and he stood now in the doorway, smiling benignly, which I found infuriating. It had meant nothing, I could see. As I pulled my car back, an arm around the headrest beside me, I looked apologetically at my old house, its brick face hard and stoic.

The apartment was clean, with new curtains and two worn rugs. I sighed deeply when I had laid down the last box against the walls, and went straight to the bathroom to run a hot bath. The tub was small, but as I eased my way in, and my skin contracted, pulled tight right to my scalp, covered in goosebumps, I felt myself relax. I lifted a toe under the tap to catch the last drops onto my toenails. I took a breath and submerged my head into the water, feeling a momentary panic, and then a great ripple of shivering relief when I pulled myself out again. I wondered where my heater was, packed in a box full of screwdrivers and kitchen utensils and other unrelated items. The window above me had steamed over, and I noticed how clean the windowsill was. Heard the squawk of a crow, over and over. I thought of how I had once learned about how smart crows are, how resourceful. I laced my fingers together and smiled at having space of my own.

And so when, two weeks later, I discovered that I was pregnant after making an appointment for a blood test to rule it out, I was shocked that something had still managed to slip under the rug of my privacy. I believe my face froze, my whole body still, while a nurse told me the results, her face a mask of solemn professionalism. My first thought was that it was a good thing

I had been so careful for all these years, because obviously, I was fertile ground for bad ideas. Next, I planned on erasing it, striking this fateful diversion altogether, to hell with Hattie and Jameson, the king and queen of St. Margaret's. It wasn't fair, and I would take care of it, regardless of Hattie and her stupid plans to have a baby.

I stood in front of the mirror after another bath, holding my breasts in my hands and gauging their growing size and sensitivity. If I'm honest, I did feel smug. It was my turn to get something—there, I said it. And then, like a subconscious ghost, I saw Buddy smirking behind me in the mirror reflection, lighting a cigarette. *You just can't let her have anything*, I heard him mutter. *Cunt. I told you: I chose the wrong sister.* I looked at myself and touched my stomach, pushed my fingers in, casting Buddy out.

CHAPTER 14

DAYS PASSED. I HADN'T DONE ANYTHING ABOUT the pregnancy yet, I still hadn't made up my mind. I paid attention as everything became hypersensitive: my boobs and my nose and my bladder. I had no one to talk to about it. This was my life, of course. I rarely had anyone to talk to about anything. Funny thing about murdering your husband: you can never really make friends after that. And whoever you once had, like sweet Sally, has to be left by the wayside. Jameson had been the exception, but he was Hattie's. There was no one I could trust, no one I'd expose anything to. Even Hattie and I were tangled up with secrets.

But now I was alone in my above-the-store apartment. So few furnishings. Everything was still in boxes, which were themselves becoming a comfort in that place. I often heard metal grinding or banging coming from downstairs. I wondered what my elderly landlord would make of my predicament. I worried about what he would think. I feared that he could read it on my face when I waved at him through the front window of the shop. I worried about that, so I wouldn't have to worry about Hattie and Jameson.

I thought about Jameson so often. I felt like I did at puberty: confused and disgusted, curious and ashamed. My body wasn't helping. In private, I was horrified by my darkening nipples, but was turned on by the sight of them at the same time. And the fact that I was avoiding him and Hattie enabled me to knead my memory of him into something fresh. At times, it was easier to resent him. All these girls and women out there—Hattie!—who wanted what I had, to conceive. And still I didn't do anything about it. Days were coming and going, a wash of grey and snow outside my window, on my way to work, waiting for a blizzard that hovered, waiting to drop. I dodged Hattie's phone calls and ignored her messages. Finally I had a secret to myself, and I had no desire to tell her; but I wasn't ready yet to decide what to do with what was growing and making plans inside me. Maybe it made no difference what I thought, maybe not. Maybe the Fates were tangled up in the course of events, no matter my opinion on them.

I wanted to distract myself. I headed into Joseph's repair shop after work. The door jingled when I entered, and I was surprised to see so many people there. Buying weird little hinges and copper parts, waiting in a small line to have their keys cut, holding them out like they were going to open doors in succession. Joseph busily moving around, chatting to everyone he saw. He smiled and hustled over, put his arm around me. Once again I felt myself sag under his warmth.

"Penelope Grayson, you vision!"

"Hello, Joseph." A nervous finger over my ear. "Your store is busy."

"Oh, yes, yes. And what brings you here?"

"Nothing, really. Um. Do you need any help?"

Joseph laughed, and his face crinkled all over, and my own smile faltered. But yes, he said, of course. Come on back behind the counter. I grinned, and my lip cracked.

Joseph gave me an apron, asked me if I knew how to operate a cash register. I did, having worked at a deli as a teen, although now it took a couple of customers before I got comfortable. I marvelled at the small and large things that Joseph had repaired for the people of St. Margaret's: toasters and fans, alarm clocks and even regular clocks. His workshop, which was a thick, wide table behind us, was littered with springs and whirring remnants of time and habits and memory and stubborn refusals to give up. Between cutting keys, Joseph chatted with friends and strangers, handing over repaired household items that had been wiped clean and given life. I fought a cynicism that asked why people didn't just replace their broken things, and certainly in time feelings like mine would win over, and shops like Joseph's would cease to be. But more than his craftsmanship and stick-to-it-ness, I admired Joseph's ease with people. Something I've never had. I am proud and defensive, always a second behind on the smile and just not quite warm enough. I would love to have that easy way with people, that magnetism. Hattie had it. Joseph softened me, and I bonded with him so quickly that it startled me.

The change rang through the register, the sun sank, and soon it was time to close up the shop. I was more tired than I wanted to admit. I flipped the sign from Open to Closed and turned the lock on the door with great satisfaction, while Joseph tallied up the till.

"Thank you, Penelope. It was so nice to have some company."

"My pleasure. Thank you. I needed that, too."

He raised his eyebrows, but said nothing. Reached under the counter and pulled out a pack of cigarettes. "I hope you don't mind if I smoke. Would you like one?"

I declined, but inhaled longingly while Joseph lit his. I smelled his aftershave and felt that cozy comfort of daughters and fathers, and something inside me sighed. Joseph smiled, watching me kindly. He was taller than I had thought at first, and strong, but so much more, so many other things. He was the last of his kind.

"Do you have children, Joseph?"

"Yep. Two daughters. Both in their thirties, but they're still my little girls. You know how it is. I'm sure your dad feels the same."

"Yes. Well. My father left when I was young, and my mother died a number of years ago."

Joseph bowed his head and said how sorry he was, like someone who says that kind of thing often. I figured that Joseph had lost a lot of people in his life. Or maybe he just was really good at being sympathetic. I thanked him. Changed the subject.

"So." I looked around the store. "So I'm, uh, I'm pregnant." I chuckled like this was a funny thing. A funny thing; not a scary, sticky, troublesome thing to me, and a possibly wonderful blessing to my sister. "Ha ha. You must think I'm a real fuck-up. Sorry—excuse my French."

Joseph ashed his cigarette in a bean can in front of us.

"Wow. That is a pretty big deal, darlin'. Lots of questions, none of them my business. But the number-one question is, are you okay? Want to sit down? You've been standing for hours." He pulled out a stool and wiped his hand over it, sawdust clouding his arm hair.

I laughed. "Thanks, Joseph." I sat down, felt the relief immediately. "I'm only barely pregnant. Like, this thing is microscopic, it's just a dot. I don't even, you know," I looked out the window at a man walking a tiny dog, "know if I'm going to keep it." I looked quickly at him. "I'm sorry if that offends your moral or religious views. Please don't kick me out." I smiled sheepishly.

"Are you kidding? I may be old, Penelope, but I'm not old-fashioned. Now: Do you want a beer? No judgement here. I happen to have a small fridge here under the counter for just this sort of emergency." And he rooted around under there, pulling out two cans of beer. God, I loved him. I heard a phone ring-ing somewhere and realized it was probably mine from upstairs. Hattie, undoubtedly. I had no friends who would call. I sighed loudly and opened my beer, hand cold around it.

"What about siblings, Joseph? Do you have any of those?"

"Sure. I had four, but my sister died. She was the oldest, and she got sick. It was very sad. My three brothers and me now. It's not the same. She really looked after all of us. We're all old men now, but I miss her." He paused and drank. "What about your sister, Penelope? Can she help you out? Does she come visit? She's very welcome."

"Are you new to St. Margaret's?"

He smiled. "I moved here after my wife passed away. Four years ago. I know it looks like longer by the state of the store."

"No, not at all. I love it here," I said, looking around the shop I'd grown so fond of. And I told him about my mum, about that bee that stung us out of adolescence, and about my husband dying in a fire, about living with Hattie, about my barn. I left out Jameson, which is what I had planned to do from now on. And I left out the part I played in Buddy's death. I worried he would be able to tell, anyway. But Joseph saw only the good in me. He squeezed my hand and said, "So, what, the whole town knows about you girls, except me? Is that what you're saying?" He pro-duced some peanuts from under the counter. "What a crap time you've had, darlin'. That's no joke. And now this?" He sipped and pointed in the area of my stomach. "Well, I'm happy for this place to be your hideout, whatever you decide."

"Joseph, I thank you." I raised my can and clanged beers with my friend.

* * *

LATER, I LAY ON MY BACK AND WEIGHED MY OPTIONS. I could terminate the pregnancy and move on, like it had never happened. I knew that would be, without a doubt, to punish them, even if they never learned of it. On the other hand, there was something here that I was relishing. This thing, this tiny achievement—having nothing to do with any skills of mine, but at which I had bested Hattie.

I did not want a baby, not to hold and feed and nurture. I was not torn about giving this child, should I let it come to that, over to Hattie under the pretense of generosity and to undo the ropes of debt that were wrapped so tightly around us. I didn't fear that I would grow attached to whoever this was. Foolish, perhaps, but this thinking propelled me to accept the terms and conditions of the deal Hattie had set in motion so long ago. Tit for tat. I imagined the pair, in Hattie's house, turning my room into a baby's nursery, becoming Mom and Dad while I was able to step out of the role I had been forced into. I thought that as a mother, Hattie would no longer be a liability, she would be stable and calm and I could bury the bee and the fire once and for all. I could be free. And so, when I think of it now, I realize that must have been it: I was drawn to the chance of a real private life, the one I had wanted so long ago, the possibility of secrets that could be, again, my very own. I could leave town, even, and I could put a real distance between Hattie and me. That was when I decided I would carry this child to the end, that I would let it occupy my body, so that I could pass it on like currency: the exchange of services rendered. To even the score.

I called home when I knew Hattie would be out, but Jameson would be in.

"I want to tell Hattie that we'll try her idea," I said, when he answered.

"What? Are you—first of all, hi, Penny. I mean, it's been a long time. How are you?"

"I'm pregnant, Jameson, so try that on for size."

"Jesus Christ."

I let it hang there.

"So, you want to go through with Hattie's plan to cover it up, is that it?"

"I am happy to just abort it, Jameson, so let's not quibble over who's going to benefit here, since I don't think it'll be you doing the pushing."

"I know. I just—" I heard him exhale, and I relished making him weigh it all.

"I don't want to hurt her, Penny."

"You fucked her sister, Jameson."

"Yeah, I know, Penny. I have been dying inside. I can't believe we did that. Look—I know I've—I've been a coward. I've avoided you, I avoided it with myself even. I can hardly look at myself. It was a mistake. The biggest mistake I've ever made."

That stung, and I said nothing. I let the pause stretch out.

"If you want a baby, I can help you out."

"Jesus. I don't know."

"I'll take that as a yes."

HATTIE WAS BIZARRELY HAPPY WHEN I TOLD HER THE following day that we would try. In her strange, toxic mind, this was the ultimate gesture, the means to a beautiful end. I balked at her thanks, felt nauseous, the betrayal kept at bay by the affection. She thought I was paying her back for her loyalty and devotion and love, and I let her think that, because I needed her, too.

And there was a thread of love there, but it was not my love for Hattie that wove itself through the tangle of flesh.

Hattie planned it. The curator of our catastrophe, she needed a role, needed to be the director of this epic tale of familial love and fucked-up priorities. She wanted Jameson and me to increase the chances of success by having it all happen within minutes, if the baster was, so to speak, fresh. She decided she would go out with her friends for a "girls' night" and leave us and a turkey baster in the house together. She planned to do her hair, dress up, booze up, flirt, distract, stumble home, celebrate the planting of a poisonous seed that was really already a sprout.

Jameson and I made dinner. We sat on opposite sides of the table. I put on a record. We opened a bottle of wine and hardly touched it. We refused to ignite the electric current between us, and so we played Battleship and talked. It was worse than a fuck; it was a date. I couldn't help myself: I felt alive around him, and something in me died because of that.

"So . . ." he said, awkwardly, "kind of hard to get back into the swing of things, isn't it."

"Well, it's a bit weird." I laughed. "But it's good to be here. I've got to admit: I've missed you, Jameson."

He smiled kindly, like a brother.

"We've missed you, too, Penny."

CHAPTER 15

TOLD HATTIE THAT I WAS PREGNANT AS SOON AS would be reasonably possible. She wanted to move me back in immediately. I hadn't accounted for the fact that she would feel entitled to me again, now in a new way.

"I'm fine, Hattie. I'm going to stay where I am. I like it here."

She ignored me and clapped her hands together.

"Oh my God, I can't believe it, Penny. I am so happy. Thank you so much. I will be forever grateful, we both will be. I knew we'd get our own baby somehow. See?" she shouted at Jameson, almost hysterical. "You both thought this was a crazy idea, but it worked! And it's going to be so perfect." Jameson smiling benignly behind her. Embracing again, I breathed in the smell of her and my stomach turned. I was becoming accustomed to how certain deodorants and shampoos triggered nausea, and this was a new thing, to find Hattie, her baby-powder freshness, so off-putting. I put my hands on her small shoulders and pushed her back. I looked away and offered them tea, heading into my small kitchen. Joseph's machinery was grinding quietly below us, and I wondered if he had seen Hattie and Jameson come in.

I hadn't told Joseph any more details about my pregnancy, although I had spent a great deal of time with him of late. In his quiet, calm way, Joseph offered solace that no one else could. He was, I suppose, a kind of father figure, and I needed him, and that was all. I had taken to working at the shop after coming home from the daycare, and I was learning things about basic electrical work, repairing, soldering. Joseph had tried to pay me, and I had refused, although I knew he was putting the cash in a coffee tin under the workbench, saving it there for me. We sometimes ordered dinner into the shop, and other times Joseph went into the back, where he lived, and warmed up something or other for us to eat. The building itself was one of St. Margaret's original old brick houses on our quiet Main Street. The main drag was populated by shops and the occasional diner, a hardware store. It took five minutes to walk the length of it before you came upon houses with larger and larger plots of land, turning quickly to farms. Joseph's place was a large and rambling thing. The shop was in the front, and he lived in the back. The front hallway and stairs had been cordoned off, and made up my private entrance to my upstairs apartment. Joseph's living space was, in some ways, an extension of the shop; he kept an overflow of gadgets and mechanical artifacts there, alongside lamps and books and pieces of his life. The effect was cozy and welcoming. I loved it there.

"Pretty loud up here, don't you think?" Hattie remarked, settling into one of the chairs I had brought with me from the house. There was, in actual fact, quite a racket going on in the shop, a rapid banging that stopped as abruptly as it began.

"I don't mind it."

Hattie nodded primly, sipping at her tea.

"Have you been to the doctor yet?"

"Why, is there something wrong with me?" I smiled, and Hattie did as well, tightly.

"Okay, Penny. But when you have doctor visits, can we come?"

"Let me think about it." Absolutely not.

"Hattie, let Penny be. Lay off a little, okay?" Jameson bridging between us, and I knew he didn't want Hattie to figure out the difference between the real conception and the one she knew about. "You do whatever makes you comfortable, Penny. Seriously. We just want you to be healthy and happy. This is a big deal. And we know," he reached out to Hattie with his eyes, "that this isn't easy. And that it might be harder when the baby's born."

"I don't want the baby, Jameson. I never did. And I won't."

"Okay. I just want us all to be prepared for how, I guess, unpredictable these things can be."

Hattie nodded, and said, "And I'm sure it'll be a little awkward with other people. I don't think St. Margaret's has seen too many turkey-baster babies." She smiled and reddened. I looked anywhere but at the two of them. Into my cup. Away from thoughts of that night.

"Oh yeah, a turkey-baster baby is plenty weird for this place. We'll be the local science experiment." The tension broken, a chuckle, someone changed the subject. The sound downstairs started up again, and Jameson stood up and began thumbing through my tapes.

Eventually they left. There were hugs from Hattie, and Jameson and I embraced, although I stiffened, and he released me, nodding formally. Hattie said goodbye, loudly, to my stomach, and I couldn't wait to close the door behind them.

Sometimes, when I look back at that period in my life, I cringe, my hands shaking, knowing what came later. And I would do it all again if I had to.

After Hattie and Jameson left, I went down to the shop. I decided to go out onto the street and back through the jangling shop door. A scene change. It was a chilly February, and snow had gathered and then been shovelled away from front porches and walkways. There was a fan shape carved over the sidewalk from the door opening and closing. The glass door was frosty, and a child's hand had finger-drawn faces in the fog on the bottom half of it. I was reminded of what it had been like to tag along with our mum on chores and errands. An endless shop-hopping of high counters and things I couldn't touch. Going to big department stores so you could squeeze in some clothes shopping on a busy day. The dry heat of those places. Hiding inside a circular clothes rack, sitting on a dark carpet, watching the hems of skirts swish around me like deep sea waves, hearing the clack of hangers moving as women browsed the wares. Wanting to go home. Whining that I was thirsty, bored, tired. Sometimes childhood felt like an endless parade of waiting. What I wouldn't do to wait for her now. To slow down time. To have protected her, from that tiny thief that stole her life through the palm of her hand.

It was Sunday. Joseph kept his shop open on Sundays, claiming that it was because it was harder for people to come on a workday, although I suspected he was prone, as am I, to a kind of Sunday melancholy, and needed to be surrounded by work and people. He chose Mondays as his day off.

I could smell a roast in the oven when I entered the shop, a smell that will forever make me feel ill, but I smiled, knowing that Joseph would likely invite me to stay for supper, perhaps as well as some other folks: maybe he had asked a couple of his friends. I had met these men on other occasions, and found a kind of lonesome solidarity with them, those hearty seniors. Sometimes they played poker and I read in a corner under a light that had been cobbled together out of an old colander and some wire. Other times I joined in, when they needed a fourth, and I knew they went easy on me. I was wondering if I had anything in my fridge that I could bring to contribute to the meal, as Joseph waved at me, then returned his attention to a woman with a temperamental alarm clock. There was music playing out of a silver ghetto blaster plugged into the end of the workbench, and a CBC broadcaster updated us on the news of the hour. I suppressed a chill, a relic of a feeling I'd had since the fire, a fear of hearing about myself on the news. That the juicy details of my plotted revenge would be piped into homes across the nation still raised the hair on my arms.

I looked out the window and froze at what I saw. Officer Moore was standing on the sidewalk in front of the store, hands crossed in front of his chest, talking to Mac Williams. Mac was gesturing wildly, which wasn't unusual, but I felt a shiver of panic at the sight of the two of them together. The window was foggy and I craned my neck to see the men more clearly. Suddenly Mac broke off with a dismissive wave and stormed towards the shop. I turned my back quickly and busied myself tidying a shelf.

I heard the door jingle behind me.

"Dirty Penny." A chuckle. I turned to face him. A stocky man, Mac wore layers of flannel and a puffy vest, his greasy dirty-blond hair hanging from under a deer-hunter's cap. I shuddered at the sound of his and Buddy's old nickname for me, although sometimes it was "Lucky Penny" instead. There was a glint of furious mischief in his wild eyes today, and I felt my hands go quickly to my middle.

"Mac. How are you?" I looked over his shoulder and saw Iain Moore peering in. He caught sight of me, and I turned my attention back to Mac, who was following my gaze.

"You know that loser? He was in our year at school. He's always sniffing around like a fucking choir boy."

This town was so small, so few pieces in the game, but they were always rolling just out of my reach. I calmed myself with the thought that after the baby was born, I could leave them all for good.

"No, I don't know him. Not really."

"'Not really.' Yeah, okay. Like I believe that shit." He sized me up. "You look good, Penny." His eyes lingered on my breasts. "Been a while."

"I know. Thank you." I avoided his gaze. He stood beside me, fingered the steely contents of a box, picking up items and inspecting them vacantly. A look back outside told me Iain Moore had moved on.

"Keeping that hair short, eh? I always like it long on women, myself."

Joseph was looking my way, eyebrows up the way he did. Asking if I was alright. I nodded, smiling.

Mac looked about, grasping for something else to say.

"I seen your sister hanging around with that one-armed China-man. What the fuck is that about?" He looked thoughtful. "Always liked your sister. Red. Spitfire." He looked behind him through the window again, where Officer Moore had been. "She knew how to party, your sister. You always seemed a little too much of a goody-goody." His eyes hardened, and he lowered his voice. "I hate goody-goodies. Always makin' decisions that aren't theirs to make." He lightened his tone, then, and put his hand on my shoulder. "You might think that you're better than everyone here, Dirty Penny, but you are St. Maggie's born and raised, just like the rest of us, so don't get any ideas." He squeezed my arm hard, and I took a step back.

133

I inhaled, trying to compose myself. "Mac, I gotta go. I was just on my way out. I'll see you later, okay?"

He watched me, milky-eyed old dog letting a rabbit get away. I waved at Joseph, heard the voice of the familiar radio host lending comfort to the Sunday sadness, and I hurried outside.

CHAPTER 16

THE SNOW FINALLY MELTED. AT FIRST IN DRIBS and drabs, and then suddenly, St. Margaret's thawed, and the streams and creeks and eavestroughs gushed with a racket that signalled awakening. Birds and stubborn crocuses, trees budding, the escarpment turning green all at once. The children in the daycare made crafts about baby animals and blossoms, "Spring Has Sprung!" in large letters, tacked in an arc on the walls I could see from my office. I had started to appear pregnant, and as such, needed to let people know. Or at the very least, I figured I would tell enough people that word would roll downhill into the valleys of the town. The idea of attention made me nervous, but at least the gossips in town would be thinking of a baby, and not a fire.

I am carrying a baby for my sister, Hattie. She is unable to have children. There was something selfless and sisterly about this, something that spoke of enough love, devotion and sweetness that if it weren't for the fact that Hattie was unmarried, or the straight-up technical questions that people had, I would by and large have been left alone, if considered a bit of an oddball. Still, I was constantly robbed of my privacy and dignity while people thought nothing of touching my stomach or asking bold questions. Sally took to calling regularly and trying to set up coffee dates. I dodged her, unable to wrestle up the energy that friendship demanded. And meanwhile, I thought, Hattie was continuing on as she did: cutting hair and looking fresh-faced and happy all at once. Sure, people judged her, and certainly Jameson would eventually become the object of even more curiosity when it became clear who the "sperm donor" father had been. But mostly I felt sorry for myself. I had chosen this path despite Hattie's wishes, not because of them. Suddenly all manner of old friends, high-school teachers, elderly strangers, neighbours, customers and the parents of the daycare children offering tight smiles while asking after the baby. *Why, what a surprise!* I learned to perfect my own pious smile, emulating Saint Margaret herself, patiently explaining our "predicament," and saying some version of, *Without getting into the technical details, I'll say that there are all kinds of medical miracles you can do now.* People asked if this meant the baby was a "test-tube baby." I laughed like this was the first time I'd heard this, and quipped that I was looking less like a tube with every passing day.

And I was. As the days got longer and I opened my windows, as Joseph propped open the door to the shop in the late afternoon and turned on the rusty overhead fan, that tiny uterine plan grew into a threat, pushing out my concert T-shirts and giving me a most impressive set of cans, as Buddy would have said. Hattie had learned to keep her hands off my belly, but she was becoming unhinged with excitement. She stared at my growing bump while talking to me, and had overhauled the house to prepare for the imminent arrival, which was still almost five months away. My old room had become swathed in bright colours, and filled with baby furniture and mobiles and enormous stuffed animals. They had taken our mother's room. I hardly recognized the place, and for the first time since I had moved out, I felt a sense of longing. I moved about my family home with the recognition that there were different smells, different food being cooked, different music playing. There was a new family there now. Hattie and Jameson were a strong unit. Somewhere along the line, Hattie had let me go. And while this was what I had wanted all along, there was a real pang, a bitter sweetness that comes of feeling at once released and unneeded.

I HAD BEEN GETTING PHONE CALLS AT THE APARTMENT. The phone would ring out loud into my quiet space, putting me right away on edge.

"Hello?"

Heavy breathing.

"You bitch," the voice slurred.

"Who is this?" But then I knew. "Mac?"

"Shut up. Just—keep your trap shut. I know you been talking. It's gotta be you."

"I don't know what—" But the phone went dead.

There were a few of these calls, often in the middle of the night. I tried to calm him, while he reeled off names of people he thought I had told of one thing or another. He sounded drunk, high, volatile and paranoid. He was trouble, possibly more than I'd ever accounted for. He'd also come into the store a few more times. He never spoke to me, but lurked in the aisles, watching me. I heard rumours of him being tied up in petty crimes, fights and maybe worse.

Once he called and rambled, in a slurring stream of consciousness, about Buddy. "We used to do stuff together, y'know, and now I have nobody, no one like him. Y'know he beat up a guy in fifth grade who was pushing me around? He tell you that? Put his hands around the guy's neck until the teacher came and tore him off, but that other guy never touched me again. He would do anything for a friend and I don't have him anymore, Penny. And you don' fuckin' care, do ya. You don' fuckin' care." I listened to him crying, and then, finally, the phone went dead.

I pushed thoughts of him out and away, focusing on the present, the future. Forward, always forward.

Hattie and Jameson invited me to dinner once a week. It was always a bit of a showy affair, and an opportunity for Hattie to demonstrate how grown up she was. Jameson was a very good cook, no question, and Hattie shone as host. And so there we were, summer again. It was a different experience, enjoying the freshness and warmth of late nights outside of my family home with this duo, now that I was pregnant and sober, and now that it was no longer my home. My feelings for Jameson, which had stood just outside the thin door of love, were confused and mixed up. I almost hated being with him, I found it palpably painful. Certainly Jameson and Hattie picked up on my unhappiness and maybe they felt they were the agents of my hostility, and so they served me terrines and tarts and fruity concoctions, they hugged me and doted on me, and I acted the spoiled child, the secret between Jameson and me festering inside.

But only with them. At work, with co-workers and preschoolers, I was merry and keen to talk about the baby. The children were, in fact, among the only people I spoke to about it with any kind of honesty. These three-year-olds were wholly worthy of my confidence. I told them that I was going to give the baby to my sister, and their eyes widened like this was a fairy tale.

"Will the baby have two mommies?"

"No. My sister, Hattie, will be its mommy. I will be Aunt Penny." I silently cherished the idea of being the faraway aunt. I had been planning my escape from St. Margaret's, lying in the night while the baby rolled and kicked. I would think about where I would go, how far I could get.

"I have an Aunty Jenny, and she is really old. I think she is twenty-five or something."

"My daddy has grey hair."

"My grandma's hair is all grey."

"My grandpa has NO hair!"

Afternoons often passed with perfect, silly conversation, and no one asked me who the father was, or how we did it, or if I would be sad, or anything like that. No one presumed to know how I would feel, or what I was having, or whether I was crazy or not. I realized I had surrounded myself, in this new life, with toddlers and senior citizens, and in this way was building a fortress around me. Only Hattie had found a loose board through which she could crawl into my mind.

One night after dinner at the house, while Jameson was doing the washing up, Hattie and I sat in the backyard. The sun was low in the sky, but it was warm. She had turned on the twinkling lights around the patio, and it was romantic and soft and lovely. There was a breeze and it lifted the hem of Hattie's skirt. Her hair flew about her face, and she smiled at me, tucking it behind her ear.

"What a difference a year makes, hey?"

I nodded. "Indeed."

"I can't thank you enough, Penny."

"We're even, Hattie."

Hattie smiled and looked out across the garden. "I would do it all over again, Penny. You're my sister. I love you more than anyone." Her eyes found mine again. "If only I'd heard Mum . . . You probably never would have married Buddy had it not been for me. So yes, we're even."

I heard Jameson turn on the tap through the open window. I took a drink and looked towards the house.

"You've never said anything, have you?"

She followed my gaze. "Not a word. I couldn't. It would ruin everything. Everything else." The other secret, the one between Jameson and me, opened its eyes. I ignored it. Hattie pulled a beer bottle from a bucket of ice in the centre of the table, and popped off the cap. "I mean, there have definitely been times when I wanted to. It's hard having this one secret between him and me."

"Hattie. No fucking way. You can never. We agreed on this a long time ago."

"I know, I know. I'm just being honest with you. I'm just saying it's not easy, I'm not saying that I'll say anything."

"Well, God, I know how hard it is. But this has to be something we take to the grave. Otherwise all this can just be kissed goodbye."

"Alright. Jesus. I'm just saying." She was silent. "He would never betray us."

"Oh my God! You told him!"

"No! No, of course not. But I want you to know. You can totally trust him."

"That is not the point. I don't trust anyone with this. It's too big."

Hattie shrugged. "I get it, okay, okay."

I got up to leave and reached out my hand, and she hesitated, then placed her hand in mine. "I did not tell him, Penny."

I squeezed it, keeping her eyes on mine. *I love you, Hattie.* Little Harriet. Sister of mine.

CHAPTER 17

I WAS AT JOSEPH'S HOUSE PLAYING POKER, EIGHT MONTHS pregnant. It was finally cooling off after a hot and uncomfortable summer. The tension between Hattie and me had begun to lift with the change in weather. I carried a worry, though, that her love of Jameson would tempt her to tell him our secret. That she thought it was hers to tell simply complicated matters further. It was mine to keep, it was mine to never tell. But our secrets were now buried with secrets, and any one of them could topple them all.

And so I needed to keep Hattie close, to bring her back to me. I made a point of spending time with her, of faking myself into good moods. I smiled in her presence, thanked her, included her. I invited her to touch my enormous belly to feel the baby, who had begun to kick regularly. She pressed her face against me, spoke in hushed tones to my stretched skin. And I knew she loved that baby more than I could, more than I had allowed myself to even think of. I considered myself an ox, a carrier of precious cargo, and rarely in my waking hours did I let thoughts of the baby intrude on my day. At night, though, I dreamed of all manner of freaks and prophetic infants: from a baby with the wet, slick hair of an otter, swimming from between my legs, to a house of sticks and leaves, or rosy, bath-scrubbed beauties who would whisper terrible things into my ears, their breath sweet and their messages foul. And when the baby kicked, it startled me, physically insisting it was there.

I wasn't sleeping well and this was exacerbated when people told me, strangers all, that I should get my sleep now, *ha ha*. I felt like sitting on those people. My sheer girth made it virtually impossible, in the heat of my apartment—fans be damned— to fall into anything other than the kind of slumber where I was aware of sleep itself, fully cognizant of my turning over, my twitching, swollen feet. I did not feel that I was a radiant, beatific and glowing force of motherhood, but rather a water-logged, gargantuan grouch with a sore ass and frizzy hair. I couldn't wait to eject the thing that was occupying my body with such wakeful determination.

Joseph and his cronies, however, noticed none of this; or at least, they were too kind to say so. They tripped over themselves to offer compliments, pulled out the chair for me at the card table, and throughout the game offered to adjust the temperature, to get me drinks and food, pillows and blankets, and all but volunteered to hand over all their money and carry me around on their backs. I indulged in their fatherly tendencies, and they indulged me. I loved the evenings I spent with them, especially when they settled down their fluttering and we began an earnest and competitive game. Sometimes in complete silence, other times there was so much swearing and laughing that I almost fell off my seat.

This night. Hank, one of the younger of Joseph's friends, folded his poker hand and said to me, "I knew your mother in high school, you know."

"You're kidding," I said, shocked that this had never come up before.

"No, I did." He smiled. "I actually asked her out rather relentlessly for some time. She never did agree to go out with me."

At this, there was a chorus of guffaws and teasing about Hank's height or weight or bank account. I let this sink in, the sugar sweetness of a memory that was not my own dissolving into the mental catalogue of my parents' history. I looked at Hank in a new way, and thought that he was probably quite handsome when he was young. And in doing this, I realized how often I tried to peer into a face and imagine it in its youth. The truth was that Hank was handsome now, and that there was no reason to pity him into reverse. I wondered how often people tried to imagine if I was pretty when I wasn't pregnant, feeling as I did like a swollen and stretched version of myself, waddling and groaning with every step.

"She was a knockout. But also," he laughed, and I folded my own hand, realizing I couldn't concentrate properly, "she was stubborn as an old bull."

"What do you mean?"

"Determined."

"Determined to avoid Hank!" an Englishman named James quipped.

"In everything. She had a real belief in her convictions, Renatta did. A strong moral compass. Well. I mean not in a prudish way. She just knew what was right. Knew how to treat people."

And there it was. I blanched and reached for my glass of punch that Joseph had brought me, finishing off the rest. Maybe, were she here, Mum would think I was without that compass, like I had lost it overboard in a storm, and forged ahead, directionless. I imagined her peering at me, a disappointed look on her face. The thought of what she would have thought of this mess often sent me spinning.

There was a screech of a chair as Henry, the tallest wisp of a man, moved into the kitchen. I heard him pouring me more to drink.

"Yeah, that was her, alright," I managed.

"Sure. I mean, she was your mom, you would know better than anyone. She musta loved you and Harriet something fierce. And raising you all on her own after your dad skipped out, like she did."

"I guess. Yeah." I took the glass back from Henry gratefully, and he bowed back into his seat saying nothing. He picked his cigarette from the ashtray beside him and leaned away from me while drawing on it. He made that simple act look so gratifying and charming that I thought he could convince a whole generation to take up the habit.

"I remember this one time," Hank went on, as Joseph gathered the pot towards himself, grinning, "a group of us were going skating. We were playing hooky, you know, skipping out of class, to do it. It was thrilling, the truancy! And Renatta, your mom, she was game to do it, always up for a laugh. It really was one of those perfect days for skating: cold but no wind, sunny, still. The creek was just begging to be skated on."

I watched him, imagining just the creek, the kind of day: a chill, red-cheeked morning.

"And so when the bell rang, instead of going in, about four of us looped around behind the school with our skates over our shoulders. And there was this kid, Nicky was his name. Ugly little guy—pimples and stuff, you know. Spit when he spoke. We didn't have much time for him, you know. But Nicky saw what we were doing and asked if he could go with us. He said his house was on the way, he could go in and grab his skates."

Hank licked his lips and began shuffling, dealing out a new hand. My cards lay in front of me, untouched. "And the rest of us, we said no way, forget it. We made up excuses, you know, like that the teachers would suspect something if there were too many of us gone, and stuff. But he knew, and we knew, that it was because he wasn't popular enough, that we were put off by him. And I guess Renatta thought that was mean." He laughed. "Well, obviously it was. And she told Nicky that not only was he welcome to come, but that she would accompany him to his house on the way. I mean, we were all shocked. Your mom, Penelope, she was a real attractive young lady. Any of us would have died if she'd talked to us like that, so nice and everything. And that was it. She and Nicky went ahead of the rest of us and met us at the creek, where she spent the morning skating only with him. Made his day, I'd wager. Made the rest of us pretty jealous, too." He heaved a sigh. "That's what she was like. Big heart and no muss. Did not suffer fools."

My stomach clenched and I smiled at Hank. I lost the next few hands but made a comeback at the end of the night, whether on my own, or because of the generosity of my friends, I do not know.

I wished them all goodnight and wobbled upstairs, my hand on the stair railing. My room was quiet.

I loved that space. Against Hattie's wishes, I had firmly decided that I would have the baby in my apartment with a midwife. Hospitals, doctors, they were too close to the world of officials, law and order. I would do this my way, then leave the rest to Hattie and Jameson.

I turned on a small fan and pointed it towards the bed, where I lay down, listening to the movements of my body. Wondering who was in there, and what would come.

Hearing the story about my mother had jarred me. She had always looked out for people; even, in small ways, sought justice. I ignored the simmering shame of everything that had happened until now and focused on the fact that I was giving Hattie a child. If our mother was here, would she be glad of the outcome, despite how it came about? Would she tell me to strike out, finally, on my own? Maybe she would see that I deserved it, after all I'd been through.

Thoughts about leaving St. Margaret's had long been taking shape. They seemed like a real possibility, now that I was closer to the end. I began to put my plan in motion. An escape, a getaway, because what I needed more than anything was a way out.

CHAPTER 18

HATTIE AND JAMESON GOT MARRIED, RIGHT AT the last moment. Right when I was ready to burst. There were only three of us there for the ceremony, which was in the same church where I was married. I looked around at the chapel, the almost empty pews, save for a couple of curious strangers. It was a day so vastly different, so wholly apart from my own wedding day. Here I stood, the fabric of my autumnal dress pushing out in indecent floral, and there were Hattie and Jameson, she holding his hand in both of hers, and facing each other in absolute devotion. She was a vision: her hair folded up into loose knots, a simple cream lace dress that looked like it had been dropped from above, hanging just so on her slight curves and bones. Jameson, in a linen suit, grinning like a fool, that almost-father. I stood to the side, holding the flowers, holding the baby inside, holding it all in. Tears running down my face for all the wrong reasons. I let myself think of my night with Jameson. What if she knew what he'd done, I wondered. But she couldn't know, if only for my own self-preservation. He'd chosen her, anyhow, and I grieved this in the face of the celebration. The stained-glass windows filtered the October sun through rich jewelled colours. A bird flew by, casting a dark shadow for just a moment before the light shone again.

Afterward we went for lunch. We laughed, and ate to the point of bursting. It was, by all three accounts, a most wonderful day. *Soon*, Hattie said, tipsily raising a glass, *soon the baby will be here. Soon we'll be a real family.*

Jameson stopped me as I came out of the bathroom. I stood close to him, aware of my girth between us. He looked at my belly, pushing its way between us. I smiled, and heard someone laughing in the other room.

"Penny—"

"Want to feel it?" I lifted his hand gingerly and placed it on me, covering it with my own, feeling the warmth between us. "That's us in there, you know." Whatever else she had, this was ours.

He swallowed, surprised. A moment passed between us, and then he moved back slightly, pulling his hand away. "Penny." He looked at me, his eyes worried. "She can never know."

I almost burst out laughing. We all think that we are too good to be bad, to have these kinds of skeletons. But here we are. There we go.

I smiled. "Of course, Jameson. I know. I agree. It's our secret." Ours.

Something borrowed, something blue.

THEY CALL IT GIVING BIRTH. GIVING THIS BIRTH OVER, finally giving way and giving in, it struck me like a hammer. I crouched on my side, my knees drawn up under the pain. Sheets around me, a swirling undertow. I cried out. And then it stopped. Labour is such a curious thing: body-bending pain, and then nothing. Nothing between the pains. No throbbing, no sting, no residual memory of pain, until it strikes again, over and over, teasing a pause before the next, and the body almost forgets for minutes at a time what it feels like, finally learning to gather strength, to prepare for an onslaught, a gathering wave that feels it will almost drown you, and then suddenly you are breathing again.

I was scared like a panicked child, a cornered cat, by the increasing pain, and was unable to prevent the yowls that escaped me; they came from some bottom body place, rising and falling as my body squeezed itself unconsciously. So strange to have your muscles working without your brain telling them to, to have all your strength whirled into a motion over which you have no control.

I heard Joseph rapping at the door below, then fumbling with some keys. A small flush of embarrassment about my ratty night-gown, my braless, terrified state, before another contraction hit, and I yelled out. For an older man, the rapidity with which he hustled up the stairs was astonishing.

"Penelope? Penelope! Is it happening? Can I come in?" He was, at this point, already in, on the threshold of the living room, hardly containing himself as he leaned around frantically looking for me. He caught sight of me holding on to the door frame of my bedroom, pushing my back out in a way I found instinctually offered some respite during the pain. I laughed, in spite of myself.

"Yes," I panted, "I believe it is happening."

"Holy Jesus! Oh my Lord, here, lemme," and he rushed over to me as I howled and sank to my knees. "Lemme take you to the hospital, Penelope, okay, here, let me. Where is your bag?"

"I'm not going to the hospital. The midwife is on her way."

"Midwife? Are you—isn't that kinda—okay, whatever you say, oh, hang on there, what can I do, does this help?" He held my hand and rubbed my back in circles. I wanted to punch him.

"No. Just. Can you just—be quiet. And push against my back as hard as you can. Yes. That's it. Lower. Yes. Thank you."

Kneeling behind me, smelling like cigarettes and beer and sawdust, he leaned against me, and I felt a dim appreciation.

"I need you to call Hattie." I gasped, as Joseph called out the minute number between contractions. I heard the midwife closing her car door out front.

"Okay, darlin'. I can do that. Hang on there, I think what's her name is here." He hurried downstairs and let the midwife in, both of them returning in no time. A dynamo with dyed-blond hair in a punk cut, Alice, my midwife, was at once professional and comforting. The air in the place seemed to quicken and slow at the right times while she prepared my bed for the birth. She spoke to me in firm, calm tones, orchestrated the events with a way that made it seem she had some control of things. I almost cried with gratitude.

Then Hattie came. A force of nature, a rainstorm, making me thank God that this debt to her would finally be paid. Up the stairs, pounding frantically, calling my name, urging Jameson to come on, *come on*. Alice took one look at me and understood how to handle her. She gave Hattie jobs. It was the best thing to do, give her seemingly important tasks to keep her away from me but make her feel integral to the birth. When I think back to those hours, Hattie was like a whirring, ticking machine in the background, calling out at me occasionally with axioms of love and encouragement.

Jameson stood in a corner with Joseph, neither of them sure of what to do, where to go, if they were needed. I whispered hoarsely to Alice to send them downstairs, and she did, deftly guiding them, to their great relief, making it sound like it would be an enormous help if they left. "Maybe make a pot of coffee. Or something stronger!" She smiled kindly and saw them down the stairs.

It felt like hours and then like it took no time at all. The bodily force, the impetus to keep going, it was like time was contracting along with me. Alice described it as work, and a job I had to do. I screamed wildly as my body focused, taking over, whipping my midsection into a fury of tightening, tightening like a giant fist. My hair was drenched and I was naked on the bed, a wild thing. This is what it took, this was my penance. I know now that some scores can never be settled, but there I was, pushing through to some other side, to a new life.

And when I finally, at last, pushed him from me, that squirming red and wrinkly boy, when I pushed him out and away and into Hattie's waiting hands, to her wailing delight, I threw back my head, and I cried.

PART **TWO**

CHAPTER 19

IT IS REMARKABLE HOW SOMEONE WHO CONSIDERS herself normal can rationalize a decision, finally, to murder. But everyone has their price. Everyone has their breaking point. And the price might be the nightmares, which even followed me to Paris, but I still believe they are worth it.

When I read about heinous crimes taking place in the city around me, in the most romantic city in the world, those that took on the Gothic black of their Parisian settings, I wondered if the psychopaths here were all that different from the ones at home, in small towns, in St. Margaret's. But was I the psychopath or the victim? Maybe our actions define who we are, but maybe it is the actions of all those around us who make us. Mum made me good, and then she was gone. Buddy made me bad.

That day. I had waited until the time was right. Until my collarbone had healed. Until I was strong. That morning, a kind of adrenaline protected me, and from the moment I woke, the morning of Buddy's death, I was ready. I was sure. I was in control, on some kind of autopilot, almost as though driven by another person altogether. Maybe that seems like an excuse. Perhaps it is. What choice do I have now, now that it is done, but to present my course of action as the only possible one?

I woke facing Buddy, and as I took in his face, a part of me said goodbye but another part told him he'd asked for it. I hardened. I am a hard woman still. I pulled back the covers gently on my side, and mentally set things in motion, like turning a crank. I planned my day. I took one last look at my home, which had never been a comfort, but a kind of cell. I assessed the flammability of every article: wood, textiles, rugs, pillows. I did, I remember, feel the softness of my sheets between my fingers with regret, despite the fact that that bed had never softened the brutality of my nights. They were nice sheets.

I had told Hattie my plan the day before. I called her up while Buddy was out. I was smoking, something I never did; I was shaking and nervous. She wasn't home. I waited half an hour and called her again, letting the phone ring over and over. Finally, with a breathlessness that told me she was just in the door, putting down her purse and smiling into the receiver, she answered. She sensed my tension right away, pausing, asking, with a stillness she brought on our trips to the emergency room consoling me over burns and bruises, if I was okay. And I told her: *I am going to kill Buddy, Hattie, and I need your help.*

There was silence on the phone, but I knew she was there. I heard her pull out a chair, and in my mind's eye I saw the cord of the phone, which had been stretched and tangled over years of teenage bids for privacy, dangle lifelessly at her side. She started to say something, my name, then stopped.

"Okay."

"I'm going to come over tomorrow afternoon. We can work on that quilt you're making. We'll have dinner together. I'm going to sleep over because we're going watch a movie and catch up."

"Okay."

"But listen. I'm not really coming until after. Until after it happens. But I need you, listen, Hattie, I need you to make it look like I was there. Two plates, two glasses, everything. Watch the movie, okay? Are you listening? Make it look like I have been there the whole time."

Her voice shaking. Just a kid. "Right. I get it."

"It's very important, Hattie. And if anyone calls, you tell them I'm there, okay? Or if you talk to a neighbour, tell them I'm going to be coming by that afternoon. I'm going to walk there."

"What are you—how are you going to do it?" A delicate, fragile, porcelain whisper.

"There's going to be a fire."

She was silent.

"Hattie?"

"Be careful. Please be careful, Penny." Her voice caught. "I can't lose you, too."

"I will be, alright? I'll be careful. I need you to just be strong, just wait there for me, got it?"

"Yes. Alright. I'll do that." Her voice shaking, crying almost-silent tears.

"I'm going to be fine now, Hattie. You're going to help me. I need you."

I heard her pulling herself together. "I'll be here."

AND NOW, HERE I WAS. I HAD TO LEAVE HER. I HAD TO make a clean break. I had delivered the baby, paid my debt, and little Elliot would be there in my stead. He would fill my void.

I went to France. It was exactly far enough away and struck me as exactly the kind of romantic and self-serving leap I needed. Hattie couldn't reach me there; she couldn't visit, not with a new-born. I may as well have chartered a rocket to the moon.

Bon voyage! Hattie had cried, tearfully, waving Elliot's small hand frantically as I walked through to my gate at the airport. The minute they were out of sight, I exhaled and smiled. Freedom.

I stayed. One month turned into the next, and soon I had been there for over a year. And Paris became, in its anonymity, in its urban strangeness, my new home. Having never had a real home outside of ours, everything was a discovery. I got a job at a small florist shop in a touristy area. It was mindless and exactly what I needed, the pay being enough to keep me comfortable in my minimalist life. The flat I had moved to after my first year there, leaving behind the temporary one I found on my arrival, was perfect for me. It was clean to the point of being sterile, completely white, with old fixtures—chandeliers, light switches and heaters—all white as well. The landlady was a severe woman in her fifties, and I was fascinated by her, not that she'd ever let me spend more than five minutes in her company. I admired her tough, frank nature, and her commitment to her opinions, because despite those few firm decisions in my life, I have never felt very sure of anything. She reprimanded me regularly, and scoffed at my French, which was Canadian-schoolgirl French, rather than France—let alone Paris—French. Undeterred, I was always pleased when I encountered her outside the building, or when I had an excuse to call her on the phone. Mme. Durant was her name, and she tsked quietly, her tongue chastising me delicately, whenever I said it. A little clicking, so much judgement.

I had furnished the place sparsely but carefully. I bought a large rug, which cost me a great deal, but of which I was proud, and it made the entire flat come together. It was woven in rich jewelled colours, reds and burgundies, purples and dark blues. I often sat crossed-legged on it like a child, trying my hand at reading the Parisian newspapers, my back up against a chair. Other than that, my furnishings were strictly functional and plain, not unlike my encounters with people there. I secretly hoped that Mme. Durant approved of this no-nonsense approach to decoration, although I never got that sense from her. I was, as I had planned, entirely alone.

Hattie and I spoke semi-regularly, at first. We had a standing date to speak on the phone, with its strange long-distance pauses and the cost that overshadowed any frivolous talk. She was busy, with the harsh newness of motherhood, and eventually the calls became more infrequent, and soon they were only occasional. She mailed pictures of her son, a serious-looking baby with a thicket of black hair, and kept me up to date on his progress as though reporting to a teacher her own progress. I kept an interested distance, couldn't bring myself to look too closely at his pictures for fear I might feel something.

"He's not quite walking, but I can tell he really wants to, he's *dying* to! Jameson says I worry too much about his milestones, but I can't help it."

Hearing Jameson's name always struck a chord of pain. I was hurt, and angry at him for forgetting me so easily, for moving on in his role of husband and father. And I missed him terribly. I thought I could get away, but distance wasn't enough. I kept myself busy. I distracted myself. And still I thought of them all. I had dreams about the baby: that I was pushing him in a stroller, that I had come home to my apartment and he was there, gurgling on the carpet, or cooing in a high chair. In the daytime hours, I pretended none of it had ever happened.

"I'm sure you're doing great, Hattie," I told her. She seemed to think that by giving birth I had some innate knowledge that she didn't, and I was constantly reassuring her. "I know nothing about babies, but he sounds like a good one. You're a great mom, Hattie."

"He looks just like Jameson, you know."

"I noticed," I remarked, holding the phone under my chin, the cord pulling over to the sink, where I was washing dishes. I glanced at a picture of Elliot on my fridge.

"Except when he cries. He actually looks like you then." She laughed.

"Glad I could give him something." A twinge, an ache. I laughed it off.

"He loves daycare. We send him twice a week, you know, to give Mommy a break," she said, her voice faltering a little. "It's not the same here. Especially without you. It feels like insult to injury. Please, just come home, already!"

I deflected these regular pleas, trying to convince her that I was happy with my new life.

"One day, I promise. But I really love it here."

Hattie had left the salon when Elliot was born and had then gotten a part-time job at the library, which satisfied her desire for stories and to be surrounded by books. Soon she was hired by an eccentric writer who frequented the library and had her doing research for his next book.

"On lady spies of the Second World War!" she trilled down the phone line. I could hear Elliot gabbling happily in the background with Jameson.

"Right up your alley," I said.

"The pay is good, too. Better than the library. And since Jameson has been full time at the school for a while now, we don't have to worry as much."

Our conversations skimmed the surface, too much else churning below, too much left unsaid. It was a relief to all of us when they began to diminish, as time and space invariably worm their way into any relationship and expand. I didn't even have to avoid her calls or find excuses not to reach out. I thought of them all a little less, as they no doubt thought of me less, my solitude in a foreign country stretching out like a blanket of fog.

A call from Hattie after a long period of silence. She sounded so cheerful that it was almost brittle, talking quickly about Elliot's advanced progress and all the fun they were having.

Until she said, "A lot of people are asking after you."

"Oh yeah?" I put the kettle on the stove and withdrew a mug from a cupboard. There was a pause on the phone that was characteristic of the long-distance connection at the time, but also felt loaded between every exchange.

"Yeah. So . . . I ran into Mac Williams the other day. He looks like a bag of shit."

"That's not new."

"Yeah, well. He looks worse. Apparently he's been in prison. He asked me where my 'frigid bitch of a sister' had gone."

"Wow. Nice guy." A shiver ran up my spine, and I pictured Mac loafing about town like a ticking bomb.

"Yeah." She put her hand over the phone and I heard her tell Jameson to take Elliot for his nap. I heard her wait, then return, and whisper into the phone.

"There's more. Remember Iain?"

"I could hardly forget," I said drily.

"He's a detective now, big promotion, but I wanted to tell you, he came by the house."

"Why?" I was standing frozen, with my hand on my tea mug.

"He brought something for you. Said he was," she paused, and dropped her voice, "looking through our file. He thought you'd want it. It's your wedding picture from the house. I guess it survived the fire. I sent it to you, but Penny, why was he looking through the file?"

After I hung up, I remained in the kitchen, standing still for a long time. The thought of Officer—or Detective—Moore filled me with a cold dread, and the room around me seemed to freeze into hyper focus, even the fan seemed to hold still. Why had he been looking through the file? Why had he kept that picture of me and Buddy? I knew the picture, and as promised, it soon arrived in the mail. I studied it for a long time: Buddy grinning at the camera. My gaze was out of frame, I had glossy eyes and a worried mouth. Mum's green emerald earrings sparkling in my ears. In the background, someone was dancing. The camera had caught the hem of a party dress, an arm thrown back in gleeful celebration. Was it Hattie's? I thought of her saying, all those years ago, that Buddy had it coming. The last straw.

Collarbones themselves are like straw: sitting like fragile frames around our stronger bones. They shouldn't be crushed in a fall or feel the bottom of a boot.

What was my last straw? Was it the same for Hattie?

Hattie had been avoiding coming to the house I shared with Buddy. She felt guilty for the attention he was paying her, and worried about how I had read it. Did I think there was more there? Sure, part of me did. I wasn't certain. Hattie's loyalty was, as always, reassuring to some extent, but I had become suspicious of everyone.

And then. Buddy happened upon her one night. She had been picking up extra hours at the local bar, Dusty's. She was gathering up darts, and when she stood up, Buddy was standing over her, she told me after. Suddenly too close to Hattie, the wall behind her, the darts falling sharply. A mumbled slew of comments on her body, her youth, her hair, what they could do together. His rough mouth on hers before she knew, and then her nails in his arm, her knee in his crotch, but not strong enough to help her get away. Not if they'd been alone. But they weren't, and there were shouts of *Alright, alright, Buddy* from Mac, who pulled Buddy away from Hattie, chortling. *Take it easy, would you, Hattie? He's married.* The two of them laughing as they lumbered away and left her against the wall.

I woke to my long hair being snatched, lifting me off the pillow, knocking me onto the floor, my collarbone breaking as I hit the cheap hardwood beside our bed. I would never have long hair again after that. It was a noose, a weapon against me. My scalp throbbed. Buddy's angry breath as he pulled down my pyjamas. Taking what he deserved. Every thrust like a jolt through my body as my neck and shoulder howled.

He put his hand over my mouth and called me Hattie.

Hattie.

Hattie.

He climbed into the bed and passed out. I lay on the floor, in the dark, where I heard her name over and over, ringing in my ears.

Hattie cried at my side the next day, at the doctor's office. *Shh, Hattie. Shut up, Hattie. It's okay, Hattie.* She told me what had happened, how he'd kissed her, but she had hated it. *I believe you,* I told her in a choked voice, trying to push the image from my mind. *Of course you did. I trust you, always.* She blamed herself. She never thought that he could be like this. She was sorry. I said, *Don't worry, Hattie. I love you, Hattie. It's him, not you. We stick together.*

I stared straight ahead. My collarbone sang furiously, but my mind went calm. In the face of roaring evidence, I had to be still while I took stock, counted out pieces of fury, my currency of justice, tucked in my pocketbook of madness.

A sling. A haircut. A plan.

* * *

HATTIE HAD NONE OF THIS CHEMICAL, EMOTIONAL PREP-aration, no protection. In the end, the role she played had a ripple effect that I hadn't foreseen. She came undone, laces of her life lying around, and I was the one to tie her back together. She clung to me to help her breathe. She was broken inside. And Elliot, the boy, the bodily distraction of parenthood, was an attempt at repair.

I hoped, as I turned the key and locked my flat, so far away from her, that she was whole now. But that wasn't all that hung in the balance. Iain Moore, the file on our fire: my worries starting to unspool, threads running away, out of my control.

CHAPTER 20

DIDN'T GO HOME FOR ALMOST FOUR YEARS. IN THE rare times I spoke to Hattie, her voice had changed, like something had slipped sideways for her. At first it was little things. She missed the life she and Jameson had before Elliot's birth. But then she claimed her little boy hated her, that he wouldn't hold her or cuddle her, but demanded all her time, that she wasn't a natural mother, that I would have done better. I brushed off these comments about my being Elliot's "real" mother, such was the weight I gave her feelings. Or mine. I had almost convinced myself that I hadn't given birth to him, anyone, that it had never happened. My stomach was stretched but I pretended not to notice. The dreams I had about going into labour became more frequent, but I forced myself to forget them when the sun came up, putting on the radio and allowing the kettle to whistle loudly and for too long, trying to put the thoughts out of my mind. So much time had passed. More, I put so much faith in Jameson's ability to steady Hattie that I hadn't accounted for the fact that he might not want to.

And one day, I heard his voice on the other end of the line.

"Hi, Penny. It's Jameson."

I felt the familiar ache that Jameson provoked in me and my resentment. Even after all this time.

"Is everything okay?"

"Everyone's fine. Nothing has happened. Well. Everyone's fine."

"Okay . . ."

"Okay, look. I'll just get right to it. Hattie's really not in a good place, Pen." His familiarity with me still gave my stomach a jolt, and I tried to stay focused.

"What do you mean? She seems fine," I lied.

"Well. It surprises me to hear you say that. She's not. And look, the last, and I mean *last* thing I want to do is go behind her back—"

"*Again*, you mean," I said, but my barb reached him at the same time that his voice came to me with the phone delay.

"I mean, she's not good. Things are not good with us, she's not happy. Half the time, I bet she's drunk when she calls you."

This, I knew, was true. I hadn't admitted it to myself, hoping that she was sounding simply tired and overworked, but I had known the telltale sound of Hattie after a few drinks.

"I don't know if you can call it postpartum when your kid is almost four, but she seems to be in a very dark place. She's angry, and to be frank, pretty nasty sometimes. Not to Elliot, not really, but she's stopped trying . . . or something. She'd be really great with him if she'd give herself a chance."

"I'm so sorry, Jameson. My God. I had no idea."

"I mean, it's not bad all the time or anything. But I needed you to know. Maybe you can talk to her. She doesn't even want to be near me anymore. She has accused me of not knowing the real her, of never really knowing her."

My eyes widened. Risk. I felt the risk. I felt the immediate and painful surge of needing to be back with her. For her sake and mine.

"Oh, Jameson. This is terrible. Is she still working?"

"Yeah. She still goes to work. She's working all the time for that author-researcher guy. He's a bit of an old piss tank too, if you ask me. I don't know how he can afford to pay her, she seems to be paid just to organize his life and his crap. Half the time she doesn't come home until after Elliot's gone to bed. There's nothing fishy going on with him, I'm pretty sure he's not even into women, but she seems to fall down a hole of old papers and photo albums, and sherry, and then comes out hours later not knowing who she is."

I heard him sniff into the phone.

"I don't know what to do. I think she might leave me and Elliot, to tell you the truth, Penny. She's becoming so withdrawn and so private, but then she goes out a lot of nights."

"She goes out?"

"Yeah, you know, she goes on walks and hikes, or to catch up with old friends or whatever," he finished lamely. Hattie didn't have any old friends. I pictured her, going on hikes alone, up near the escarpment. Her fears propelling her higher and higher into the rocks.

"And I know that Elliot needs her."

"Of course—"

"I mean, he's fine—totally a happy kid. You would love him. I know you would. He's funny and smart and creative. He's the best. Did Hattie tell you how much he looks like you? I'm sure you know all about it. People are always saying so."

I said that yes, I'd heard, but my mind was racing. I needed to reel her in again. I'd been pretending that a taut line hadn't connected me to Hattie all this time. As though I could ever get away, or trust her to go on without me. She was my burden, my responsibility.

"Maybe it's time for me to come home," I said, surprising myself.

There was a pause, then, "Really? For good? Oh, Penny. Thank you. I feel like you're the silver bullet here." He laughed. "But, no pressure."

"It's time. I was thinking of moving home anyway," I said, looking around my apartment and wondering how quickly I could leave.

"She'll be—we both will be—so glad to see you."

She was drawing me back to her, and I was powerless to resist it. She was my sister. She was my own dear heart. And she was a risk.

CHAPTER 21

THE AIRPORT WAS BUSY AND FULL OF CHEERY transition. I didn't have a lot of bags, having given away most of my old things to second-hand stores in Paris, and keeping only those things I really felt I needed. I had a large knapsack on my back, and while it was bursting, it really wasn't a lot, considering I was restarting a life.

I handed over my passport and waited. Watched the face of the woman at the desk, wondering if the impassivity of her expression was what they were taught to do when flagging a criminal for security. I stood still, fighting off the urge to look around me, listening for the footsteps of authority, but they never came.

"*Je rentre chez moi,*" I said, smiling. *I'm going home.* Took my documents and walked away, my hands shaking at my sides.

PERHAPS IT WAS THE JET LAG OR THE SIMPLE FATIGUE OF travel, but I hadn't given Elliot much thought as I wheeled my suitcase into the arrivals area, foggily sweeping my eyes across the crowd for my sister. And then there was Hattie, waving energetically with one arm, and holding the hand of a child with the other.

I wasn't prepared for him, this little person I had steadfastly refused to visit. He looked not only like me, but like our mother and grandmother, and Jameson, and was an echo of all the people I'd loved and those I'd lost. My heart clenched like a fist, and I coughed to stop the pain. He shyly held out his hand as I knelt down and shook it, his palm warm and damp. *How do you do, Elliot.* He was wearing a cape made of green velour that was tied in a knot at his throat. Black curls in all directions. People jostled and hugged around us, and I was right back to the night I'd given birth, to handing the wriggling baby to my sister. And now he was this lovely boy. And in spite of everything, I started to cry. I covered it up with a laugh and stood, burying myself in a hug with Hattie, who was beautiful but a little more tired, her hair mussed, bags under her eyes.

"Welcome home, Penny."

"Thank you, Hattie."

And at first I thought it was mouthwash, that minty pungent whiff in her kiss, but it was more, I discovered later. It was the smell of coping and forgetting. She took up one of my bags and hustled us all, in a wave of happy homecoming, to the parking lot, Elliot's cape catching a bit of air as he ran.

Hattie at the wheel, occasionally handing snacks back to Elliot, who chomped solemnly while playing with two action figures.

"How's Jameson?" I asked.

She looked in the rear-view mirror and changed lanes.

"Oh, you know. Fine, I guess. He's always in my face."

"What do you mean?"

"Who's face?" Elliot piped up from the back seat.

"No one, Elliot. I'm trying to talk to Auntie Penny, please. Here, here are some stickers. You can decorate your cup." She thrust a pile of stickers at Elliot that she had uncovered from an overflowing space between our seats. She rolled her eyes at me as she did so. I looked at Elliot, who took the stickers silently, his eyes on mine. I winked at him. He regarded the plastic cup lying on the seat beside him, evaluating if and how to decorate it.

She continued. "I feel like he's breathing down my neck all the time. Judging me."

"I'm sure that's not the case, Hattie." I turned again to Elliot, who returned my smile with a stony face. I looked at Hattie. "We can talk about this later. I'm exhausted. Not retaining much right now, and, uh, I don't think we should talk about this in front of him, do you?"

"Whatever. If we waited until we were alone, I'd never get to talk to you," she said darkly.

And yet I had energy enough for the joy I felt when we pulled up to the old house. Our childhood homes, don't they carry that irreplaceable spot in our hearts? That house is still the setting of most of my dreams. I know the hallways, the lighting, the dark corners and the bright places where the sun comes through in the morning. I know the view from my room when I first wake up, the rustle of leaves outside my window. I will always remember these things, they are as much a part of me as a birthmark.

I stayed in the car while Hattie unbuckled Elliot, who was whining about having to pee, and I watched her gently tug him up to the front door, struggle with my bag, drop her keys and snap at him. She left the door open, and a whirl of leaves circled into a frenzy on the porch. I closed my eyes and fell almost immediately into a slumber, the autumn breeze touching my cheeks, my hair, through the open car window.

Soon Hattie shouted my name, and I woke, disoriented, my mouth open. She was standing there with her arms out as though to say, *Really? Come on!* and she turned in a haze of red hair and went back inside. I gathered my things and followed her, shoes scuffing on the driveway gravel. The sun was a bright blur, and my eyes watered as I went up the front steps, regarding the door like a soldier home from the front. I smiled to myself. Home.

Jameson met me with an enormous hug. I grinned and saw Hattie over his shoulder, and she rolled her eyes and proffered her hands in a *see?* gesture.

"Let me get your bags," he said, while I looked a little closer at the face I hadn't seen in far too long. He looked like a worn and frayed version of what I remembered.

"I already did it, Jameson," Hattie grumbled from the kitchen. Jameson shrugged, smiling, and patted me on the back, unable to hide his relief that I was there, swooping in to rescue . . . whom? Hattie? Him? Myself, once again.

The house was a mess. Mostly, I suspected, it was messy due to the busy nature of life with a young child. There were books and clothes, newspapers, craft supplies, little pieces of construction paper everywhere like confetti, lifting off tables when someone walked by, floating to the floor. Trains and their tracks littered a round braided rug that I didn't recognize, and there were also random things like some large buttons, the eye of a toy that stared up at me from the floor, and a large bike horn, which gave me shivers to think of the noise it could make.

Under this, though, there was another kind of mess. The leaving it in the sink for too long, sad kind of mess. I noticed a few empty red wine bottles and a very stained glass pushed to the corner of the counter in the kitchen. Hattie had never been very tidy, Jameson not much better, but there was something here that pushed me into the edge of worry. Jameson caught me looking and rushed to the kitchen to clean. Elliot chirped happily around the house. Hattie found reasons to bicker with Jameson. I watched them all, this family. My family. I kicked off my shoes and joined in.

When I had told Hattie I was coming home, I was very clear that I was going to find my own place; see if Joseph would take me as a tenant again, or maybe even shack up in my barn for a while. But she'd insisted, on the verge of a shrill beg, that I stay at the house, at least temporarily. I had relented, and was relieved. I needed to keep an eye on Hattie, and, now that I'd met Elliot, on her son as well. My old instinct to keep my family close had kicked right back in. And I was tired. Tired of pretending and trying to start again. It's difficult to reinvent yourself. There are parts of you that won't change: made of something hard like a bone that just won't bend another way. And you can chip at it, you can break it altogether even, but you can't take it out. It's there. And it was there for me. Home. And walking through the foyer, hearing Hattie's nattering from a room over, touching chairs and opening windows just to hear the creak they made, I was happy. Happy in a travel-weary, tired-drunk fog. I wilfully turned away from that whispered sadness that I knew was there, pretended not to hear it over the chatter, pretended not to see it, that under-painting beneath the whole picture. And it was because of that haunting underneath that I needed to keep an eye on Hattie, to be there. Because I loved her, sure, but because there were more people at stake. Little Elliot, Jameson: this family needed stability. I could help.

Hattie offered for me to sleep in her old room, as Elliot was in what used to be mine, and she and Jameson were in our mum's room; we couldn't seem to shake the set-up of our childhood,

if in name only. My room. Your room. Mum's room. But I pre-
ferred to sleep in the cool basement, off and away, on a pullout
couch with the promise of silence and darkness. And that night,
as I fell flat into dreamlessness, sleeping like I was being lifted
into the air, I was sure I would never leave again.

CHAPTER 22

AND SOON, WE THREE, WE WERE BACK. ALL OF us, Hattie, Jameson and me, on our best behaviour at first, doing this dance to which we all knew the moves. Forward, back, side, side. We were partly pretending, but it was hard not to resist the fantasy that we could go back in time. It wasn't as bad as I'd thought, not what I had anticipated after deciding to return. Hattie stayed in most nights and was glad to have me there. I was so relieved to be welcomed. These two were my people, and after being alone for so long, I was blindly relieved to be home again.

And then there was Elliot. He, I discovered, was not at all what I had expected. He was serious and silly, manic in his moods, sneaky and conniving, and when he napped, with curls damp to his forehead, I thought I might be sick with love. I was not prepared for this. I was ready, in fact, to be impervious to his charms, to find him sticky, bothersome, annoying. I was not his mother, I insisted to myself, but his aunt. And an estranged one at that. The whole town, as tight and tiny as it was, seemed to have taken a vow of silence on Elliot's and Hattie's behalf. Hattie was sure Elliot would never know. Hattie was his mother, and I was his aunt.

But there was something, I am sure of it now, that snuck in there, some kind of subconscious fevered connection. Not that I thought I deserved any role or name or position that sounded of family, to say little of recognition or closeness, let alone mother- liness. I was prepared to be on the fringe: a friend from afar who was staying for a while.

But there is a motherly instinct, isn't there? We couldn't keep from each other, he and I. Couldn't be expected to. Much as I didn't want to, I loved him profoundly, violently.

Morning after morning, Elliot padded down the stairs to see me. He climbed onto the pullout couch, and it squeaked under his weight. He lifted the covers of my sleeping bag, and moved in close to me, with sweet boy breath and rosy cheeks after sleep- ing through a hot summer night, breeze through the windows, his pyjamas warm, and his hands, which he sometimes—more and more often—clasped in mine, were hot and damp and perfect. He wanted to play: first thing in the morning, after breakfast, all day, right until bedtime. We spent many early mornings, often with Jameson, who was an early riser, making train tracks with wooden pieces that wove around table legs and underfoot, drawing dig- gers and cranes on coloured construction paper and cutting them out. Tiny triangles of red and blue and yellow falling to the floor beneath us, as the mornings stretched into afternoons and weeks.

"He's really taken to you," said Hattie, one evening, her voice with a slightly hard edge.

"The feeling's mutual. He's so great, Hattie, really. He's a great kid."

"Yeah. Well, I don't think I have had much to do with that, frankly."

"I'm sure that's not true."

"I'm so glad you're home, Penny. It never felt right without you here."

And I know she had been glad, initially, for there was something in the newness, the relief, the sheer change from the monotony of her life that lifted her, however briefly, out of the heavy sameness of having a small child that appeared about to pull her under.

Three adults are better than two when it comes to children, and everything took on that familiar feeling of play, of comfort. It was autumn, and while summer was our season of preference, we warmed to the darkening days, retreating inward, under blankets, warm drinks in our hands. At first, Hattie brightened, lightened, laughed easily. Tried to carve out some fresh happiness with me, now back in the house. At first, it was so nice and easy. Too easy, though, as I should have known. I had readied myself for what Jameson had warned me against, but Hattie's kindness upon the first blush of my arrival had deceived me into trusting that all that was needed was a little help.

Hattie had changed, however, and within a short expanse of time, it began to become apparent. Parts exaggerated, made bigger and bolder. When she went to bed early, it was because her mood had become sour and angry, and she often disappeared on the heels of a perceived slight. We—Jameson and I—brushed this off. Flipped the tape to the other side, kept chatting. When she stayed up late, a darkness settled around her, and she invariably snapped at Jameson or me. The next day she would be a sleepy and sullen contrarian. It was as though we were seeing the other side of the coin of our first summer. It reminded me of when she and Jameson had been trying to conceive, but louder, worse. And that conception, that secret, loomed over me when I was with Jameson. Did she suspect, or was I being paranoid? Jameson himself never let on that he thought of it, never brought it up—as though it was so long ago that he'd forgotten. But how could I forget when we lived under the very roof where he had touched me with such tenderness? Whatever resentment I had for him was washed away with being near him again, and I felt myself leaning towards him and away from Hattie.

Hattie constantly picked fights with Jameson, and I soon saw what he had meant when he'd called me in desperation. She was cruel, loud, self-pitying, and he was helpless at defending himself. He seemed so lost to me. The ground had shifted under him, the balance tipped. I often stood up for him when Hattie accused him of any number of character shortcomings, which I see now was the wrong tack. Jameson would look between us, unsure of what to do. Eventually Hattie would nod her head in what I thought was a conciliatory way, but was really her confirming what she understood to be a conspiracy against her.

"I thought you came here to help me, not him," Hattie muttered mutinously at me after a particularly tense evening. Jameson had gone upstairs quietly after Hattie had blamed him for Elliot's wilful nature, an irony apparent to all but her.

"I did, Hattie. But come on. You're being awful to him."

"You don't understand. He's my husband, Penny. I think I know him better than you. Plus, you haven't even been here." This was always her first defence. That I had gone, left, and so could never understand.

"Yes, I know." I paused, reaching out a hand. "But I'm here now, Hattie, for you. Truly. And Elliot. I want to help."

She sniffed, and looked at me with watery eyes.

"Okay. I know. I'm sorry."

"I'm not the one you should be apologizing to," I chastised.

But she continued to push him. For so long, and so hard—I had witnessed half a year of it since I'd arrived—that during one fight when she told him she hated it when he was home, he caved in.

"Maybe I should move out," he offered. I could see that he was close to crying, and my heart broke for him. "This is no way for Elliot to grow up."

"Maybe you should," Hattie countered, her face hardened.

I leaped to my feet. "No! I should leave, if anyone should."

"No. She needs you here," Jameson said gently.

"Fuck off, Jameson, you don't know what I need," Hattie snapped.

"Hattie!" I cried. "Please. Let me be the one to go. You two work things out." Did I mean it? Part of me thought perhaps I was interfering, but I had hoped no one would take me up on my offer to leave.

"No, no. Penny," Jameson said gently, putting his hand on my arm, "this is not because of you. This is a long time coming. I think maybe we need time apart." Hattie scoffed and lit a cigarette. He continued, quietly, "You two need to spend some time together, also. Without me here."

"Elliot needs you, Jameson," I pleaded.

"And he will have me, just as much," he said, with the first note of strength I'd heard all night. "I will get a place nearby and see him just as often. Without," he waved his hand around the room, "all this."

And then, as it always was, there were three.

I OFFERED TO LOOK AFTER ELLIOT A COUPLE OF DAYS A week, and on the others, I took him to the daycare where I had been rehired at my old job. I saw Jameson there, as the daycare was next to the school, and my heart ached when we made small talk at the end of the day, when we traded Elliot between us, and behaved like the fragmented couple that we were in some ways. We shared something, he and I. A secret. A son. His goodness, his dignity, rubbed off on me in those moments.

Hattie often slept in past her work time and rose in the late morning dishevelled and irritable, hardly acknowledging us before leaving for her job at the library or with the author in the big house down the road. She said less and less to me as time wore on, as routine settled in. Even after Elliot went to bed, if she was home, she sank into dark moods, staring out the window at the night, at nothing, as though I wasn't there at all. She kissed me on the cheek occasionally, as though just noticing me for the first time that day, and thanked me, her voice scratchy and small. She was disappearing, vanishing in sighs and coughs. Elliot spoke of her hardly at all, but when he did, he did so as though he, too, was talking about someone in convalescence, in childlike, hushed tones.

"Mommy doesn't have scissors that I can use," he'd whisper.

"Don't ask Mommy, she's tired."

"Mommy doesn't eat with me, she's always full."

And I thought of Hattie, pushing her food around her plate, sullen as a child, thin as a shadow.

When Jameson came to the house to pick up Elliot occasionally, I knew how the house would appear to him. Seeing its slow decline, like that of our red-headed wonder, whose hair and shiny Hattie-ness seemed to be fading into stringy disrepair. I cleaned up as best I could before he came, made excuses for where Hattie was, when oftentimes she was not at work at all but moping about in the next room, a kimono housecoat wrapped loosely around her thin frame, eating something out of a jar like a stray cat. He was polite enough to pretend not to see a swath of fabric moving between rooms, or to hear a self-pitying sniff from somewhere. He nodded, and smiled, and thanked me very much for caring for Elliot, *like he's your own*, he said quietly one day.

CHAPTER 23

JAMESON WAS GONE, BUT THE FIGHT WAS STILL IN her. She hadn't wholly disappeared into quiet sadness, but had taken to erupting when I least expected it.

Hattie's erratic bouts of energy were becoming tinged with something toxic, and I noted the change with rising alarm. Her boisterousness that was, for so long, a quality that gave a rush, made one feel daring and part of something fun, was too much now, too potent. She was a darker version of herself, and I was fighting to keep her happy, but there was Elliot now. I had a child to protect. Not quite mine, maybe, but I needed to look out for the lives that still mattered. I had started helping out with Elliot to keep Hattie grounded, but the result was that she was becoming redundant. A swaying figurehead. In those early months and years when I grew into my life with Elliot, Hattie became like a drunken will-o'-the-wisp, soft hair and lips one moment and all claws the next. She reminded me, in those awful moments, of the other unpredictable force of my life, Buddy. I found myself frightened in a place deep inside me, but that only served to make me steel myself against it. She was a terrible pixie queen, and my hold on her—the thing in our youth that had kept her so close to me—was slipping. So, too, was her place in my heart. That third person: my boy, he became my first. She needed me, though. She needed me to care for Elliot and saw that I was doing this with growing interest and love every day.

She watched me, I knew. A cigarette in her fingers, keeping tabs while I taught him to tie his shoes, made his lunches and practiced reading. She made excuses not to come to his first day of school when he was five, and so Jameson and I, something awkward and unsaid looping through us as we held Elliot's hands on either side, took him down the same sidewalk that Hattie and I had taken as children. She watched from the curtains, sunken, sad eyes brimming with anger. I wasn't taking anything of hers. Not the way it seemed. She was unfit.

There was a building pressure in the house. There were days when I thought she was about to throw me out, but then she would snap at Elliot instead, and he was confused and unsettled. His loyalty, too, was divided. He wanted desperately to please Hattie, but would always ask for my assistance and came to rely on me, regardless of whether Hattie was there. She became like a dated caricature of a father—short-tempered and uninvolved in the daily goings on of the house.

"Where did all this food come from?" Elliot asked me once, marvelling at the store of food in the fridge. "We never have this stuff."

Elliot went to the school where Jameson taught. We took the short walk together in the mornings, and afternoons I waited for him to run happily out of the school with a skip and a crooked smile. My boy. And there it was. He had moved into my heart, my mind, taken up residence, occupied all my plans. I had no choice in the matter. Mothers know. That soft, fleshy face, the lovely hair at the back of his neck, his tiny mouth, his wide eyes and husky laugh. Elliot. I had started to breathe his name, and all the rest, all the sadness and bargaining, the bitterness and ratio-nalizations, broke into small pieces. Mine.

Hattie had faded out of our day-to-day lives for the most part. I didn't account for where she might be, who with; I didn't worry or wonder. My life was Elliot now. I should have taken more notice. She was out there, her hold on our lives—and our secrets—loosening.

Once, on my way home from running an evening errand, I saw Hattie on the patio at Dusty's, giggling into the ear of Mac Williams. I slowed my car down to watch, in shock. She put her hand on his arm, and turned to look, catching my eye. She hardened. Someone honked their horn, and I started, hitting the gas.

"WHY AM I EVEN HERE ANYMORE?"

Hattie, sitting in a wingback chair, after I had dropped Elliot at Jameson's townhouse. I closed the door, placing my keys care-fully down. I said nothing.

"Seriously. What the hell am I here for? You obviously don't want me here."

"Hattie."

"What? Am I wrong? You came back and took over. I see you, the way you've just moved into my life. You're gonna tell me I'm wrong? You're not waiting for the day I up and go? You and Jameson? So you can do what you'd always wanted to do? You took my life, Penny!" She banged her fist on the arm of the chair, and it made me jump. "You fucking took it all."

I kept my voice calm, but I knew. There was truth in all of it. She had always been able to read me. And worse, now she was unafraid to say it.

"I never wanted that," I said, quietly. "I told you that from the beginning, Hattie. I came back for you, for God's sake. Again. I came back for you. I am only trying to help, while you—"

"What? While I what?"

"I don't know. Get back on your feet."

"What the hell is that supposed to mean? You think you can do better, right?"

"God, you're paranoid." I paused, staring at her, and shook my head slowly. "Jameson was right."

"Excuse me?" She whispered.

"He called me back here. Because you're a mess. You're not in your right mind at all, and a—well, you're a mother if you've forgotten, and you can lash out at me if you want, but this is the bed you've made, and now you've pretty well shit in it."

Silence. And then a hissing, whispering strike.

"Fuck you, Penny, you fucking bitch." She inhaled and stared at me. "My bed? This is my bed? Funny, because I really feel like it's your bed I've been lying in all these years."

I froze, the memory of Jameson's body on mine. "I don't even know what—"

She stood up quickly, and the chair nearly toppled over, teetering back then forth, on an ornate wooden leg, for an extended moment. "I'm sick of the sight of you," she spat. She padded out of the room, and I heard her climbing the stairs. And maybe I should have cared what she thought then, but I didn't. All that mattered now was Elliot. I was mildly aware of an itch, though, a thought that she might tell me to leave, and I rolled over in my mind thoughts of custody and of how I might keep the boy, my boy, Jameson's and my son, close.

And if anything surprised me about that fight, it was my own fury, my own protective rage. I did love the life here, and I did have a claim to it now. I had earned it. I had fought for it. She was too weak to keep it.

Later, Hattie emerged clean and smartly dressed to tell me she was picking up her son from Jameson's. She slammed the door, and I watched her pass in front of the house. Long, thin strides, her anger unfolding in waves behind her. I felt it coming, a manic wind, a change. I knew something was going to break, and I needed to be careful. And it struck me, this coming and going, this helping and hurting, that Hattie and I had been dancing about for our lives.

I was terrified that she was going to take Elliot away. The fear struck deep inside me, and I wrung my hands and waited, the clock ticking loudly, for his return. When I heard him coming down the street, I rushed outside, my feet moving before I could think, and he ran to me. I saw Hattie walking slowly behind him, watching all the while. Our eyes met. I did not look away.

I knew, in that moment, that I didn't choose her. I chose my son, I chose my life. This life. I would push her out, if I had to, to hell with the consequences. That was the moment. With the sun high in the sky and our mother's picture on the mantel, a blue jay on the porch and the house creaking its approval, the moment I said to hell with you, my sister, my heart, my darling love. I'm taking what's mine.

For all her bravado, she looked away. She knew.

She was gone the next day.

At first I wasn't so sure, although something nipped at the heel of my mind. The house was quiet, but then it always was in the early morning. Hattie usually woke long after Elliot and I had gotten up and sometimes didn't stir until we had gone to the school. But there was something. In the same way you can tell, sometimes, when someone is in a house, you can also feel it when

185

they've gone. There was a dry stiffness to the place, a space that echoed lightly with Hattie's voice.

"Where's my mom?"

Elliot pulled a banana off the counter and tried, in the way that children are never successful at, tweaking the stem, frustrating himself by smushing the top of the fruit. "Is she still here?" Something about the question made me think that she wasn't still here, wasn't here anymore at all. I tore open the banana and bit off the mushy top, handing it back to Elliot, who walked away, his hair in all directions.

"Will you draw with me?"

My boy was an exceptional artist with a bright imagination, and yet he loved for me to copy pictures he would find in some of the old books and magazines that Hattie had brought home from her job with the spy-specialist author. There were books of war planes and tanks, of submarines and spying technology that looked to be a jumble of wires and buttons. The books smelled of old cigarettes and bookshelves, that dingy sour scent that makes the book a repugnant treasure. Our dining-room table was a mess of discarded paper and pencil shavings, piles of books with dog-eared corners, as we drew out new worlds of unimaginable secrecy.

I put on the kettle, stood still for a moment, listening. She was gone, I was sure of it. *Gone off in a huff,* our mother would have said. Hattie was always doing that when we were kids: storming out and away when she knew she was beat. We learned from our father how to run away; we learned from our mum how to stick it out. When she was a girl, we'd find her in cupboards or in the basement, or, once, having tea at an elderly neighbour's house. But now she was gone, and I had stayed. I didn't know for how long she'd be gone, or where she was. I knew that she was enraged and embarrassed, that her well of sadness was deep, and that she might exact some kind of revenge before returning, if she ever did. But that wasn't for now. Now was for me, and for Elliot.

And then my hands, shaking just a bit, took a pencil and pulled up a chair with my son.

CHAPTER 24

I SAT AT THE TABLE ONE EVENING AFTER HATTIE LEFT, Elliot tucked into bed, and read the local paper. So little had changed in St. Margaret's since I was a child, and I couldn't resist the town paper for all of its articles, notices, classifieds, garden sales and photos of local kids with painted faces at one festival or another.

There was a stillness now in the house, now that Hattie was gone. I couldn't relax, not fully, but I tried to let myself enjoy the silence, and tried not to wonder where she was or what trouble she could cause.

There were the usual wedding announcements with black-and-white photos of smiling young couples, as well as obituaries and anniversary notices. There were a few for stag and does, small-town fundraisers for couples raising money for their weddings. The more people, the better; cheap drinks, loud music and it gave folks something to do on a Saturday night. The couples in the paper were familiar faces from our high school. I immediately pictured Hattie out with them all, slinging back shots with Mac Williams. I told myself that was ridiculous but couldn't shake the feeling of suffocation. I stood and folded the paper, heading down the stairs, as deep as the house could hide me from my fears.

The basement, where I was still living, was teeming with boxes of our things, mine and Hattie's. Records and books, stuffed animals, clothes, letters, magazines, all closed off in the playroom where no one played anymore. A mausoleum of childhood. Nothing was even really organized, since neither of us was inclined to give anything away, although I do have a dim memory of one of Mum's friends haphazardly packing up my room and taking boxes downstairs after the wedding, when Hattie was staying at the house with all its hauntings. And now that the tables had turned once again, and the plates and cups and all else were in my lap, I looked around me.

I wandered into the large room where I hadn't ventured for at least a decade. I opened the doors, smelled drywall and the dust that was hanging in a scant sunbeam coming through the window at the far end. A ping-pong table, its net hanging limply in the middle, dominated the room, and I thought of the occasional evenings of boredom in my early high-school years. Hattie and I had challenged each other with nothing else to do, snow built up to the window, soon fiercely in the game, competition raising the colour in our cheeks, batting the ball crazily until one of us lost, the only sound our heaving breath as we battled it out.

I ran my finger through the dust on the green tabletop and wondered why Hattie hadn't brought Elliot down here. It seemed a trove of exploration potential, a place where children in the middle of playing had up and left. She had no real instincts for children, Hattie. Maybe it was my years working at a daycare, but all around the house I saw missed opportunities where she could have done more with Elliot. Part of me thrilled at the thought of my days ahead with him, while pushing down a wave of guilt.

I lifted the lid of a box full of stuffed animals, their eyes staring vacantly in all directions. A box of cassette tapes—mixtapes with happy faces scrawled beside the titles in my and Hattie's handwriting, early seventies hits, the soundtracks of riding in our mum's old car, of sitting in our rooms. I found a neatly folded bag of clothes, and I pulled out pieces, remembering times I'd worn them. Unlocking rooms of memories that I had long since forgotten. I sat down and leafed through badly written poetry and diaries full of angst, collages made from cut-out pieces of magazines, photos of Hattie and me that our mother had taken. And so I found that once I'd started, I couldn't stop because here it was, my life, her life, laid out before me; and if I could have gone back to any of these moments—the firecrackers in a jar, the tiny teeth and bones for drawing, the beads and crafts from Hattie's necklace-making craze, the experimental photos of the trees in the yard, letters from me to Hattie when I was away at school. If I could go back to all of this, would I do it differently? Could I find the spot where it veered off track and change the course? *Maybe you could, Mum. Maybe you think that I tied rocks to Hattie's kitten feet, but don't you know that she jumped in on her own?*

LATER, THE PHONE RANG. IT WAS HATTIE.

I asked where she was.

"I'm in the city, staying with a friend for now."

"How long are you planning on staying?"

"Until I can find my own place."

I exhaled with a chuckle. "You really are more like our dad than I thought. Are you even going to ask about Elliot?"

Elliot was in the backyard playing with one of his little friends. They kicked a soccer ball between them, their feet dancing around the ball.

"I dunno," I heard her murmur defeatedly, almost to herself. "Maybe it was all a mistake." Then, to me, "You're right. I need to sort my shit out, Penny. I rushed into having a kid. Well. I mean, you know. I want to get my head on straight. I'm not good for him right now."

"How nice for you."

"Sorry?"

"How nice for you to be able to choose that you're not good for him so you are going to take some time. I'm sure there were times Elliot would have left you, given the chance. You're a mother. Get your head out of your ass."

I hung up the phone feeling a rush of smugness, then guilt, but it didn't last long. In fact, I didn't even really want her to return. I opened the door and called the boys in. Sunday night, an early dinner before Elliot had his bath. A treat, to have a friend over on a school night, but I allowed it, trying to encourage new friendships that had begun to blossom in his first-grade class. It was November, and their cheeks were chilly and their breath husky when they ran in, huffing and puffing and making a mess of kicked-off shoes by the back door. I was his mother. This was my house.

"Jamie, do you want to play Sorry! while we eat?"

Jamie, a cautious child, looked at me for permission, and I nodded, smiling.

"Okay," Jamie said, wiping his hands on his pants after washing them in the bathroom. Elliot grabbed the game from the sideboard and began setting it up between the plates of spaghetti on the table. I brought over glasses of milk.

"Are you his mom?" Jamie asked me, making, I was sure, the connection between food and parents. *Yes. Yes. Yes.*

"No, sweetie. I'm his auntie Penny. His mom isn't home right now."

"Oh."

"My mom has to work a lot, but she's really nice. You'll meet her one day," Elliot explained, straightening the Sorry! cards and slurping noisily at his milk. "My dad lives in another house. With a tree house! Auntie Penny, can Jamie come there one day?"

"My dad isn't at my house, either," said Jamie. "My mom sometimes goes on dates."

"Sure, Elliot—I'm sure your dad would love to have Jamie over."

There was, in fact, a pretty fantastic ship-shaped tree house already at the house that Jameson was living in. I suspected that was part of the reason he'd rented it in the first place. It was nearby, and he'd made sure that Elliot's life was as unchanged as possible since he had moved out. Maybe he thought it was temporary, hoping she'd come around. He hadn't pushed for custody or any formal legal agreement. Hadn't even fought for more time with Elliot, but made sure it was split almost exactly. He knew that I was here now, and I think he hoped this would help Hattie, help bring her back. When in fact, it did just the opposite.

Happy chatter, games. I wiped down the countertop and felt a little like I was playing house. Earlier in the day, I had brought up from the basement trove a few of our old toys and games, and shown them to Elliot and his friend to wild delight. I felt in this moment that I could do no wrong. With the sun setting early and the leaves flying around in the wind on the driveway, with two kids gabbing and laughing at the table, with the dryer tumbling warmly in the other room, I was a making a home. Was it someone else's? That was a trick question. My house, her house, our house. My son, hers. I had staked a claim now, though. I knew what was best. *Who* was best. I pulled out some bread and peanut butter to make Elliot's lunch for school the next day and thought of Hattie, wherever she was. I didn't allow myself to think of all the secrets, of Buddy and Jameson, but they were there, lying beneath the surface like bodies under water. I was still worried that she would tell someone, that it would all come out, that our secrets would unravel after that and I would lose everything, but here we were. Almost like the fire had never happened. It was, after all, so long ago: *that thing that happened.* It was hard to imagine crafting anything like that now.

I spread the peanut butter, poured a little honey in, and closed it up with a soft piece of bread. Jamie asked for more spaghetti please. Elliot asked for just meatballs. Hard to imagine saying such a plan aloud, let alone pulling it off, pulling it out like a terrible magic trick of flaming red scarves. *Thick as thieves,* Mum used to say, that we sisters were thick as thieves. I looked over my shoulder and saw that I had pulled off a master heist.

Bath time, story time, bedtime. Routine, for Elliot and me. A life that felt like it had alway been this way, even though I'd only been with him for two years. In the quiet evening that followed, I opened a beer, sat in the old wingback and called Jameson.

"Have you heard from her?" I asked.

"Yeah, she called me. Nothing much to report." He paused and said, "It's so frustrating. I'm so disappointed in her, Penny. She's abandoned her son. And I mean, what irony, right? After how much your dad leaving messed with you two?"

"I know." I sipped at my beer, letting the silence stretch out between us, feeling for that connection that I was sure had never disappeared completely.

"If it's okay with you, I want Elliot to keep living there, with you, half the time. The less that things change for him, the better." His voice dropped to almost a whisper. "He loves you."

My heart leaped, in spite of everything. I smiled, shyly.

He paused, then, sighing, "God, I hope she figures herself out."

"I think she will. She just needed a break. Motherhood is hard," I said, knowing that in this I was serving to protect us both, Hattie and me, again.

I moved on to the logistics of the following week, to pick-ups and drop-offs and the sticky business of keeping the family ball rolling. I was so grateful to Jameson. He was such a calming force amidst this storm. He was my family, the father of my child, a dear friend, and under it all, I felt sure there was more. I couldn't blame Hattie for assuming there was more than mutual respect between us, for of course there was, more than she knew.

"Thank you, Jameson," I managed to say.

He laughed, and said that he clearly owed me more than I owed him. We chatted some more, shared some funny stories about our son, things that only we might find charming and brilliant and witty. I finished my beer and said goodbye, putting the phone in the cradle and listening to the silence of our old house. My house.

I stood, hands on hips, and surveyed the room. I had won. I was back where I belonged, and all was good. Fortune had smiled on me because I knew, truly in my heart, what was right, what was *my* right, and I took it. It was hard-earned, of course. Hattie was a formidable opponent; I had always known that. I was the only one who had ever recognized what she was capable of, how her actions threatened the safety and happiness of our home. She wasn't up to it, but I was. I always had been. Life was as it was fated to be now, and it was because I had fought for it. I knew it would work out.

I hadn't been rash. I had thought carefully, not impulsively. I had paid attention, I had listened and watched, and I would not be taken by surprise.

I had kept my eye on Hattie at all times.

Mum could be proud of me now.

CHAPTER 25

MONTHS HAD GONE BY WITH NO WORD FROM Hattie, but we were getting along just fine now. At first, Elliot had woken some nights, crying for his mom, but I was there now, and his nights were peaceful. I woke one morning to the sound of Elliot calling me from the main floor. I sat straight up in a panic, then lay down again.

"I'll be right up, darling."

"Okay. Auntie Penny, can I have some cereal?"

I heard him rooting around in the boxes, then the telltale sound of cereal pouring all over the counter. I smiled as he called to me again. To be needed, isn't it one of life's pleasures?

On the way to drop Elliot off at school.

"Hey, I don't know if your mom told you, but I have a farm."

"A real farm? What kind of animals are there?"

"Okay, so, none, but there is a barn. Do you want to go there with me sometime?"

"Why don't you have any animals?"

"I do. His name is Elliot."

A giggle, a shove against my side.

"Want to see it? After school, maybe?"

"Can we get ice cream first?"

"I fail to see why you'll need ice cream to see the barn."

Elliot's toothy grin, different now that his big teeth were coming in. "Ice cream is very important."

"True. Smart kid. Although maybe you can help me figure out what to do with the barn. Put in a swing or something?"

"Okay!" A skip to his step.

There were leaves spread out beneath us, and Elliot picked many up, asking me to save them for later, which I did. A collection gathered inside the door of the house, and a musty autumn smell, as they curled and dried out, losing their sheen, their impossible loveliness, but I couldn't bear to throw them out.

I kissed him at the door to the school, where he hastily ran after Jamie, whom he spotted by the portables. His knapsack thumping against his back as he went. I had the day off, and I turned and caught sight of Jameson pulling up on his bike. He dismounted gracefully, deftly handling it with his one arm, and walked over to me. We hugged and something inside came unclasped. Relief.

"Plans for the day, Penny? Your day off, right?"

"I think I'll go visit Joseph. It's been a while. You'll come get Elliot after dinner?"

"You got it."

"Do you want to come for dinner? We'd love to have you."

Jameson smiled, and demurred. "No thanks, Penny. I've got some marking to do, so I'll just grab on the go." *In time.*

I left, the fall breeze blowing my hair off my forehead. It had grown a lot, waving somewhere near my chin. Echoes of Buddy and his preference for long hair had faded, mostly. I saw him in my dreams still, a shadowy and frightening presence who usually strode in from somewhere else, lighting a cigarette and tossing a net of obscenities. Sometimes the dreams would end with me cornered by him against a wall or a bank of cupboards, trying futilely to push back, my fists useless, and I would wake with a start to the sound of my alarm. But he felt like part of another life. For so long, he, the torment, the fire, had become so firmly entrenched into my being that I thought I'd never move on. Yet in the same way my childhood had drifted into a foggy memory, that middle part of my life had become a barely perceptible scar. I marvelled sometimes how easily I had been able to move on; I had survived. Made it.

THERE IS SOMETHING ABOUT MAKING FRIENDS WITH older people that makes it all the more heartbreaking to witness their aging. Joseph was losing weight, and his skin seemed to hang on his large frame. But he was still wiry and strong and tall, and when he grinned, his eyes sparkled. But he was tired, and now had a stool with him at the workbench, whereas I had only ever known him to stand in the time before I left. But he greeted me as he always did.

"Oh my darling, Pen-entine," he sang out, the door jingling merrily behind me. There was a cracked-open toaster in front of him that he was fixing—these machines were his bread and but-ter, he used to joke.

"Jay-sus, Mary and Joseph," I called back, walking around the counter to accept a fuggy hug of aftershave and mechan-ical grease. It rang through my heart like the best kind of love. I breathed in the smell of my old friend, pulling up a dusty stool with a torn leather cover.

"Where's the wee one?"

"At school, Joseph. It's not like when you were there and kids played hooky just 'cause it was Monday, ya know."

"Right you are, Penelope. Keeps him out of trouble. Would hate for him to get up to any kind of mischief." His eyes twinkled. "But you know, if he happens to get bored," and here he rooted in the drawers of his work table, pulling out a dusty old package of small firecrackers. "I found these, and thought the lad would like to experiment with them—you know, under supervision."

I laughed and took the little paper bag. "Thank you, Joseph. I appreciate your continued horrible influence on my nephew."

"Your 'nephew.' Bah." He waved a hand. "He's your son through and through. And," he put up a hand as I began to protest, "that is not because you've got a biological bond. Nope. You're his mother because you bloody well act like it."

I put a finger to my lips, and Joseph zipped the imaginary zipper of his own.

I had, over a number of months, brought Elliot many times to visit Joseph. The two of them had sat side by side surrounded by tools, the old man's hands guiding Elliot into exploration of nuts and bolts, wires and thingamajigs. I had alluded to my sister's demons, and Joseph had woefully shaken his head, giving Elliot handfuls of candy as we left.

I wondered, for the hundredth time, where Hattie was now, and with whom. Something dark worried at me, gnawed at the edges of this new life. I saw her around every corner, often hearing her voice in a distant laugh or shriek, with every call and cry and giggle. She had become a child to me again, in some ways, and when I thought of her, it was of her over the years: as a kid, as a grinning and rebellious teen, as a tenacious youth, as a friend, as a foe, my blood, my poison.

"No offence to your sister, you understand," Joseph said.

"Of course not." I paused. "So, I'm thinking of taking Elliot to see the barn today."

"Excellent idea. Kids love barns. Nice day for it, too. Maybe take him out early?"

I chuckled, and pointed to a toaster. "So, what have you got here? A four-slicer, I see."

We chit-chatted, I helped him with some of his heavier tasks in the back room, and did his dishes as well. Threw in a load of laundry and opened his windows a crack to let in the warm fall. I visited with townspeople who needed keys cut, were picking up fixed fans and VCRs, laughed happily at all of Joseph's corny jokes, swept the floor and soaked up the time with this man who was the nearest to family that I had. He had rented the apartment out to one of his poker buddies, Sid, who shuffled downstairs around eleven o'clock, raising a withered arm in a wave to me before taking to the sidewalk for his daily walk around St. Margaret's.

"Grumpy bugger," Joseph grumbled, not looking up as the door closed behind Sid. "Nothing like you, Penelope, I tell you."

"You tell me all the time, actually."

"Well. It bears repeating."

"At least he's not having babies up there. I mean, that's a bit disruptive."

"You haven't heard him on the old commode. Sounds like he's giving birth half the time!"

THE FIREWORKS IN THEIR PAPER BAG SCRUNCHED INTO my purse, I picked up Elliot from school. Hattie had taken Mum's old car with her, and I had gotten myself my own little beater. I had come to love the cantankerous sound it made when I started it. I rooted through the tapes in the glove compartment and pulled out one that I hadn't heard in a while. I pushed it into the tape deck, and it took a tipsy second to catch up to itself mid-song. I rolled the window down even though the day had become cooler as it wore on.

"Did you bring me a snack?" Elliot asked as he was buckling himself into the back seat.

"I did. Here." I tossed an apple from a fresh bushel that I had picked up earlier. It was giving the car a new, un-Hattie-like, autumnal smell. He caught it and grinned, surprised at his reflexes.

I drove to the barn, to the site of my old life, ashes to ashes. We climbed from the car, the doors slamming into nothingness, echoing the silence. Elliot followed my cue, keeping quiet but for his crunchy apple. My skin was tingling. Since I had returned to St. Margaret's, I had made pains to avoid this place. Even when it made sense to take this route, I found another way. I hadn't been here for years.

It had grown wild and had an abandoned, lonely air about it. Grasses and weeds and wildflowers sprung in all directions. The barn, except for one large graffiti tag, was largely untouched from the outside. I had half-expected it to be gone: razed to the ground, burned down, blown away in a freak wind of change. But it stood, steadfast and true, waiting.

"Is it a grass farm?" Elliot asked, lifting his legs through the wild grass towards the barn.

I laughed, lifting him onto my back. "No, we're not growing grass to harvest it. I just haven't come by in a while."

"It's pretty crazy here, Aunt Penny."

"You can say that again." I got a hold of the sliding door and gave it a large tug. I knew Elliot was smiling.

"It's pretty crazy here," he repeated, laughing at his wit.

And then there it was. It stank like cigarettes and booze and piss. I thought of Mac and wondered if perhaps this had become his haunt on a more permanent basis. It needed a good cleaning. But it was my barn.

"It stinks in here," Elliot said. I nodded.

We agreed we needed a swing.

"And a slide," Elliot said, "from up there." He pointed to the rafters.

"A swing's enough for now." I was surprised to see some of my things were still there: pots and pans, a can opener, things that I imagine had been made good use of by others who were looking to skip out on their lives for a spell.

"Did you used to live here?"

"Not really. Well, I would camp out here sometimes."

"With my mom?" And there it was: I saw in Elliot that same urge to learn about, to keep love lit, for his mother that Hattie and I had as children for our dad. More and more often he had begun to ask me to fill in blanks in family stories with colour about Hattie. It hurt, that she was gone. It was a familiar sting.

"No, honey. By myself. But I did live here in a way. There used to be a house over there." I pointed through the opening of the door, the sun in my eyes as it made its way down. "Where all the mud is. Shall we get those sparklers?"

"What happened to it? To the house?"

"There was a fire."

I hadn't meant to tell him. In one of those moments that is over before you can stop it, I just said it. Would I change my answer now, given the chance? I doubt I could have stopped myself. Secrets have a way of fragmenting like a kaleidoscope.

"A real fire?"

"Yes."

"How did it happen?"

"A cigarette."

"Smoking is bad."

"It is, yes."

"Is that why there was a fire? Did God make that happen?"

I knew that Hattie had occasionally taken Elliot to church, and I could see the echoes of my own childhood obsession with retribution.

"No, sweetie."

"But there was a fire because someone did something bad."

"I—"

"Where is the house now?"

"It's all gone. The fire took it, Elliot."

"Did anyone die?"

He stood rooted to the spot, as though moving would make it happen all over again, like he could keep us safe by staying still. The apple in his hand, brown creeping into the white.

I nodded. He stood perfectly still. His face was a white mask.

"Who?"

I took his hand and broke the spell. Walked with him out the door into the failing light towards the car.

"His name was Buddy. He was my husband."

CHAPTER 26

FIRST HE HAD THE DREAMS. THEY BEGAN WHEN he seemed to accept that his mother wasn't returning, not in the same way. He would tell his friends, "My mom doesn't live here anymore." He seemed fine with this. But sleep knows better. Dreams have a will of their own.

More like night terrors: Elliot woke yelling about fires. The first time it happened, he had walked in a glassy-eyed haze down to the main floor, crying out for me in a sleep stupor. When I finally woke, and rushed so quickly I slammed my shoulder into the railing as I fumbled up the stairs, I tried to snap him out of it. His black-brown eyes wide and horrified, he covered his face and wailed. The next day he remembered nothing of it. Over and over this happened, and, Jameson told me, at his house as well. There would be a span of a few weeks without them, and then the terrors would start up again, always with the garbled moan about *fire fire fire*. They haunted me, these panicked, middle-of-the-night fire dreams. I had my own burning ghosts to contend with, those that Hattie had so often comforted me out of. But we held each other, Elliot and I, and soon, he'd fall back into fitful sleep.

It had been a couple of years now since Hattie had moved out. She rarely visited or called, her appearances frantic and stressful for me, fraught with expectation for Elliot, who saw them as monumentally important. She whirled into our lives, bringing gifts and taking Elliot out for dinners, then spun away again, leaving a cloud behind her.

Christmas came. Hattie called to tell Elliot she was going to visit in the new year. I spoke to her briefly. It sounded as though she was on a bar pay phone, chatter and clinking in the background, a pause as Hattie covered the mouthpiece and said something to someone. When I hung up, I expect she replaced the phone into the metal cradle and lit a cigarette, swinging her hips on her way back into the spotlight, her shoes on a sticky bar floor. I bit my lip, fretting over loose lips, wondering when she'd come.

But there was life to be living. Elliot, and Jameson just out of reach. Christmas lit up our lives with Elliot in it. I wrapped presents, hung holly, filled Elliot's stocking, which I had found in a box under the stairs with all of our family's Christmas decorations, including those Hattie and I had made as children. There were times, and Christmas decorating was one of those, when the house was like a museum that I had stumbled into by accident. All those old memories packed in cardboard boxes.

For Christmas, I bought Elliot a real sketchbook and a long, flat tin box of differently graded pencils. His eyes shone when he opened the lid, and we tested the softness of the pencils on the white paper that had protected them. Our fingers smudged, we ate chocolates and watched *It's a Wonderful Life* until Elliot fell asleep against my shoulder, his mouth lolling and his cheeks glowing happily. I carried him up to bed, in the room that was once mine, and crawled sleepily into bed in Hattie's old room so I could be nearby. He was having such nightmares I couldn't continue to sleep in the basement. It was my room now, it had to be.

HE BEGAN TO DRAW FIRES.

I tried to steer him back to battleships and spy boats, but they held none of the draw of a fire. Almost off the page, black smoke as dark as he could make it without tearing the pages, his hands charcoal black moving across the pages. Pages and pages of them. Famous fires, house fires, forest fires and river fires. The fires of London, Boston, Chicago, Rome, wars, battles, car fires and gas fires. I found the drawings around the house like terrible talismans pointing to the disaster of my life. They unnerved me so, those sketches of smoke curling away in dark scribbles. Elliot wanted to know everything about fires: how they could start, how to prevent them—if being "good" would stop them, famous fires in history, and most terribly, everything I could tell him about what he called "your fire." My fire. I had spent years running away from that fire, its sparks nipping my heels, only to come back home and be haunted by the imaginings of my son. I wanted to snap his pencils in two.

"Were you sad?"

"Terribly sad. But not anymore, Elliot. You make me so happy."

"You're lucky you weren't there."

"Very lucky."

"Were there any animals?"

"No, sweetie."

"Was the house all gone?"

"Mostly, Elliot. But, I don't really like to talk about it, honey."

"I know, but, was it, like, all gone?"

"Yes, mostly."

"What was left?"

"Me. I was left. Let's talk about your day at school."

Jameson noticed it, too. Felt sorry for me; knew this fascination would drudge up old memories I didn't care to remember. He tried to discourage Elliot from asking me about the fire, "my fire," because I had lost my husband there.

"You didn't lose him, though."

"That's what they sometimes call it when someone dies."

"He would have been my uncle, if he was your husband, right, Auntie Penny?"

And here I almost laughed in spite of it all. "Yes, honey. But he's gone. And can I tell you something? He wasn't all that fun."

"What do you mean?"

"Just that, I don't know that you would have liked him all that much."

"Oh. Okay. Because he was bad?"

"No, honey."

"It's still sad, though."

"Yes, still sad."

And I felt, with my arm around my son, like the worst kind of monster, like the best kind of saint. If Mum were to catch my reflection then, would it be of a mangy-haired, clawed and toothy creature, wrapping her murderous arms around an innocent child? Or of an angel who had rescued herself and then her son from the clutches of a desperately sad life? I kissed Elliot's head, trying to ward off I don't know what, to protect him from the deadly secrets of a life like mine. He turned a page to a fresh sheet in his sketchbook, sharpened a pencil and began again: drawing out my demons. Fire-breathing dragons. Their snouts just outside the frame, flames filling the white of the page almost all the way to the edge and onto the table. A dark curling madness filling the open, cloudless sky. An evil no one sees. And there, if you look: A tiny house at the bottom of the page. A triangular roof. A chimney. A square window with little curtains. A smudge of the pencil here and there, a carelessness, a trick of the light, and there seems to be a tiny shadow in that little window, just inside. Arms raised.

And then, just as quickly, dark hair hanging in his dark eyes, tongue sticking out in concentration, the fat of Elliot's hand slips across the page, and in an instant, it is snuffed right out.

OUR LIFE WAS FULL OF THE KIND OF HAPPY REGULARITY that sometimes dips into monotony, not that I very often took life with him for granted. I still felt like I'd won a bet, gotten away with the easy end of a dare, slipped away with the loot while the other party wasn't looking.

Raising a child in a small town is a wonderful thing; it was nothing compared to growing up there, for me. My perspective had shifted to include hikes in sprawling parks, visits to farms, fort-building and swimming in the lake—all of it close to our house.

On one occasion, my arms wrapped around me in the cold, watching Elliot play with some other kids at the creek in a large park, I saw Iain Moore, out of uniform, opening his car door in the parking lot across the way. The kids were hitting the lightly frozen water with fallen tree branches, the ice snapping under their blows. He paused. I knew he had seen me, but there was enough of a distance that I could pretend I wasn't sure who it was. He tilted his head, considering something. Then, looking in the direction of the boys, he got in, closed the car door and

backed his car away. I returned my attention to the children playing, the loud cracking of their sticks sounding suddenly frightening to my ears.

HATTIE CAME TO VISIT. SHE ARRIVED WITH THE NEW
year, on the heels of a cold snap, with an overnight bag.

"It's me. I'm home," she called out.

I heard the declaration and the door slam almost in the same
loud, banging moment, and felt a chill blast through the old vents
and up my arms. I was in the laundry room, taking a load out of
the dryer. Heard the keys drop on the bench by the door with that
familiar jingling finality. *It's me. I'm home.*

I took a breath and lifted the laundry basket, carrying Elliot's
and my clothes in a warm bundle, up to greet Hattie.

"Oh," she said coldly, surveying me with a wry smile, "there
you are. Still playing house, I see."

"Welcome back, Hattie." I put down the basket and took
a step towards her, then stopped, my arms dangling lamely at
my sides.

She chuckled and said, with a new, quiet fury: "I don't bite."

She embraced me. She was home.

I began to worry. Hattie was a louder caricature of her former self. Her red hair was brassier, her make-up applied with a
broader brush, her voice husky, her jokes crass. She was there
somewhere, my little sister, under the boastful bravado she was
using to bury everything that had come before. I tried to be
patient with her, to cajole her, but there was anger there that I felt
it unwise to provoke. She tried, in subtle and bold ways, to assert
herself in the house, to tug at the edges of my insecurities. She
knew I was nervous about her being in this space again: lifting

up objects and inspecting them like the mother-in-law in an old TV show. It was laughable that she would hold how I kept the house to a high standard given the state it was in when she'd left, but she still waltzed around the house some days with a removed and judgemental air about her that I'm quite sure she knew set my teeth on edge.

There were other times when I saw my poor old Hattie— and she was regretful, sad, ashamed, swallowing her pride and trying to push the clock back. In those moments, when she was reading with Elliot or trying to help with dinner, I felt such a grieving sadness in my stomach, wishing it could all be as it was. But when? It had never been right. *I know I never should have asked for her help years ago, Mum, but what would you have had me do?* Maybe she had been too young, too fragile, and it had frozen her in time. I had tried: it wasn't just me, but Hattie I had tried to save, hoping that the fire would keep her from harm as well, forgetting how embers smoulder long after a fire goes out. And as I watched her, trying to recover something, the sun coming through the window and touching that red hair I loved so much, there were times I wished she'd never leave.

But then it started to go sour. It's difficult to find the exact moment when things changed and I could no longer keep the balance—but something was pulled below the surface with a jerk, an undertow, when Hattie learned that Elliot had a preoccupation with fire.

Elliot and I were entwined like a secret and its keeper. We had an unspoken ease together, were similar in the peaks and valleys of our personalities; we spent hours in happy silence or in excited storms of imagination. We had long ago transformed the barn into a place for him, for us, for solace and company, and it was now the most perfect hideout for an almost-eight-year-old: with swings and ladders, a trap door and a switchboard I'd found at the dump that I screwed in under a steering wheel.

There'd been no whiff of Mac Williams there for a long time; perhaps the childlike presence had spooked him, but at any rate, it was a happy place.

Elliot had a small group of close-knit friends: three boys, including little Jamie, and a girl. They plotted and ran about, riding their bikes on our street after a day of playing at "the barn," muddy and sunburned during the summer, rosy-cheeked and frozen in the winter. I was friendly with the parents of his friends, but as they mostly ended up at our house, I felt like I was mother to them all: handing out Band-Aids and popsicles and hot chocolate.

Elliot's preoccupation with fires, with "my" fire, continued. Most disturbingly, I had once found a drawing of what looked like our barn with a fire blazing in the background. My heart swelled, a large, breath-stopping thing, and I felt dizzy. It was too close. I wanted to scorch the memory, the history. I wanted to tear up his drawings so no one would ever see—Jameson, Hattie, no one—but was almost afraid to touch them at all, like they contained a kind of mystic magic that would ruin everything if I went near them. And so they continued to appear on tables and surprise me falling out of the pages of books, and I left them there, and they stung me with random irregularity. I started to feel jumpy, nervous, easily startled. The house, which had offered so much comfort, was making me feel trapped. I lightly suggested to Elliot that other people might not enjoy the drawings of fire as much as I did, that perhaps he should keep to doing them only when he was at my house. My home, holding in everything it saw.

And then, on one of those days, a day in late August, Hattie took a closer look at a pile of Elliot's drawings as they lay, those ticking, cross-hatched time bombs, on a bookshelf.

There was silence where moments before she had been humming to herself, a cigarette in between her fingers, the smoke whirling away from her. I was washing dishes, she was on drying. I turned to see where she'd gone. Her back to me, a towel slung over her shoulder, her hair up in a messy bun. I turned off the tap. And then.

"What's this." A mutter.

I said nothing. I'd worried it would happen. I knew she'd see them. I don't know why I hadn't tried to hide them. Elliot was outside playing. It was a Sunday. We were going to have burgers for dinner. There was a bottle of wine open on the counter. End of day.

"Your *son*," she said more audibly, "he's quite an artist."

"Don't call him that, Hattie."

"How does he know about the fire?" She still had her back to me, was rifling through the drawings now, pausing occasionally.

"I told him there was one. When I first took him to the barn." I stopped, then, "I told him my husband had died."

"Died, eh?" She ashed her cigarette on the floor.

"Hattie, please. I had to say that."

"You sure like your secrets, Penny." She shook her head slowly. "But of course. He can't know the truth about the fire. No one can. But boy," and here she dropped them all, some of the drawings floating gently to the floor, others gusting across the room, "it's such a good story." And then she just walked straight out of the house.

HATTIE BEGAN TO NEEDLE, TO PUSH, TO PLAY WITH ME, through Elliot. She took a sudden interest in his fire drawings, encouraging him, inquiring about them, teasing out conversations, asking how he knew how to make them so realistic, how did he manage to capture that movement so well? She took him to the library to take out books on famous fires, to the fire station to talk to firefighters in person. She fanned the flames of his obsession where I had tried to dampen them. *Fire is so . . . alive, isn't it? I can see why you're fascinated by it.* I wonder sometimes if Elliot's interests were encouraged by Hattie's urgings. If things might have ended differently if she hadn't pushed him like she did. It wasn't right, what she was doing. She bought him paints, and then the images were alight with action: fiery yellows and oranges bursting off the small canvases she'd provided. Once she pulled out her lighter and lit a small piece of paper while she was sitting with him, his eyes suddenly aglow, the two of them watching it dance threateningly before she dropped it into a water glass with a laugh. "Boy, we're like two peas in a pod, aren't we?" And Elliot had laughed, revelling in this time with his mom, while I stood wringing my hands behind them.

Late last night, while we were all in bed (dum dum dum)
Old Lady Leary lit the lantern in her bed (dum dum dum)
And when the cow tipped it over, she winked her eye and said,
It's gonna be a hot one in the old town tonight—Fire Fire Fire!

Hattie, singing that goddamn song, "Old Lady Leary," about the woman whose cow started the Chicago fire, over and over, whistling the tune at all hours, bursting out with the end bit, startling me when I didn't know she was there. *She was making me crazy, Mum.* She had changed. Something had snapped in her. What a hoot, Elliot must have thought, what fun. His mother was back, and they had a sudden kinship. "I'm not afraid of fires," she'd tell him, "but don't bring them up to your aunt. It will only upset her."

I snapped at Hattie in these moments, found myself short tempered with Elliot. She just smiled at him and shrugged, provoking him to follow suit. She had done it; flipped the switch and put a gulf between us. I was unravelling, Hattie holding on to the thread of my sanity.

All she needed to do was pull. And if I'm honest, in my very heart, I wished her gone altogether. I fantasized about her death, about her dying, and having Elliot to myself. We'd gotten away with our secret, but now there was so much more at stake than law and liberty. Our son, my son. And so, yes, I thought of it. I lay in bed and wished she would just choke on her own vomit, would trip down the stairs. I'm a monster, perhaps. Once a murderer, always one. But I'm a mother now. And wouldn't any mother kill for her son? I lay and wished away my darling girl. I even saw myself, grief-stricken at her funeral, genuinely heartsick about her death. I love her, I loved her, I hate her, I hated her.

CHAPTER 27

WHEN ELLIOT WAS TEN, JOSEPH DIED. Quietly, and in the shop, after he pulled down the Closed sign one last time. I came to visit him the next morning, and he didn't open up. Whenever this happened, I had felt panic rise in my chest, and this time, what I had been fearing all this time was waiting there. I used the key I had for the shop, my hands fumbling. He was sitting in his recliner in the back. His mouth and eyes open. It scared me terribly. I cried out, yelling uncontrollably. Finally, his tenant, Sid, old as time but alive, came in and closed Joseph's eyes, like he'd done that before, held my hands firmly, calming me down almost silently with the great care of an almost stranger. Would I never grow accustomed to death?

Elliot had never been to a funeral, but he insisted on coming to Joseph's. The two of them had a strong bond, Joseph had been like his grandfather, and Elliot took the death badly—heaving in my arms. It is so painful, and we never do get used to that horror, that shock, the injustice of being robbed of happiness and normalcy.

Elliot had been going through a difficult time, something to do with being his tender age, I guess. He was, like all kids, sometimes lonely and misunderstood, angry and unique. He still had the same friends, his best being Jamie, with whom he had bonded over having a "broken" home. Jamie's mother, however, had recently remarried, Elliot had told me. I hadn't met the stepfather and really only knew the mother by phone, keeping my distance, as was my wont. Elliot spent a lot of time at Jamie's house now, for dinners and sleepovers and after school. I was glad for him that he had someone, because when he was home, he was often sullen and preoccupied.

Hattie didn't come to the funeral, although she was home again. She was working at the Driver's Licence Bureau, which she said was ironic given that she'd been charged with a "tiny" DUI last year. After coming and going on a whim for two years, staying for sometimes short, sometimes long periods, she claimed she was finally back for good. She said that she would find her own place, but I had insisted, feeling I'd rather know where she was. There was plenty of room at the house. Here we were again: my sisterly conscience, my dark heart, was in the house. At home, she had said. Her anger had dulled somewhat. She seemed to be surrendering something, was tired. Was giving up.

ON THE WAY TO THE FUNERAL, I TALKED TO ELLIOT.

"How are things going with your mom, El?"

"It's okay. It's nice, actually."

"Yeah. It's good having her home."

"She had dinner at Dad's with me the other night," he said.

"No kidding? Did your dad know she was going?" I felt a twist in my belly.

Elliot smiled. "No, but he was happy to have her, he said."

We didn't talk for a bit. We were pulling into the gravesite and I looked at Elliot, his baby-face, freckly profile. A bird swooped low in front of the car. I ached thinking about Joseph. His empty bed, a book open on his chair.

It was April. Chilly and wet, not much in the way of sunshine. Crocuses peeping through the mud at the gravesite. Jameson had parked close to my car, and he walked with us, and stood between us during the burial. Standing close to me, his arm around Elliot. I thought about all the single gloves he didn't use. I watched, detachedly, as dirt was thrown on the grave. I was crying, and Elliot, too, his head turned into Jameson's chest. We three, like a family, standing among Joseph's poker buddies and lifelong friends, daughters, customers and the people of St. Margaret's who knew Joseph, the repairman. That was the end of that kind of thing in our town. Soon a time would come where people threw it all away, all their useless things, just buy a new one of whatever it was. Broken toasters rusting in the sun on heaps of garbage.

Someone read a line from *The Giving Tree*, and then it was over, and we were all making a lonely shuffling line back to our cars. Poor Joseph. The thought of his store, in all its immaculate chaos, saddened me, and I rubbed my arms to beat off the chill.

Elliot walked ahead of Jameson and me, and in his retreating figure I saw so much of my own sullen ten-year-old self that my heart swelled a little for him, but really for me. Watching your child grow up is a life flashing before your eyes, a sentimental death by a thousand cuts. The endless stream of little bath toys and scribbles, of homework and broken zippers, tears and confessions and then suddenly-finally, they are there walking ahead of you, their figure getting further and smaller with every step. What would I tell my mother about him if I could? *Your grandson, who is the son, by way of this strange life, of your two daughters.* I was proud and protective of him but also scared for him, because he was dipping his toe into mischief now. He was failing and flailing the way so many kids do but the way each parent thinks is unique. We fought more, and not the frustrating bickerings of a young child and his parent, but some knock-'em-down rows that ended with his door slamming and my head in my hands. *You're not my mom!* Grades and friends and teachers and getting into trouble, getting swirled into a tangle of best intentions and poor judgement.

But still. He was a small boy to me in so many ways. Prone to tears occasionally, his face scrunching up and looking just as it had when I had first met him and something hadn't gone his way.

Sometimes I walked with him to school, still, and hugged him well before the entrance, heading back feeling I'd stolen a moment. The days and months were slipping so quickly out of my reach, and so was his childhood. One of those days I had seen Iain Moore driving by in his cruiser, and I raised a hand in greeting. I felt a shiver run down my back at the sight of him but smiled. He gave a cursory nod and drove on. I dropped my hand lamely at my side and went straight into work, losing myself in busywork as a distraction.

NOTHING STAYS THE SAME. MOTHERS AND SISTERS KNOW this. Autumn comes.

There was an incident.

One weekend afternoon, there was a knock at the front door, and when I opened it, Iain Moore was there, with Elliot. I couldn't hide my shock; my mouth fell open. Elliot stood sheepishly behind Iain, who was out of uniform and just in plain pants and a golf shirt, and I tried to understand what brought them there together.

"Penny." He nodded. And then, looking past me into the house. "Is Hattie here?"

"What? No. What is this about? Elliot, are you okay?"

"May we come in, please?" Iain asked curtly. "We need to talk about the fire."

I staggered against the open door. Iain came into the house, moving past me to sit down in a chair in the living room, Elliot on the couch.

Elliot spoke up. "This is Jamie's stepdad. His name is Iain."

And my life's parts began to bleed into one another. Jamie and Elliot had been caught trying to start a fire in a nearby forest two weeks earlier, which Iain thought that Hattie and I would have known about already as Iain had made Elliot promise he would tell us. My ears were ringing as Iain explained that the two had been getting into mischief lately, staying out late when they were meant to be coming back to Jamie's—and now Iain's—house, and that while the attempted fire had been too damp for any spark to take, Iain insisted Elliot needed more discipline, that Hattie or I needed to enforce this, he needed to be made to understand the dangers of fire.

"I'm sure you've told him about the frightening potentials." There was an edge to Iain's voice, but I nodded dumbly. "This isn't arson, but it's careless, and I needed you, as his guardian, to know. And Hattie, too, if she's here. I had a feeling he hadn't told either of you, and he confirmed that today."

I sat numbly through this brief meeting, feeling a frightened fool, quietly thanking Iain when it was over, and ushering him out of my house, trying to arrange my panic, quiet it, calm it down.

I didn't tell Hattie about it for fear that she would take advantage of the information. I was losing track of what I told her, what I kept to myself. A secret-keeper's burden, and they were stacking up for me: what Hattie knew, what Elliot knew, the one Jameson knew, but others didn't. I had become so dishonest, such a hoarder of untold truths.

"ELLIOT, WAKE UP."

"I don't have to go to school today, it's Saturday."

"Get up, Elliot. I have work for you to do. Up and at 'em." I pulled off his covers.

"Penny!" He groaned angrily.

Elliot hadn't called me Aunt Penny in a very long time. It was too fussy a name, too much distance in its formality, stretching between us and not accounting for the role I played, and for me, who I really was. So I was Penny to him, although more and more there was distance between us anyway, and lately he was using the fact that I was his "aunt" as a tool in his arsenal.

Afternoon. I had given Elliot a hot and punishing chore, outside in the fall sun: putting the garden to bed, raking up the summer and tucking it into a series of bags and piles, tying up the tender trees with burlap. I folded laundry and watched him through the window, marvelling at how this boy had come to be in the yard of my childhood, where Hattie and I had run around, made forts, dug holes. Where he had done the same. Small for his age, spunky, strong, kind and sometimes cruel. This house that had held up so well through the years, that housed us all and provided warmth to murderous parents and blackmailing sisters, to love and sex and infancy. When we were gone, who would live here, and what more would it know?

Houses, homes: they kept our secrets. My house with Buddy, in its clean modest floors, its curtains and linens. No one would have known the smash-'em-up, burn-'em-down fights that took place there. No one knew how it haunted me still.

I pulled a shirt of Hattie's out of the basket and carefully folded it, started a pile for her clothes. Sorting, separating. *Look out for your sister*, our mum had always told us—*she's the only one you have. Look out, Hattie. Look out, Penny.*

Elliot had raked the leaves into a giant pile. The yard, which was more of a sprawling property, was deep, and so it wasn't until I smelled it, coming through the open windows, that I realized what he was doing. I went onto the back porch and saw a column of smoke at the far end of the yard, a black and orange pile. Burning leaves. I called out to him, and he lifted his head but didn't respond or wave.

"Didn't you learn anything?" I shouted at him, rushing outside. The same question I could ask myself.

LATER, WE SAT AT THE KITCHEN TABLE TOGETHER.

"I don't think you know how dangerous it is," I said.

"Penny, you're making too big a deal of this. I was just trying to get rid of the leaves. People do it all the time."

"Don't give me that. This is not a coincidence. I don't think you know how quickly those things can spread. Where did you even get matches?"

He ignored this. "Look, I know you're paranoid about fire. I get it. I understand, okay? God, Jamie's stepdad gave us a lecture already. All about some disgusting corpse he found at a fire once that they'd never solved, which I didn't really need to hear. I get it. I'm not some pyromaniac."

The image of Buddy's body before my eyes. My mouth went dry and I felt my breath quicken. Never solved.

That night, I woke in a sweat, dreaming of Buddy on fire. He stumbled out of his chair, flames licking his arms and hair, and bellowed my name. I sat up, gasping, my throat burning for water.

I FRETTED THROUGH CHRISTMAS, WATCHING HATTIE and Elliot constantly; I kept my worries to myself. Winter, that season of shutting doors and drapes, of keeping secrets tight, and yet I felt a growing sense of the potential of a crack in the foundation, where something might get in or out.

In February, a letter came home from school. There had been a few small fires in the children's playground. Someone or some people had started them inside the playhouse, the only dry part of the park, which was mostly covered in snow. It could not be used until it was repaired. If parents knew anything about the incident, which the school was taking very seriously, they were to contact the administration.

We were shovelling the driveway. Elliot was at Jameson's house. Hattie mostly stood smoking with her hands on the handle of the shovel.

"I saw that letter from Elliot's school," Hattie said.

"Yeah. Pretty upsetting. They were talking about it at the daycare." I had thought of little else; my fears and nightmares were crossing into my daily life. I hated that Hattie was looking through the mail but said nothing about it.

"Why didn't you tell me?"

"What?" I stammered. "I don't know. I didn't think to."

She nodded.

"He used to love that playhouse when he was in kindergarten," I said. "I remember having to drag him out of there after school sometimes."

I thought of little Elliot, his black curly hair under a newsboy hat, hiding in a little house. And Hattie, too, in those days, when she was hiding in our house. The shovels scraped against the packed snow. It had been a cold winter, but this was the first snow we'd really gotten. I marvelled that the fire could have caught at all, in these elements.

"Who would do something like that?"

"Kids, I guess."

Hattie laughed. "They think they're all different, but they're all the same. We were the same." She stood, breathing heavily, leaning on her shovel. "It wasn't El and his friends, you don't think?"

"I hope not." And yet. I knew. Something tickled the hair on my neck. These moments, when Hattie and I tried to parent together, both jockeying for position, trying to act like we weren't. I rejected her question, assuming I knew him better. But there was something there, and I thought of the day Iain Moore had come by. I pushed it away, hoping it would pass, impotent in the face of only this thing—fire—to act.

Hattie, for her part, mostly deferred to me on issues around Elliot. Since she had moved back in, she had quieted. She drank a little less, and she dangled our secret in the open more infrequently. But there was still a way about her: the sense of only just holding it together. If she was tired, if she was drunk, it came out: the sneers and the snarls, the quips and judgements. Today she was managing it well, though, and she looked at me thoughtfully.

"Didn't you say he'd been getting into trouble lately? And," a twitch of a smile, "he still loves fire, doesn't he?"

"Hattie." I stood facing her. "Iain Moore, the detective . . ." I watched her face and suddenly she was listening carefully. "He's Jamie's stepdad. He—he came here one day. Told me about a fire the boys had tried to start—just a small thing, like a campfire,"

I rushed out, while she stared at me. "But he—Iain—told Elliot about a fire he'd been called to once." I swallowed. "Where a person had died. He even told him what the body had looked like." I loosened, showed her my vulnerability. "Hattie, he said it hadn't been solved." My voice cracked. "I'm afraid."

She stood stock still for a moment and then shook, almost like shaking me off. Inhaled her cigarette. Stood taller. Looked away.

"Yeah. I would be too, if I were you."

THAT NIGHT, LONG AFTER HATTIE HAD GONE TO BED, I wandered into her room. She had been sleeping in our mother's old room, the largest bedroom. She looked so small there. I watched her, her chest heaving like a child's, her mouth open slightly, her hair thrown around her in a net. My heart swelled with memory and love, with the weight of our lives, and I carefully lay down beside her, feeling the rhythm of her breath. Her face was turned to mine. I swept a stray hair off her cheek. She closed her mouth and swallowed, smacked her lips like a baby. *What happened to us, Hattie? What if I'd never known you?* I thought of how easy it was to snuff out a life—as easy as a pillow over a mouth—but how hard it was to move on afterward. I cried, silently, then. And while the tears rolled between us, I curled my hand into hers, my Hattie, and I fell asleep.

CHAPTER 28

I T WAS A DRY AND QUIET SPRING, AND THEN A SCORCHED, rainless summer. The years were passing, and while part of me felt grateful for pulling it all off, I was left with a deep worry, a sadness. School let out and time opened up. Summer left me with a thirst, a loneliness: Elliot was pulling away, uninterested in our life, our home. I busied myself with outdoor projects while Hattie sat on the patio and watched me. I felt like I was under glass, hot and suffocated, but desperate to keep my family close. I was irritable, jittery, easily startled. I hadn't been sleeping well; my mind, day and night, felt filled with smoke. Elliot often asked to go to friends' houses, and I felt like I was losing him. He was surly and distant; he'd become a stranger. Jameson visited semi-regularly to check in. He wanted us to keep an eye on Elliot, knowing that there was mischief afoot that had less to do with experimentation and more to do with trouble and danger.

St. Margaret's was beset by a fear of fires. The town itself was a tinderbox. There was a fire ban for campfires. The whole place could go up with a spark, it felt like. There were a series of small fires to start—garbage dumpsters and rubbish piles—no one knew what was accidental or deliberate. There were occasional larger, more dangerous fires in sheds or bushes. People were frightened; the town chatter bubbled over at the market and school with talk of "the fires." The local paper was plastered with photos of burned-out piles of ash.

I didn't want to believe it was him. I knew that it was.

"Have you asked him, Penny?" Hattie asked, pouring herself a large glass of wine one afternoon. Her hair piled on top of her head, wet tendrils hanging down in the heat.

"He flat-out denies it. And I believe him," I said, stiffly.

She nodded, sipping. Then said quietly, "He could get hurt, Pen. You know how dangerous—"

"Of course I do," I snapped. I looked at her and she held my gaze. It was all I could do to stop from bursting into tears. I swallowed, pushed it down. "I'm keeping an eye on him, Hattie."

"I'm sure you are," she murmured, turning away, heading to the backyard, where she spent the better part of the afternoon flipping through magazines while I moved around her, keeping house. Keeping my house.

Jameson called after a couple weeks and told me that he was worried. He was, he said, refusing to let Elliot go out with his friends while he stayed there, but Elliot was becoming hostile. I sympathized with Jameson, told him he was doing the right thing, but I continued to watch as Elliot came and went with growing independence. He had changed so much. He was becoming taller and more sinewy, growing into an eleven-year-old, losing his baby fat. He was transforming before my eyes, his childhood in his wake like a pile of broken toys.

"El, I want to talk to you about what's going on in town," I got up the nerve to say to him one day while he wolfed down food at the table. "The fires."

He slammed his hands down on the table, exasperated, in a way that made me jump. "Penny, not again! This has nothing to do with me, I swear!" He looked up at me, saw my surprise, and softened. He bent his head. "Okay?"

Anything. Of course, okay. I would have done anything to keep holding his hand, to keep him close for a little longer. And to do this, I was gullible, permissive. Go, go out, I trust you. Hattie watching from a doorway as I waved goodbye, Elliot walking to Jamie's house, hands thrust in his pockets.

"What about Iain?" Hattie said. "Think he's just ignoring this, too?" She was drinking more. Filling her cups with smugness. Her smiles were crooked. She was enjoying this but was worried, too, I could tell. *Not my problem,* she often said, except that it was. She and I both knew that. It was a problem that was growing, and swelling, and threatening to pop.

Iain Moore, detective about town, it turned out, was not ignoring anything. And one day, late in the afternoon, he arrived at the front door. I almost didn't hear the knock, it was so faint. I was so unused to people visiting. But then Hattie was there, pulling the door open, like so many years ago.

"Iain!" she trilled, tucking a hair behind her ear.

His face was impassive.

"Hello, Hattie. Can I come in?"

"Of course, please." She stood aside, faltering at his briskness.

I had watched from around the doorway and now tried to put a smile on my face.

"Hello, Iain." I went into the room, where he sat, and so much was suddenly the same. Hattie and I, in the two chairs, facing him. Except that he was no longer the nervous young man. He was sure of himself. He avoided Hattie's eager smile and looked right at me.

"Penny," here he nodded at Hattie, "Hattie. I'm here about Elliot. I'm concerned that he's getting into trouble." He reached into his pocket and pulled out a small brown leather jewellery box. I recognized it immediately. He opened it towards me, and my mother's emerald earrings winked up at me. Hattie and I exchanged a look.

"Where did you find those?" Hattie asked.

"A local pawnshop called me about a kid trying to sell them there. The shop had taken down Elliot's name in case. Are these yours?"

I inhaled sharply. "They were our mother's."

Iain's voice softened. "I told them I knew the kid, and that it was a misunderstanding. But," he handed me the box, "this isn't good. Curiosity, mischief maybe, but it never ends well when it starts out that way. Seen it a thousand times." I nodded. He continued. "Jamie told me, Penny, that Elliot continued to want to make trouble long after I put a stop to Jamie's involvement. After you and I spoke. The fires in town are pointing in one direction."

Hattie leaped to the defensive.

"What, you're telling us that the fact that the two of them are inseparable doesn't suggest they are both getting into something?" she quipped, her mouth turned up into a slight smile.

"Elliot hasn't been to our house in a long time, actually. I forbade Jamie to see him a while back."

I felt a fool but still said, "But he goes over there all the time."

Iain shook his head. "No. Sorry, Penny, he doesn't. And I just wanted to warn you that the police department is handing the recent fires over to an arson specialist."

A cold feeling ran down my arms, and I felt Hattie's eyes on me. I felt her fear pass between our chairs. All these years later.

"I wouldn't want to have to bring in a kid. Especially one from a troubled background—" Here Hattie blew out her cheeks. "I like

Elliot. But it's headed that way if these don't stop." He looked hard at us both. "I don't have to tell you what a fire can do."

He took a deep breath. "I've never really felt right about your house fire, Penny. I, well—I have wondered for a long time if there was something I missed. It was one of my first cases, and I was young. I didn't do right by you, I know I didn't."

We two sisters, in that moment, sat still like two foxes at a hunt, and time stopped. Hold on, Hattie, just hold on.

"I dunno," he said, sounding less sure of himself, "I had my suspicions about Buddy's friend, that Mac Williams. He turned into a proper criminal down the line, and I just never felt right that I hadn't pursued things more thoroughly at the time. I had been distracted." A look to Hattie. "So, I think I'll pass that file on to her also—the arson specialist, that is."

I nodded dumbly, and Hattie cleared her throat as though there was anything she could do.

Iain stood up.

"Well. That's all I had to say." He nodded to me, ignored Hattie completely, and turned, closing the door behind him when he left.

AND FROM THEN ON, THE TWO OF US IN THE HOUSE, THE threads of our secrets breaking, we began to panic, to snipe at each other. We were worried for Elliot, for ourselves, for the past and the future. Time was marked by arguments and drinking, and the other side of the coin of our summers past: days and nights no longer stretched out in the lazy beauty of the sun but closed in on us like a trap.

I grounded Elliot, demanded he stay within my sights, but he was like living with a slippery wild thing, and sometimes he would leave in spite of my protests, saying he was going to Jameson's, slamming the door behind him in a way that was a relief and a damnation at once.

Hattie was coming undone. Drinking more, falling into her familiar tracks and traps, dropping dangerous hints and veiled threats. The pressure was undoing us both and I feared it was going to burn right out of her. I couldn't trust her anymore to understand the importance of our secrets, of the fire, of Elliot's birth. She scoffed at me whenever I tried to tell her to keep her voice down.

We lost track of when Elliot was home, so tied up we were in our own scraps, me trying to wrestle fate to do my bidding, Hattie allowing us to be its plaything. I avoided leaving the house, afraid of the town, afraid the smell of smoke would get into my head, drive me mad. Hattie crashed about, reclaiming the house by leaving pieces of herself everywhere. It felt smaller, messier, like a war bunker, like a shelter that turns into a bomb.

CHAPTER 29

EVENING. WE PACED THE MAIN FLOOR, EXCHANGING swipes. Elliot was at the library, working on a school project.

"Well, you've done it now, Hattie." I slammed a cupboard shut. All the slammed cupboards, I thought. Existing only for the furious emphasis of all the women who had lived in this house.

"Oh God, what now, Penny?"

"Everything! You are a menace. *You* did all this—all that fire talk! You think you're so sly, but you're like a bull in a china shop. Don't you realize how serious this is? How much there is to lose?"

She spread her arms.

"All this, right? Your hard-earned life." She laughed derisively. "I would hate to be the one to sully it, but sister, this is yours now."

She shook her head and went back upstairs. The silence in the house was a blessing, a curse, a gift and a threat. The sun was setting.

I called Jameson and asked him to come over. It was urgent, I said.

I heard his car and went out to the back deck, wringing my hands. I remembered when it was good. When he was such a welcome sight. I called out to him, and he came in the open gate.

"Penny? What is it?"

Hattie appeared in the doorway, her hair a mess, her eyes impassive, waiting.

"Ah. The other excellent parent," she said.

"I just think we need to talk about what to do, about Elliot," I said before Jameson could respond.

"Now? Why, what's happened now?"

There was a strong summer wind kicking up, the sky was uncharacteristically dark. The leaves were rustling loudly, a rose-bush that should have been trimmed scratching against the windows. I shuddered against the noise of it, despite the warmth. My collarbone was aching from that old break, as it often does before a storm.

"Nothing. I—I'm sorry. I just—I am afraid something bad is going to happen." I don't know what prevented me from being more frank about Elliot. I was afraid Jameson would judge me, afraid, ironically, that he'd find me untrustworthy.

Hattie walked slowly outside. She was coming, spoiling for a fight, her hair whipping around in a frenzy. I wished then that I had left well enough alone. But I never learn.

"Something?" she said. "You think 'something' is going to happen?"

"You okay, Hattie?" Jameson asked, cocking his head to the side.

"Never better. Now that you two are here to save the day together." She plopped herself in a deck chair and smiled at him. A memory flickered in my mind, of the three of us, all those summers ago.

"Elliot is getting into trouble, and I'm afraid he's going to get hurt," I said.

"I've talked to him," said Jameson. "I think he gets it."

"Yeah, you guys really have a handle on things, don't you," muttered Hattie.

"Shut up, Hattie," I said.

"What, am I wrong? You mean, you two—'Mom and Dad'— you don't have it under control? Wow," she said, "parenting really is a bitch."

"Someone is," I said.

I could hear the gate creaking, and the trees sounded like waves as they bent against the wind. Blustering leaves and broken branches on the driveway.

Jameson put up his hand.

"Look. Yes, he's having a little trouble staying on the straight and narrow. But maybe we have all had a hand in that, Hattie, not just me and Penny. All the change he's had to adapt to? It's got to be confusing for him, not sure who he's supposed to listen to, who his parents are." He ran his hand through his hair. "I dunno. I think, maybe, it's time for him to know the truth. About us. About who his birth mother is. Someone's going to let it slip in this town, and it should be us who tell him."

"The 'truth'?" Hattie scoffed. "What a novel idea, 'the truth.' I'll leave that one to the real parents, I guess. The biological parents. Step down. Abdicate my throne." She grinned nastily. "Leave it to the prom king and queen."

"Enough, Hattie." Jameson raised his voice loudly and pointed at her, surprising me. "I have had it with you dangling that around like you're jealous. Like the whole thing wasn't your idea to begin with." Louder and louder, his arm outstretched. This shy man, reaching his limit. "That is the truth, Hattie. That is the real truth. Penny and me? That was your idea. You forced me into it."

I felt these words like a hammer in my mind.

"What?" I heard myself saying, the words out of my mouth before I realized. "What do you mean? You—you told him to sleep with me?" I staggered, this knowledge hitting me to the core. "What the fuck, Hattie. That is diabolical, even for you."

She and Jameson froze. Shock in her eyes. He closed his own in defeat.

"You slept with him?" she whispered.

My mouth opened and closed. "I—"

"Jesus, Penny," Jameson murmured, shaking his head. Hattie gasped, and I heard a small sob escape her mouth.

"Hattie, look. It was—"

"Oh my God," she whispered.

"Like you didn't push him to me, serve him up on a platter!" I panicked, saying something I hardly meant but hoped to be true. I was sweating, horror creeping into my thoughts. I felt hot despite the darkening sky, the summer storm coming in.

"Oh my God," she repeated, staring first at Jameson and then at me. She stood, and her chair tottered, then tipped, clattering to the ground. She was breathing quickly. She stared at Jameson. "You fucked her." Then to me, "Penny, you did that to me? You did. You fucking did. Elliot wasn't premature, he was right on time. Because you were already pregnant when— my God."

Jameson had been staring, mouth open, and he walked quickly towards her, but she shoved him away, and wheeled on me.

"And you thought I *asked him to*?" She exhaled, hard. "Only you, Penny. Only you are capable of being that kind of monster."

"Hattie, I'm so sorry," I breathed, my voice cracking.

Jameson turned sharply over the fence to the driveway, his eyes widening in shock.

"Elliot!" he shouted, and I looked in time to see my son, his eyes on mine, his hands on the handlebars of his bike. He turned and sped away, those untangling truths chasing after him.

CHAPTER 30

RAN TO THE DRIVEWAY AFTER HIM, THEN PULLED MY own bike out of the shed, and rode out to find my son, leaving the wreckage of my life behind me, Jameson and Hattie calling after us.

I circled the neighbourhood, calling out his name. I was rusty, not having ridden in a long time, pumping my legs hard to get speed and balance. Soon I was taking turns boldly like a kid, taking shortcuts between streets, enjoying the feel of it in spite of myself. These were my streets. How often as a child had I careened around these corners, grinning, cool air on my teeth, wind making my eyes water. I had peddled faster and faster, out-riding Hattie in an instant, leaving her spinning her wheels in my dust, heedless of my mum's plea to keep her in my sights when all I wanted was to be out of sight. Gum popping in my back teeth, knuckles cold around the handlebars. Life seemed hard but it was a breeze then, wasn't it. The world turns and now we were barely hanging on.

Elliot, Elliot, Elliot. With each burst of calling his name, I felt I loosened my grip on him, on myself.

Past the school, where Hattie and I had grown up and where Jameson worked, where I had taken Elliot by the hand.

Schoolyards look so desolate at night; perfect for melancholy teenagers, but there were none there. I rode down the main drag, where there were two pubs, neither of them good, but always full to the hilt with those people who, like me and Hattie, had never gotten out of here. There were a couple of men walking away from Dusty's, towards a parked car, towards me, and as I got closer, I locked eyes with Mac Williams, twirling his keys around a finger. He looked surprised, then called out angrily, "Dirty Penny! Hey, you fucking bitch," and I heard in the echo of that boozy bellow how our fates had crossed. I had underestimated St. Margaret's, its players, how they could trip me up. This is the school, this is the pub, this is the church, this is the steeple and then there, at the end—the Grayson house. Home is where your secrets are. That huge brick vault, keeper of lies, witness to death, protector of the guilty, and home, home, home. I veered dangerously close to them, to Mac and his friends, and screeched to a halt.

"Have you seen Elliot pass this way?" I asked, gasping for breath.

He laughed bawdily. "You lookin' for your boy?" He looked at his friends, elbowing the one closest to him. "You can't seem to keep a hold of the men in your life, there, can ya?"

"Fuck you," I spat, my fear glad to have found a target. "Fuck you and your sad fucking life."

His laugh turned to a snarl.

"You'd better watch yourself, Dirty Penny. People will start to talk. Your kid and all these fires . . . People are going to come after you, like they came after me."

"They went after you because you're a criminal." Done with him, I lifted my head, looking, looking. And suddenly I knew where Elliot was.

Mac started towards me, his chest puffed out. "Oh, is that right? You know, maybe Buddy just didn't hit you hard enough. Maybe you need a couple more knocks." One of his buddies pulled at his arm, as if sensing danger, but Mac snatched it away. I put a foot on my pedal, just as he grasped my wrist, hard. I tried to yank it away, but he held firm. Wrists are delicate—I remember this. There are things that you will always know after, and one of them is how fragile your body is. So much was the same, but now so much was different. I felt my body tense in fury. His friends hung back, their bravado stripped away, calling lightly for him to come on. He ignored everything but me.

"You know," he said, tightening his hold on me, "maybe the police've been barkin' up the wrong tree all along. You're a hothead, and you've got a crazy family." His voice dropped to a whisper. "God almighty, you probably had something to do with Buddy. I mean, hell, you act like you don't even care he died."

I leaned over my handlebars. It was worth it, even if it took me from Elliot for this glorious minute. I hissed like a wild cat.

"I *didn't* care, Mac. You're right. I was *glad*. And do you know what? You haven't got a *clue* about what really happened."

His eyes widened. Something Mac couldn't bear was being taunted. He bared his teeth, I reeled back, and I spat in his face. He loosened his grip long enough for me to snatch my hand back, and I launched away, furiously pedalling, fear galloping in my chest.

Mac screamed after me—*I knew it! I knew it, you bitch!*—and soon I heard his car screech away from the curb, coming up behind me quickly. I hopped onto the sidewalk, peeling away. I took a route that a car could never take.

I raced towards the property. *Elliot. Elliot.*

Then, over the trees, a tiny orange spark flew on the wind, and suddenly I was there, through the trees, and it was, too, all around me: a blaze. A barn burner. My barn, my sanctuary, Elliot's hide-out, up in enormous flames. I stood, my legs straddling my bike like a teenager, stunned at the furious beauty of it, at the power and momentum of this thing. This thing, all over again.

It came back to me in an instant: that one terrible, wonderful day.

I HAD PREPARED.

I had roasted a chicken for dinner. Carefully, expertly, I had washed the cavity, pricking a lemon with a fork and pushing it inside with a handful of thyme and rosemary, resting it on carrots and potatoes in a large roasting pan. I had sliced some onions in quarters, pulled two garlic cloves from a bulb I kept in a small ceramic cup with a broken handle that I liked. The smell of it, as it cooked, wafted through the house.

I WAS MOMENTARILY TRANSFIXED. IT WAS A BEHEMOTH of fire: a dazzling, dizzying force. And then, I began to scream for my son. I threw my bike down, shielding my eyes, and ran towards it.

I heard something. Muffled yelling. I turned all around, unsure where it was coming from, and I saw Mac's car parked at a crazy angle halfway up an overgrown path. He had come a different way, taking the old road that led to the back of the barn, the one he and Buddy had always used. I ran around the barn, calling out against the smoke that was filling my lungs. Calling *Elliot. Elliot.* Screaming his name until I was choking on it, on the smoke, my eyes streaming. And on top of it all, above the crackling and smashing of wood coming down, that sound that has haunted me for years, that sound that brings me to a stand-still no matter where I am: sirens.

I HEARD HIM COMING UP THE STAIRS. I HEARD THE DOOR opening, and tried not to think of all the things in the house that I loved. Insignificant things, really, when it comes down to it, but the things we surround ourselves with: soap dishes and favourite sweaters, a fork with a pretty handle, juice glasses etched with snowflakes, paintings and framed pictures of family, soft leather Mary Janes, a flowered scarf, a hairbrush. There were so many more things: things that I had forgotten about but would dis-cover later in the smouldering ash. The roasting pan itself would be found essentially intact, sitting on top of the stove, with an uneaten chicken in it, looking almost untouched while the house around it had curled into brown lace.

He stumbled in, leaning in the doorway. His voice was gravelly and already thick with afternoon beer that I had stocked in the fridge. He took his position in his chair, barely acknowl-edging me. A shrug when I reminded him that I would be going to Hattie's house to catch up, that he should eat. He waved me off. I offered him a beer, everything heightened into technicolor focus: the beads of sweat on the can, my hand, the sound of the can opening. And soon another, into which I had slipped three sleeping pills, the small orange ovals he took regularly, my heart beating in my chest as I saw them fizzing just inside the mouth of the can. I kissed the top of his head, a guilty gesture maybe, and he dodged me, irritated, turned up the baseball game. The crack of a bat, the commentator, in my ear like a megaphone. Focus,

focus. I puttered in the kitchen, I tidied. I brought him another
beer. Time roving in haphazard speeds: too fast, slow motion, and
my own body like a robot. The sun had set; it was night. Four
cans on the table beside his chair, his cigarette burning in the glass
ashtray. Earlier in the day I had gone to the basement, where we
kept a cookie tin of dead batteries that Buddy took to dispose
of periodically. I switched two dead batteries with the ones in
our fire alarm. I lit a cigarette standing on the chair beneath it,
holding the match in my hand long after the cigarette was lit. The
smoke curling into the yellow-white device, a silent accessory.

ELLIOT. ELLIOT. I RAN TOWARDS THE FIRE. AND THEN I
saw them, framed in the doorway, their skin lit up by the blaze,
Mac incandescent with rage, screaming into Elliot's face.

"This is *not your place!*" he bawled. Elliot stood, frozen with
fear, seemingly unaware of the size and danger of the fire growing
in strength behind him. "This is *his*, you little shit, *it's Buddy's*
place! Where is Penny? Where's that bitch?" He was sobbing and
yelling, Elliot staring in shock. I lurched forward, stumbling and
running. My boy. My son.

HE CRACKED ANOTHER CAN OPEN. I WENT UPSTAIRS AND
packed a bag. Came down and heard him snoring. A loud, wheezy,
noise. His chest rising and falling. Breathing. Life. I stood still. A
fly ball on the TV, players rushing, running, looking up, up, up.

Maybe he didn't deserve it. Maybe no one does. Maybe he
always begged my forgiveness after our fights, maybe he said he'd
change. But some things need to come to an end. Sometimes you
need to force somebody's hand.

It had to look accidental, and so there was a chance it wouldn't work: that Buddy would be woken by the fire, that our neighbours would see the smoke or flames sooner than necessary, that the capricious Fates would twist and bend and break events so that I would wake the next day with a furious and injured husband, no home, and no new life. I tried, in my planning, to prevent this. I figured if I set the fire at the far end of the room, a wall of smoke would lull Buddy into death before the flames entered the picture and took hold of his body.

I watched him snoring. It was late now. People were sleeping all over town. I collected myself in the doorway of the living room, waiting. I had taken a long fireplace match from the box on the mantel, and I now held both the match and the box in my shaking hands.

And then I saw myself, my reflection in the window across the room. Sometimes that image floats into my dreams; me, standing like a ghost girl, a scared face.

I SCRAMBLED TOWARDS THEM, AND WHEN HE SAW ME, Mac grabbed Elliot, pulling him out of my reach, his eyes on me. No. No. An enormous piece of wood broke off above us and came crashing down, separating me from them. Elliot struggled against Mac, this man who he didn't know, this terrifying person I had underestimated just like I had the rest of this town. The firetrucks were arriving around the other side. The sirens blasting above everything else. The heat was overwhelming. The smoke blinding and choking. My terror was pulsing like it had a heart-beat of its own. My head throbbed. *Elliot. Elliot.* I held out my hands, trying to calm Mac, to reassure Elliot.

"Mac, please," I said, firmly. Elliot's eyes were locked on to mine. I took a step forward.

Mac pulled him further from me, deeper into the barn.

"Tell me the truth! It was all your fault, I know it!" he hissed, and I tried again to reach for my son, but Mac pulled him away, light as a doll, and my voice broke into a sob.

"*Please*, Mac!"

"What did you do to him? What did you do to Buddy? Tell me!" he thundered, his voice cracking. I heard more noise around us, the yelling of firefighters. I felt the space change as huge bodies crashed towards us. And then I saw that face, Detective Moore, and other officers, firefighters, and Mac turned and saw them, too. The who's who of the people in your community: police, firefighter, murderer, criminal, son, sister, daughter, mother. What will we be? What had we become?

"No!" Mac screamed, holding Elliot in front of him. "Not me, *her*!" He wailed like a spoiled child, pointing at me, Elliot crying in earnest now, limp in his arms, "I know what she did!" But they were all over us in an instant, Iain tackling Mac, and a firefighter scooping up Elliot in his arms. Someone's arms around me, rushing me into the breathable air.

We were far from the fire now, at the edge of the woods, an ambulance parked nearby. Elliot was sitting with the ambulance some ways away, with a silver blanket around his shoulders. He was drinking water and being checked over by a paramedic. I knew he would never touch a match again for the rest of his life. We were alive. We were exhausted, in shock, but we had survived.

Mac was gone, pulled away in handcuffs by Iain Moore and handed off to another officer. I had watched him, spitting out pieces of my secret behind him as he coughed and ranted into the darkness. What would he say? What would anyone believe?

Hattie and Jameson had arrived just as we'd come out of the fire, Hattie hysterically pushing past anyone who tried to stop her, her tiny arms encircling Elliot fiercely. Then she had rushed at me, crying into my neck, her relief and her pain like a tangible thing, her arms clutching me with a strength and intensity I had forgotten she had. I had watched Jameson hold his boy, tipping his face up to his, and kissing him all over, tears running down his face. He had gripped me closely afterwards, murmuring, "You're safe. Thank God." Hattie had barely agreed to let Elliot go for him to be seen by the paramedic, but Jameson had led her away, reluctantly.

We watched as the fire was taken, watched it give up. Jameson stood a little behind Hattie and me. Here we were, after all the noise, after ensuring everyone was safe, here we were, our family: silently looking on in shock, as the barn smouldered in front of us.

And yet. This circular trick of fate had dislodged something. The fire was under control, but I could feel something else starting. A crackling, a rising tension. Hattie was pacing, energy coming off of her like sparks, her eyes darting over at Elliot and then me. She had almost lost us, and I could see that this had made her more volatile than anything else. And she hadn't forgotten what she'd learned: what we'd done. Jameson took a step towards her.

"Hattie," he said, "Hattie, please—"

"Shut up, Jameson," she snapped. She shook her head in disbelief. "I cannot believe this. Look at this. Look at you both. What a disaster." She threw out her hands to encompass the wreckage around us.

"Hattie, enough," I said. I was defeated, numb, but not ready to let her have full reign of her anger. "You don't *get* to blame him for this. For anything." She stared at me, her eyes furious. "You're the one who gave up. And yes, I am sorry. About Jameson, about everything. But it was years ago now. If nothing else, tonight should teach us that we need to protect the life we have."

"The life *we* have? It's my life, Penny! My life!" she screeched, suddenly, and I knew she'd been waiting for this. The pressure keg of her withheld anger had finally burst. "You think I gave up? Just lost interest in my son? Do you have any fucking idea what I have gone through?" Her hard eyes locked on to mine; it was me she had in her sights, only me. "It's never going away, Penny! It's never fucking getting out of here!" She hit herself hard on the side of the head with the heel of her hand. "Every day it's in my head, Penny. You left it all on me, then came back just in time to be the fucking hero again—"

"Hattie, keep your voice down. It's not like that—"

"Oh yeah? Do you think you know what it's like? You think you know how it feels to be me? To live with what I've done?"

And then I saw Iain Moore. He was talking to Elliot. He was looking our way. It was happening too fast. Too slow.

DOES HATTIE REMEMBER? I DO. WHEN I WAS FIFTEEN and she was twelve? It was summer, glorious summer. I was parched. Parked my bike against the garage and cracked open a sweating pop can I'd bought from the corner store. I lifted it to my forehead, I remember, and closed my eyes for a second. Took that first sip as I walked in the front door. That's when I first heard her crying. Hattie. I stood, listening. It was from the kitchen.

"*I'm sorry, Mamma. I am. We would be a real family if it weren't for me. He would have stayed. Penny said—*"

"*Never you mind, Hattie. Never you mind. That is not true. Look at me, darling, look at me.*" I heard Hattie sniff. "*That is not true. It's a lie.*"

245

My skin went cold all over, the hairs on my sweating arms standing up. I tiptoed towards the kitchen and peeked my head around the corner. She was something, our mum. So lovely in an eyelet dress down to her ankles.

And then Mum turned to me, the look on her face like she'd never loved me at all. Like she'd be happy to never see me again, I swear she did. Holding onto Hattie like she was precious gold. Red gold.

"Penny," she said, calm and cool, and Hattie looked over in surprise, her eyes fearful, but locked with mine, secure in Mum's arms, "get out of my sight."

COULDN'T MUM SEE? THAT HATTIE ALWAYS HAD ONE over on us? That she had it in her to ruin absolutely everything?

I saw in my reflection in the glass that night, that same girl I was, second-best. I couldn't forget. He'd called me Hattie. He'd put his hand over my mouth. He'd called me Hattie. Now I had to save her, again. I looked at Buddy, lying in the chair.

Why did I have to do everything for her? It was her turn now. She owed me.

Buddy snored. The TV rattled on. There was the phone on the wall, the cord dangling low and twisted. I lifted it to my ear. I dialed.

"Hello?"

Her voice, young and quiet, tender.

"I can't do it," I whispered. "Hattie, I can't do it," and I began to sob quietly. She was silent on the other end. In that pause, what could have gone differently if I had spoken again, if I hadn't waited for what I knew would come?

"I'll do it," she said. "Come here. I'll go there. I'll do it for you, Penny."

246

She hung up. I held the phone limply. I froze. I didn't call her back and talk her out of it. I hadn't said no. No, Hattie. Yes.

Seconds passed. And then I came to life. Life, not death. I leaped into action and ran out the back door, leaving it open, not taking a backwards glance. Go, go, go.

I got out of sight.

Over the fence, through the bush, the forest, the back way, running, running, leaves under my feet, the fastest, the quietest I'd ever moved. A murder of crows erupted overhead. Did they see those two sisters, those loose threads, pulled in opposite directions, passing each other within a few blocks of one another? Switching places, trading fates. *I'll do it for you, Penny. For you, Penny. Pound pound pound* went my feet in the dark, and my heart and my breath, and the noise of my panic was like a death knell but I was alive, I was running away. Go, go, go.

Into the house through the open back door. Locked by instinct. Panting, my lungs burning. I stood with my back against the door. I was alone. She was gone. It was done. I remembered the plan. I took the stairs, turning off lights as I went. I had brought a small bag with me. I pulled out a nightgown and changed. I climbed into her bed and I waited.

When I heard her come in, I sat up, turned on the light. She didn't do it, I was sure, she couldn't have. Everything was too calm and quiet. Where Buddy was concerned, I thought of screaming, agony, chaos. There were no sounds. She didn't do it.

"It's me," I heard her say, her voice scratchy. "I'm home." And then, when she stumbled into the room, wild-eyed and breathing hard, her lip trembling just a tiny bit, I knew. She toppled into bed, curled against me, touched my hair: my little sister, tiny Hattie of our childhood. I heard sirens now in the distance and felt shock course through my veins, my hands shaking as I wrapped the covers around her.

247

She did it. She did it for me. She lit that match that started the fire of our lives. It never went out.

"Hattie, I know. I know. Keep your voice down."

"And so what, you know? What am I going to do about it, Penny? How can I ever be forgiven?" She was crying now, her voice hard and loud.

"Hattie—"

"No, you listen. I was okay for a while. Jameson came along and we seemed so happy, and I felt like it was the right thing. But then I couldn't have a baby, and I dunno, I started thinking God was getting me back—"

"Come on, Hattie, of course not."

She looked at me with disgust.

"I know, Penny. No one was ever true to me."

Iain Moore was walking towards us.

"I'm glad to see you're all okay," he offered, looking at Hattie and me, then Jameson. He paused. He looked over his shoulder at the remains of the barn. "I need to discuss something with you. Both of you."

"Iain, please don't do anything to Elliot," Hattie pleaded, moving towards him. "He's a good boy, and he's had a tough go. It's all my fault." She ran her hands shakily though her hair. "Give him a break. For old times' sake? Remember our friendship? You said it meant so much to you. Give El a chance." She reached over and touched his arm, and he stiffened.

"Hattie, don't. This is my job. There is no 'old times' sake' for me." He paused, rubbed his face and turned to me. "I've spoken to Elliot. I think he's been scared straight. That was a horrifying ordeal for him. But I'd like him to volunteer with us, take a fire safety class, that kind of thing. I know he's just a kid, but this has got to stop." He watched me take in this news, waiting for a reaction. I was so tired. I nodded.

"I want to ask you something, Penny," Iain said, eyes still on me.

My mind a fog. So tired.

"Yes?"

"The fire. The first one. With Buddy."

I lifted my head.

"Don't tell me you're listening to that idiot who almost killed our son," Hattie said, gesturing to where Mac had been taken away in a patrol car. Iain ignored her. He was looking at me.

"Penny," he said, watching me closely. And then: "Why didn't we find your earrings at the site of the fire?"

Something was ringing in my ears. I clenched my hands, and I swear I could feel those earrings digging into my palms, like when little Hattie had just given them to me.

"What do you mean? Who cares about the earrings," Hattie snapped. She was ramrod straight, but I felt my body losing energy, becoming limp.

"Detective," Jameson interjected, "maybe now is not the time?"

Iain ignored them both. He was looking at me.

"They were in your wedding photo. They're pretty fancy. I recognized them," he said, "when Elliot tried to sell them."

Hattie was breathing heavily. I was aware of her beside me, just like all those years ago. Alert with attention, ready to step in. Here we all were again.

"We categorized all the things we found at the fire. I went back to check the records for them. They would have been there, melted and ruined, like all your other jewellery."

He watched me. He waited. *Unless* was the unspoken word. Unless so many things. He was giving me an out. Unless I'd worn them that night. Unless, I could have said, Hattie had borrowed them. Unless I'd never done it. Unless we hadn't begun. Unless they were the one thing I took with me. Those glimmering talismans, those souvenirs of sacrifice. Packing them carefully in my bag before I called Hattie, before the unthinkable.

I was done fighting. It was over.

I shook my head, regret buzzing loudly in my ears. I could see that Hattie was shaking. Something was breaking, cracks running up and down the sides of us. It was happening. The pressure had built to the point of bursting. And I was so exhausted. I heard Hattie clear her throat, ready to speak. *Quiet now, Hattie.*

"Hattie—"

Iain watching me. I reached out and took Hattie's hand. She looked so scared. I swallowed. *No, Hattie, Yes, Hattie. Please, Hattie.*

She looked stunned. And then she murmured, quiet as a child, an almost-sob:

"Elliot." Her eyes on him, where he sat, accepting more water, looking like a small boy.

And it was then that I truly saw them: mother and son. I had so often, over the years, doubted her love for him; for her boy whom she had clawed and schemed and plotted to get. I saw now how much had been at stake, how all her threats and teasing, her tiptoeing near the edge of a deep, dark telling, hadn't been to torment me, but had been as close as she'd gotten to falling into some kind of relief. In that one phone call I had pushed her, punished her for a lifetime of sisterhood.

And now I needed to repay her. Those two sides of us.

I opened my mouth and knew I was taking fate back into my own hands. Relief. A switch. I had to let the air in for her, I had to let her breathe again, because I was the stronger sister. Putting out fires.

"I did it," I said.

"No, Penny! No," Hattie cried, appealing to Iain, "no, that's not true!"

I took her in my arms, and there was no one there but us. She was so small. *I could put you in my pocket*, I used to say to her when we were kids. I could keep you there. Her shoulders heaved, her face buried into my neck. *I'm sorry, Hattie. I'm sorry, I'm sorry, I'm sorry. A million lifetimes and I cannot make this up to you, but all the same, I'd do it again, I'd let you do it. You gave me my life back and saved your own. You gave me a son who I didn't know I wanted.*

She was light as air. All the life had been taken out of her. I had saved her: she wouldn't have to tell. I had won: she couldn't tell.

"I love you, Hattie."

And then he came over to us, our sweet boy. Elliot. His eyes weepy and tired looking. His face full of concern.

"What is it?" he asked.

LATER. HE WOULD LEARN THE TRUTH LATER. BUT IT WAS out now. Or some version of it. A release. A feeling of wickedness expelled. And yet, if you were to cut me open, the belly of the beast, wouldn't you see a will to survive that she just doesn't have? *Look out for your sister.* I had risen before, and I knew I could again. Sacrifice doesn't have to mean death. It can mean rebirth.

Iain quietly suggested that Elliot go home with Jameson, who was speechless with shock but awoken by the call of parental duty. We didn't try to stop him, to explain ourselves. We watched our boy leave.

It was done. Hattie must have felt some relief. She was free, mostly, even if I knew in my dark heart that I had taken one more thing from her in exchange. She exhaled and turned her watery eyes to me, her mouth chapped and stained, her hair madly tangled about her face. That marvel, that minx, her love for me breaking over everything, and maybe, possibly, a new life crashing in.

CHAPTER 31

THE PRISON VISITATION ROOM.

Hattie holds my hand across the table. We have chatted about all manner of insignificance. We always circle back to the same place.

"Have you heard from Elliot?"

"Not yet. He might come around. You know. We should give him some more time."

"I write to him. Has he gotten my letters? Did Jameson say?"

"I haven't spoken to him recently. I don't know." A long pause. "Actually, Jameson is moving with Elliot to Woepine. A fresh start."

"Oh. I see." This sinks in. Away from St. Margaret's, away from our house. "And you?"

"I want to stay close, so I can visit you. I want to stay home."

We are here, we two. It was always us. It will always be. Thick as thieves, even after we are robbed of everything. Hands together again, like we're praying.

And today she says, "I feel relieved. Like it's over."

"It is," I say. "And I am so proud of how you're doing," I say. And I mean it. She is floating back up to the surface, past the broken bottles and chipped dreams, towards a future.

"People are still talking about us." She laughs, darkly.

"Let them. They don't know us."

SOON THE WARDEN CALLS THAT VISITATION IS OVER, AND all around us people stand and embrace.

I get up, and Hattie does, too, our chairs squealing against the linoleum. She walks around the table and holds me close. Her eyes are watery as she looks into mine, but it seems there might just be something bright in her face again. Light coming through a thicket. It suits her, this life. It's been good for her.

"Next week?"

"Yes," I say.

She turns and leaves, and I watch for as long as I can, thinking of her red mane bobbing away out of the building, to her car, as I move with the other inmates back to my penance.

HATTIE WILL RETURN TO THE EMPTY HOUSE AGAIN. Elliot is in a nearby town but might as well be a world away from St. Margaret's. Mac Williams is in prison for child endangerment and a slew of other things they were working up to charging him with. I imagine him there; tending to his grudges, making new enemies. Jameson, who will not return my letters, but who weathered the truth we told as it whipped about our family, knocking down lamps and turning out the lights. They just need time. Time to digest the fullness of the stories of this life. "We will come out on the other side," I write constantly to Elliot. Our son.

I will keep making tiny shuffling steps towards him. I remember when I slept on the pullout couch, and his little face surprised me in the mornings. How he took a chance on me then. At night

I dream he is still small, and that I can hold him in my arms. In my dreams, sometimes he turns into little Hattie, her soft hands in mine. I wake smiling. The light flickers above me. There is no one. Jameson will write back one day, I'm sure. We might have a future together, a family together, he and I and Elliot, Hattie too.

Who knows, right? Who knows what the future holds.

Hattie will always come. *It's me*, she says, every time, her face close to mine, holding me before she leaves.

I'm home.

ACKNOWLEDGEMENTS

My favourite part of a book is often the Acknowledgements page. It feeds my curiosity, and I like to know who the people are who help authors on their journeys all the way to the last page. I am grateful to so many.

I wouldn't be a writer if I wasn't a reader. I am *such* a reader that I feel slightly panicky if I do not always have a book on my person, regardless of where I am going or with whom. To all the authors who have shared their stories with me throughout my life: I owe you a great debt.

I live in a small town. This town has the most remarkable library, which I visit every few days, and where I wrote much of this book (including this Acknowledgements page). The people at the Grimsby Public Library feel like part of my extended family. Thank you to the librarians, in particular Nancy Kettles, and to the Grimsby Author Series for their ongoing support. I would also like to thank Station 1 Coffeehouse, where I spend many a morning writing. You keep me in tea and company, and I need both.

The first time I truly felt like a writer was at the Banff Centre. I am grateful for the group of writers I met there, especially Michael Crummey, who gave me the push I needed to move to the next step. It is because of him that I met Martha Magor

ACKNOWLEDGEMENTS

Webb, my steadfast agent. I cannot describe how thankful I
am for Martha. She, however, could probably help me find the
words. She is a marvel.

Thank you to Half the World Holdings for granting this book
the Half the World Global Literati Award.

To Iris Tupholme, Jennifer Lambert, Natalie Meditsky and the
entire team at HarperCollins in Canada: thank you. The night I
heard my book had found a home with you remains one of the best
of my life. Thank you for believing in *Sister of Mine*, and in me.
Jennifer, your insightful editing has truly made this book better.
Thank you also to "plot doctor" Helen Reeves.

Thank you to Matt Martz, Chelsey Emmelhainz and the team
at Crooked Lane Books. Your thoughts on turning up the volume
on this book have made it all the better, and I'm so happy to be
working with you.

I am lucky enough to have been born into one, and then to
have married into another, incredible family. To my parents, Judy
and Phil Petrou, and my courageous brother, Michael, and to all
the Petrous, the Newberrys, and their partners and spouses, to
my cousins, who are like extra siblings to me; thank you to the
Johnstons, and, as we affectionately call ourselves, the Nonstons;
to Carolyn Johnston and Ginny Sinnot, and to all my siblings-in-
law for loving and feeding me, for making me laugh and tolerat-
ing my love of all games. My life is richer because of every one
of you.

My darling hearts, the Hydra, and the MAS, and my other mag-
nificent girlfriends. You are the people for whom I reach in good
times and bad. You are maddeningly brilliant and fearless, and I
am so lucky to know and love you: Nicole Bell, Kristen Aspevig,
Donna Maloney, Karen Stewart, Laura Noble Wohlgemut, Pilar
Chapman, Cathy Davison, Sally Gfeller, Susie Lobb, Amber Lyon

Gash, Sandra Ingram, Tracy Hogan, Danielle Dominick, Jessica Olivier, Carola Perez, Lori Beckstead, Ramona Pringle, Ann Marie Peña, Erin O'Hara, Sheree Stevenson, Giuliana Racco. Thanks also to Chris Williams and Tania Camilleri, Brendan Michie and Kim DeSimone, Mat Noble Wohlgemut, Ian Lobb, Joel Gfeller, Stephen Gash, Pat Ingram, Robert Cash, Greg Owen, Derek Hersey, Jason Book, Zac Schwartz, Steven Ehrlick, Richard Lachman, Michael Murphy, Becky Choma, Mike Blouin, Elan Mastai, Sabrina Palumbo, Susie Anacleto and so many other friends, new and old.

Thanks to my current and former students and colleagues at Ryerson's RTA School of Media: there is no job like the one I have, and it is because of all of you. Our school is my home away from home.

I am beyond grateful to Eli and Leo, who fill my days with a joy I never imagined possible. You make me want to read and write and tell the best kinds of stories. You are our wonders.

And to Jay, my dearest one: I thank you, for all the years made up of spectacular moments, for the days of laughter, comfort and love. For making them all count, win and lose.

—LP